STEVEN M. ROTH

NO SAFE PLACE

What people are saying about
NO SAFE PLACE:

Steven Roth has written a terrifyingly real bioweapon suspense novel. He has the chops to keep a reader turning pages and anxious about what comes next. *No Safe Place* alerts us to what the government has done and may still be doing to an unsuspecting and unconcerned public. Highly recommended.

—Charlie Stella
Author of *TOMMY RED* and eight other crime novels

What people are saying about
MANDARIN YELLOW

A splendidly told and sophisticated tale by a first-time novelist. The multi-layered murder mystery not only remains engaging throughout, but also offers the reader a superb primer on Chinese culture and history, particularly post-World War II history.

—News4U

If you're a mystery fan, you shouldn't miss this novel that features a Parker Duofold (the eponymous Mandarin Yellow). This is prime mystery: well plotted and compellingly written. Roth weaves a taut storyline, paces it perfectly, and wraps it in twists and turns that make no sense until you get to the end (when everything clicks perfectly into place). Along the way, he slips in all the clues you need to solve the mystery right along with hero Socrates Cheng.

—RB

What people are saying about
THE MOURNING WOMAN:

There are never enough five star mysteries out there for a dedicated reader like myself. Steven Roth has now written another in his Socrates Cheng private investigator series called, "The Mourning Woman." His first was, "Mandarin Yellow," which I thought outstanding. Both have fascinating, complicated plots involving a mix of Chinese and Greek cultures. Roth's extensive credentials in the study of these groups has provided him with a unique perspective that fits perfectly with the genre of intrigue, historical vendetta, and motives unlikely to be uncovered easily by a typical American detective.

—History Major

The Mourning Woman, the second in the series of Socrates Cheng mystery novels, is an intelligent and engrossing murder mystery that is stylish, well-crafted, and every bit as satisfying as Steven M. Roth's debut Cheng mystery, Mandarin Yellow. Roth is a great storyteller. I look forward to the third installment of the series.

—QP

MYSTERY NOVELS BY STEVEN M. ROTH

The Socrates Cheng mysteries:
MANDARIN YELLOW
THE MOURNING WOMAN

NO SAFE PLACE
Copyright 2016 by Steven M. Roth.

Published by Blackstone Press

Cover design and formatting by Streetlight Graphics, LLC

ISBN 978-0-692-77478-6 [Paperback].

ISBN 978-0-692-77415-1 [ePub]

Visit the author's website: http://www.StevenMRoth.com

ACKNOWLEDGEMENTS

Writing a novel is mostly a solitary endeavor, yet so many people played important roles in bringing this book to fruition. My special thanks go to Dominica for her continued support and encouragement; to Quintin Peterson, District of Columbia Metropolitan Police Department (ret.); to Dr. Stanley Roth (deceased) for his comments concerning the symptoms related to Melioidosis; to my friend Richard M. Wrona for his valuable suggestions concerning aspects of the military occupation of the target city and concerning sniper weapons used by Russian Spetsnaz units; to Dr. Peter Aron, MD, pediatric psychiatrist, for his valuable comments concerning General Anthony Vista's childhood; and to my early readers, Gary Griffith and Hubert Grissom, Esq., for their valuable suggestions with respect to the manuscript.

I also would like to thank noted crime novelist Charlie Stella for his helpful comments on the manuscript.

Finally, I want to thank my Launch Team, comprised of dedicated fans and friends, who offered many significant comments on the manuscript and much encouragement.

For Dominica

"A good runner leaves no footprints."

Lao Tzu

PROLOGUE

THE PRESIDENT OF THE UNITED States has a secret.
It is a secret so dark, so loathsome, that should it ever be publicly disclosed, it not only will bring down his administration, it will send the president of the United States to a maximum security federal prison for the rest of his life.

PART ONE

CHAPTER 1

THE PRESIDENT UNCAPPED HIS FOUNTAIN pen and stared at the executive order sitting on his desk awaiting his signature.

He thought about secret experiments carried out in the past by the federal government against an unsuspecting American population, all rationalized as having been conducted for the greater good of the country.

There had been the Tuskegee syphilis experiments run by the U. S. Public Health Service between 1932 and 1972, the Cold War cadmium experiments in which the Army had sprayed a toxic chemical mixture over inner-city neighborhoods in St Louis, and the recently publically disclosed 1955 experiment in which the CIA had discharged the whooping cough bacteria over Tampa Bay, Florida, causing an epidemic in which twelve people died.

Satisfied that his motives today were justified by history and by frequent and credible terrorists' threats continuously made against the United States, and firmly believing he was following the best path to discharge his oath of office as president and as commander in chief to defend the country, the president signed his name to the secret executive order.

With that simple act, the president authorized the

Department of Defense to release a deadly pathogen into the general population of an American city to be designated by the secretary of defense.

CHAPTER 2

March 02

TRACE AUSTIN UNFASTENED HIS SEATBELT and settled back into his aisle seat aboard American Airlines Flight 1992 on its way from Ronald Reagan Washington National Airport to Fort Lauderdale, Florida. He glanced across the two adjacent seats at Isabella, his wife, and their teenage son, Pete.

They sat near the back of the Airbus A319 twin-jet on their way to visit Isabella's mother, called Nanna by everyone in the family, for a two-week stay while they used her condominium as a home base for short side-trips.

Isabella turned toward Trace and smiled. "So, how's the birthday boy doing?" She reached over and squeezed his hand.

Trace blushed. "The birthday boy's feeling middle aged."

"Oh, that's right. I forgot," Pete said, turning away from the window and looking at Trace. "Happy birthday, Dad." Pete grinned. "You *are* middle aged, you know. Only one more year to the big five-O"

Trace reached across Isabella to Pete. He gave him a soft, faux punch on his shoulder.

"Did you hear from Max?" Isabella said. "I noticed he didn't call you at home this morning to wish you happy birthday."

Trace nodded. "He called me yesterday at the office. Gave me a hard time about my birthday until I reminded him we're the same age. He asked for you and Pete."

"Speaking of Uncle Max," Pete said, as he again turned away from the window and looked at his father, "I'm old enough now to know the truth. Is he really allergic to alcohol like you always said or was that just a cover story because he has a drinking problem and had to give up booze?" He looked from Trace to his mother, then back again at Trace.

"We didn't make it up," Trace said. "Uncle Max really is allergic to alcohol, deathly allergic, in fact. Even a small amount can send him into shock or kill him. He never touches the stuff, never has as long as I've known him."

"Not even when you were young and SEALs together?" Pete said.

"Not even then."

"Poor Uncle Max. What a curse.

"Enough about Uncle Max for now. Let's talk about our plans for Florida. Is my boy ready to go fishing in the Keys and land a huge marlin?"

Pete laughed. "You bet your. . . . Oops! Sorry. I mean, you bet I am."

Trace took Isabella's hand. He raised his eyebrows and slightly shrugged. Isabella put her head down on Trace's shoulder.

Pete watched them, rolled his eyes, and turned back to the window.

CHAPTER 3

I T HAD TAKEN THE SECRETARY of defense almost eight months to convince the president that the secret executive order represented the prudent and responsible anti-terrorist measure for him to take on behalf of the country.

To achieve this understanding, the secretary argued that although the federal government was reasonably prepared to prevent bioweapon attacks against American cities, the government was not prepared to deal with the aftermath of a successful bioweapon attack — the fear, confusion and chaos that would follow; the collective and individual anger that would ensue; the widespread physical illnesses, deaths, and mass psychological depression that would occur; and, the general lawlessness that inevitably would result.

The reason the United States was so unprepared, the secretary had argued, was because the government continued to base its post-attack planning on inherently flawed models drawn from several government-sponsored, simulated terrorist attacks, such as the one called Dark Winter, held in various cities over the previous twenty years.

These staged simulations, the secretary contended, were inherently flawed because everyone involved, from the highest government official to the participating man and woman on the street, had merely been role playing so that there were no genuine adverse consequences suffered by anyone. In other words, no reality. That meant there was no way for the government planners to tell in advance how actual victims and actual first responders at ground zero might react after a genuine bioweapon assault, and no way to tell how survivors might make out in the weeks following an actual terrorists' attack.

The president resisted at first, but eventually accepted the secretary's arguments. He agreed to move forward with the experiment.

The secretary of defense designated Fort Lauderdale, Florida, as the target city. He named the secret project, OPERATION TESTING GROUND.

The secretary's first act — even before he assembled his small, elite team who would implement OPERATION TESTING GROUND — was to prepare a digital file of the proposed experiment and hide the file among his personal records stored on the Pentagon's encrypted trusted-network server. The digital file would be his insurance policy in case the president ever turned against him.

CHAPTER 4

Fort Lauderdale, Florida February 22

T HE YOUNG MAN SEEMED LIKE all the other young men hurrying along the sidewalk as they made their way from their jobs at the end of the work day. He dressed like them; he wore a wig that imitated their trendy hair styles; and he scurried like them, carrying a small backpack draped over one shoulder.

But he wasn't at all like them.

Dusk. The sky above Las Olas Boulevard eased from royal blue toward black as night cycled in and puffy white MGM-type clouds yielded to high, thin wispy night vapors. The air was redolent with the scent of salt water and decaying seaweed. Palm branches swayed high above the sidewalks like the undulating wings of an albatross as the ocean breeze swooped in from the east and soared over the city on its way to the Everglades.

The young man moved with ease along the sidewalk, walking east toward the Intracoastal Waterway and the Atlantic Ocean.

He was in Fort Lauderdale to perform an assignment for the federal government. Yet his name would not be found on any federal payroll record or on a Form 1099 at federal tax time. The young man worked off the books as a freelancer, as an independent contractor who occasionally executed critical assignments for his government. Today, the young man was in Fort Lauderdale to perform a brief job and then depart the city without leaving behind any identifiable footprints indicating he'd ever been there.

When he arrived at the overpass above the Intracoastal, the young man leaned back against the iron railing and looked around. Satisfied he had not been noticed, he reached into his shirt pocket and pulled out a softpack of Lucky Strike cigarettes. He bumped the bottom of the pack against the back of his hand, mouthed the tip of the cigarette that had partially jumped the pack, then fully extracted the smoke without ever touching it with his fingers. He fired up the cigarette and inhaled slowly and deeply, fully enjoying the warmth and comfort it offered him. After a few minutes, the young man field-stripped the cigarette, shred the paper wrapping, and flicked the rubble into the westerly breeze.

The young man reached over the iron railing and placed his backpack on the ground among the uncut saw grass, then nimbly vaulted the railing, landing on both feet.

He glanced around quickly, swooped up his backpack, then sidestepped down the steep grassy slope leading to the strip of sand and structural pilings below the overpass. Once he'd again assured himself he was alone, the young man stepped under the overpass and lost himself in its damp shadows.

The young man carefully set his backpack on the sand and cautiously put his hand into the canvas bag, feeling among its contents until he found the opaque, circular Petri dish he'd brought with him. He carefully placed the glass object on the moist sand and again reached into his backpack. This time he extracted a small electrical timing device which he attached to the Petri dish. He set the timer, placed the combined apparatus near a piling so it would not be noticed in the unlikely event someone happened by, and then he climbed back up the hill to the boulevard.

Ninety minutes later the young man was comfortably seated in Business Class at 37,000 feet above the Earth on his way home to Evansville, Indiana.

Forty-five minutes after the young man planted the device, it exploded with a pop and a hiss, its sound muffled by the sand, the overpass, and the nearby sea.

The detonation shattered the Petri dish, spewing up into the ocean's breeze millions of microscopic, aerosolized rod-shaped, gram negative pathogens that were encoded by nature to infest any moist lung tissue or any open skin abrasions they might encounter during their flight west from the Intracoastal Waterway through downtown Fort Lauderdale, on their way to the Everglades.

Two days after he delivered the Petri dish to Fort Lauderdale, the young man's charred body was found in the burned wreckage of his Indiana home. The coroner's verdict was that the young man had died from burns received in an explosion and consequent fire that occurred at his house, destroying the structure. The fire marshal ruled that the cause of the explosion was unknown, but suspicious, and would require more investigation.

CHAPTER 5

Fort Lauderdale
March 4

DEREK PETERSON READIED HIMSELF FOR the evening broadcast. He ran his palms along the sides of his head, smoothing back his hair, then wiped the perspiration from his forehead and neck as he waited for his cue from the Atlanta feed.

———✳———✳———✳———✳———✳———

"Good evening, Ladies and Gentlemen. This is Cindy Kramer in Atlanta. You are watching CNN's 11:00 p.m. broadcast of the evening news.

"Tonight we start with an evolving story from our affiliate WXFL in Fort Lauderdale, at the Broward County General Hospital. We go there live now to our own Derek Peterson who is outside the entrance to the hospital's emergency room. Hello, Derek."

"Good evening, Cindy."

Derek paused briefly, then said, "A spokesperson for the hospital has just told this reporter that the hospital's available human resources — its medical and nursing staffs, its ER personnel, and all its support staff — are strained to their limits by the extraordinary number of admissions here during the past week. The spokesperson also told this reporter that available medicine is quickly coming into short supply and will soon disappear altogether unless existing stocks are soon replenished." Derek quickly glanced at his cameraman, then looked back into the camera's lens, seemingly without having missed a beat.

"The cause of the problem, Cindy, is that people have been arriving at the ER with symptoms of a previously unknown strain of late-season flu that is spreading rapidly throughout the Fort Lauderdale metropolitan area."

He paused in response to an earbud signal he received from his producer, and remained silent for a few seconds until she again told him to proceed.

"Cindy," Derek said, "we've tried to speak with someone in authority at the Broward County Department of Health, but as of now no one has taken our calls or returned them. We will bring you up to date should we eventually make contact with the authorities."

He waited a beat, then said, "For now, this is Derek Peterson reporting live from Fort Lauderdale, Florida."

CHAPTER 6

Fort Lauderdale
March 5

"**M**ORNING," TRACE SAID, AS HE padded into the kitchen, still shrouded in the fog of sleep. He wore a sky blue T-shirt, baggy, beige cargo shorts and flip-flops.

Isabella looked up from the table where she was reading the morning paper. "Morning, Dear. Can I get you something to eat or some coffee?"

Trace leaned over and kissed her cheek. "Thanks. I'm good. I'll pour myself coffee. Want some?" he said, pointing at the coffee pot.

Isabella shook her head.

"Where's Pete?" Trace asked.

"On the patio. Probably listening to his music."

"And Nanna?"

"Getting dressed. I'm taking her shopping at the mall, then out to have her hair done."

Trace nodded as he sipped his coffee, all the while watching Isabella over the rim of his mug. Then he walked over and kissed her on the top of her head, took his *Maui Jim* sunglasses from the countertop where he'd left them the night before, and stepped out onto the patio.

Pete was fully stretched out on his back on a chaise lounge, facing away from the glass patio doors, his eyes closed. Apple earbuds plugged his ears at one end, and were jacked into his iPod NANO sitting on the table behind him, on their other end. Pete drummed his fingers on the arm of the chaise, repeating the rhythm of some sound unheard by Trace as he approached him from behind. A partially opened Reader's Digest-size magazine formed a tepee on Pete's bare, hairless chest.

"Good morning, Pete," Trace said.

No response.

Trace tried again, louder this time, as he walked to the front of the chaise, facing Pete.

"Hello, Pete."

Still nothing. Pete's eyes remained closed. His fingers continued their arrhythmic drumbeat.

Trace walked around behind him, picked up the iPod, and disconnected the earbuds' jack. He never took his eyes from his son.

"What the fu—? Whoops. Sorry, Dad. I didn't see you there," Pete said, as he bolted up into a sitting position and turned around to face the table behind him.

Trace held up the iPod in one hand and the disconnected earbuds' jack in his other hand.

"Very funny, Dad. I didn't hear you come out. I was listening to music . . . or trying to." He shook his head, rolled his eyes, then slumped back down onto the chaise.

Trace handed the iPod and jack to Pete, and bent over to

pick up the magazine that had rocketed from his chest when Pete had launched himself up into a sitting position. He looked at the cover of the magazine, frowned, and handed it to Pete.

"Mom's taking Nanna shopping," he said. "Want to go to the Intracoastal, have lunch with me by the water?"

"Absolutely," Pete said. He began gathering his scattered paraphernalia. "I'm ready whenever you are."

"What's that magazine?" Trace said, nodding at the magazine Pete now held.

"Nothing. It's called *2600*. It's a quarterly magazine for computer hackers. I look at it for fun."

Trace narrowed his eyes and glared. "You're hacking computers? When did this start?" He took a deep breath and counted to four to control his rising anger.

"It's nothing, Dad. Really. I just read the magazine because I'll need to know this stuff when I go to college. Anyway, I don't really hack. I just like reading about it."

That's pretty lame, Trace thought. As if I'd actually believe that. He frowned again, looked hard at Pete, but said nothing. He would let the silence stimulate Pete to respond.

"Really, Dad. You've got to believe me. I don't steal information or anything. I just test myself to see if I can beat security in different systems. Nothing bad."

Right, Trace thought. First, I just read about it, Dad. Then, I just break into systems to test myself, Dad, but don't steal anything. I just lurk. What's next? I'm a government-sanctioned teenaged white-hat hacker? Trace crossed his arms over his chest, remained inscrutably silent, and watched Pete squirm.

He slowly breathed in, again silently counting to four, then breathed out to the same count, just as he'd been taught in SEALs' training as a way to control stress.

"Okay, Pete," he finally said, his voice as neutral as he could make it, "let's get going. We'll continue this talk in the car on the way to lunch."

CHAPTER 7

Soviet Union

1982

VIKTOR RUTKOWSKA WAS SEVENTEEN YEARS old when the Soviet military plucked him from his job as an automobile mechanic in the city of Kirov and conscripted him into the army. He left behind his elderly, infirm father and his younger sister, Svetlana. His mother had died from malnutrition when Viktor was four years old.

Viktor entered his new life as a military recruit neither quietly nor passively. Instead, he resisted every aspect of Soviet military training. He groused about the food, the primitive conditions under which recruits were required to live, train and conform, and he complained about the ceaseless brutality of the instructors. As a result, Viktor created his own self-fulfilling prophecy and frequently incurred the wrath of those same instructors. This, in turn, led him to receive ritualized beatings and other corporal punishment.

Viktor quickly became the subject of his trainers' predictions that should he somehow survive basic training — an outcome his instructors considered extremely doubtful — Viktor could expect to be posted to some remote and dangerous region of

Afghanistan where the Mujahideen would demonstrate why the harsh Soviet military basic training had serious value. This possibility — this likelihood, in fact — invariably brought derisive smiles to the faces of Viktor's trainers and fellow inductees.

It seemed, at best, that the most Viktor could hope for during his stint in the army would be a miserable, danger-filled, brief life expectancy.

Except for one thing.

Viktor, it turned out, was a gifted shooter.

Viktor first became aware of this skill — for he had never before handled a weapon other than a short knife — when he participated in mandatory rifle and other firearms classes as part of basic training. Much to his surprise, Viktor consistently scored at the top of his unit.

Viktor's instructors were skeptical at first, finding it difficult to reconcile their deep-seated antipathy for the seemingly indolent and definite arrogant Viktor with their unavoidable recognition of his natural talent as a marksman.

Even Viktor was skeptical at first, doubting that his achievements were anything other than blind luck, which, he expected, would desert him sooner or later.

His instructors and fellow inductees also believed Viktor's recent success resulted from luck, and wagered among themselves, picking dates when Viktor's good luck would finally run out. After all, they asked themselves and each other, how can someone so recalcitrant perform so well so regularly and be so gifted in weaponry?

Yet Viktor's successful path as a marksman held because it was not founded on luck. Viktor's skill was a natural quality, one he had the good sense to yield to and cultivate in the face of everything else negative and brutal about his life circumstances.

Once he discovered his singular skill set, Viktor focused on his gift, and honed and developed his shooting skills. He also worked hard to learn about and excel in his survival, tracking, stalking, and camouflage classes. Before long, Viktor found himself being groomed to join an elite squad of shooters in one of the Soviet army's special Spetsnaz units.

Viktor adapted easily to his new Spetsnaz training. Not that it was difficult when compared with basic training. Although he still trained long hours — this time with a variety of specialized weapons — he now also had the best possible food, clean quarters, excellent medical care, and high pay.

The price of failure in this special training, however, as Viktor and his fellow-trainees were frequently reminded by their instructors — the cost of washing out of this special elite grooming — could be disastrous. Failure here, even if Viktor were to survive his failing ways during training, would mean certain posting to some remote and dangerous region of Afghanistan, some place from which few Soviet soldiers ever returned.

When Viktor's former comrades and basic training instructors learned of his new posting with the Spetsnaz unit, they were certain Viktor would not succeed at this new assignment.

"He doesn't have the self-discipline," one said.

"Rutkowska will wash out in no time," another said.

"Before he knows what hit him, he'll be sitting in some shit hole in Afghanistan hoping to die."

"It doesn't matter, Comrades," said another. "If he washes out, he's screwed. If he doesn't wash out, he's screwed. The life expectancy of a shooter in Afghanistan is four months." Everyone laughed and toasted Viktor's new short life, raising their imaginary glasses, filled with imaginary vodka, in honor of Viktor's certain early demise.

But what Viktor's former comrades and instructors did not know was that Viktor was nobody's fool. When he transferred to Spetsnaz training he left behind his negative attitude and he accepted the reality of power. He yielded to the unbending will of his new trainers, to his new unforgiving regimen, and focused on becoming the best shooter in his group. Better a four month life expectancy as a sniper, he reasoned, than certain death as a common, miserable field grunt planted in some indefensible outpost in Afghanistan.

CHAPTER 8

Fort Lauderdale
March 5

EREK PETERSON ADJUSTED HIS SHIRT collar, faced the CNN camera, and waited for his producer's signal to indicate that the feed from Atlanta had been thrown to him.

When the signal came, Derek began by summarizing the information available about the current late-season flu epidemic. Then he spent one minute trying to allay the fears he'd likely stirred up, based on what he'd just reported to his viewers.

Derek concluded his broadcast by saying, ". . . and finally for this afternoon's broadcast, today the Broward County Health Department has asked this reporter to request that each of you remain aware of the tremendous strain the flu epidemic is placing on the county's healthcare resources.

"You are requested not to go to a hospital emergency room unless you have a true, life threatening emergency that cannot be dealt with by your private physician. The county's ERs are so over-taxed by people showing up with minor ailments — and the ERs are now so understaffed — that unless something changes soon and changes drastically, the county might be forced to close all the ERs and deny access to everyone. You can do your part to help forestall this," Derek said, "by avoiding the ER unless you absolutely must go there."

He paused, then said, "This is Derek Peterson for CNN coming to you live from Fort Lauderdale. Goodbye until my next broadcast at the same time."

CHAPTER 9

Atlanta, Georgia
1981

E LEVEN-YEAR-OLD ANTHONY VISTA SAT CROSS-LEGGED on the living room floor smiling up at his parents and fondling the package his mother had just handed him.

His mother and father sat on the sofa watching him, occasionally eyeing one another, and sporadically leaking restrained smiles.

Anthony held the box above his head. He rotated it slowly and stared at it as if he could determine its contents if he just looked hard enough.

He beamed, then returned his concentration back to the box. He held it alongside his ear and gently shook it.

"Come on, Boy," his father said. "Open it already." He looked over at Anthony's mother.

"Poppa is right, Son. Do it. We're excited, too."

Anthony carefully untied the ribbon and peeled away the wrapping paper, folding it into reusable squares before handing it to his mother.

He lifted the box's lid less than an inch and peeked inside as if he expected a gag toy to spring out and fly past his ear.

Then he yanked off the lid and plunged his hands deep into the cloud of white tissue paper, exploding the halves away from each other as he fanned out his palms.

"It's beautiful, Mom," he said, "absolutely beautiful." He looked up at his parents with a broad smile.

"You like it then, Anthony?" his mother said. "You're not disappointed?"

"Like it? Are you kidding? I love it. It's incredible."

Anthony lifted the sweater from the box and held it up, gripping the shoulders, showing it off to his parents as if they'd never seen it before.

"It's fantastic. It must've cost a fortune. Can I try it on?"

Without waiting for an answer, Anthony tunneled his arms up into the sleeves and pulled the sweater over his head and down to his waist. He ran his palms across his chest and stomach, smoothing the yarn.

"You look so handsome, Anthony," his mother said. "It's a blessing, this beautiful sweater for your birthday."

Anthony wore the sweater all through supper, careful not to splash food on it. He continued to wear it into the evening, interrupting his homework several times to leave the kitchen table and go look at himself in the bathroom's cracked mirror. When he got himself ready for bed, he lifted the sweater over his head, careful not to stretch or snag it, and folded it just like the sweaters he'd seen displayed on shelves at Wal-Mart. He placed the sweater on top of his dresser where he could see it from bed.

Anthony happily fell asleep that night as he anticipated wearing his birthday-sweater to school the next day.

The next morning Anthony held his shoulders back and kept his head and eyes up as he strutted between classes. It was all he could do to keep from laughing. He moved briskly along the middle of the corridor, not warily shuffling along as he usually did, not hugging the row of lockers lining one wall, as on other days.

As the morning slipped away and headed toward afternoon recess, he was aware that his schoolmates had noticed his sweater and that they sensed his recently-acquired pleasure and pride. He knew this because today, unlike all other days, his classmates did not ignore him, did not treat him as if he were invisible.

He could hardly wait to get home after school and tell his parents.

Several boys had smiled at him, he would say to his mother and father, or at least they had giggled when he walked by and caught them looking at him. At lunch in the cafeteria, he would report, two boys seemed to so enjoy his new-found pleasure that they laughed hard when they looked over at him and then back at each other. He would tell his parents that he even nodded at some boys today, acknowledging their attention, proud to finally be recognized and approved of by his classmates.

His father would drape his arm around his shoulder and say, "Good boy, Anthony. I'm proud of you."

His mother would softly cry.

Then Anthony finished daydreaming and went to recess.

In spite of his special treatment today, Anthony instinctively reverted to his usual practice during recess and warily lurked alone in the broad shadow of the school near the perimeter hurricane fence. He could not bring himself to take a chance on being turned away if he tried to join the games. Not today. Not when he finally had his classmates' newly-offered approval. He would not risk destroying today's magic.

"Do you believe that fool, Vista," one boy, who passed nearby Anthony, said to another to another boy. "Did you see him prancing around and wearing that crappy sweater Kenny's mother gave to Goodwill instead of throwing it away? What a dork."

Anthony fell back against the fence. Tears stung his eyes.

He yanked the sweater up over his head, not caring now if he stretched or snagged it. He crumbled the sweater into a ball and threw it to the ground at his feet, then kicked the balled-up sweater against the fence.

Anthony walked away from recess, away from school, and left his birthday sweater on the playground, over by the fence, the sweater now abandoned by him.

Two days later, very late in the night, after his parents were asleep, Anthony returned to the playground and retrieved the sweater. He carefully stuffed it under his shirt, close to his chest. When he arrived home, he hid the sweater in his closet.

He never told his parents why he'd stopped wearing his birthday sweater. When they asked, he said, "No reason. I just did," and let it go at that.

For now.

CHAPTER 10

Fort Lauderdale
March 5

P ETE BELTED HIMSELF INTO THE front seat of the car.
"Listen, Dad, you have to believe me. What I do when I hack
doesn't hurt anybody. It really doesn't. There's even a name
for it. Ethical hacking. You break into networks, find security
holes, then point the flaws out to the system administrators so
they can plug them before the bad guys find them and get in.
Everybody does it."

"Everybody? Have you ever pointed out a security flaw to
an administrator?"

"Not yet, I'm not that advanced, but I will be someday.
Technically, I'm not yet a white hat hacker because I haven't
been a black hat hacker. I'm just lurking in the networks.
There's nothing wrong with what I'm doing."

"Yes there is, Pete. Just doing it is wrong. Legally and
morally. And now that I know you're doing it, I'll worry you'll
get caught. You could spend years in federal prison."

Trace paused a beat to decide how hard he wanted to come
down on Pete this first time around on this subject. He decided

to be blunt, but not rough. "I want you to stop hacking, right away, not sometime later. Stop today. Promise me."

"I won't get caught, Dad. I'm careful. Don't worry."

"If you keep it up you will be caught. It's just a matter of when, Pete, not if. Besides, you're knowingly breaking the law. That's not the way your mother and I've raised you. He paused, waiting for a reaction from Pete that didn't come.

"I wasn't making a suggestion about stopping or giving you an option. I expect you to stop."

"Come on, Dad, will you? Just lighten up."

Lighten up? I hate that expression, Trace thought. "No, Pete, I won't lighten up. Not about this. This isn't a game. I expect you to stop hacking, and I want you to promise me you will."

Pete scowled. "You don't understand hacking at all, Dad. It's not what you think."

Trace swallowed his laughter and suppressed his smile. "I understand it better than you know."

Pete glared at Trace. "What's that supposed to mean?"

"It means when I transferred from the SEALs to the regular Navy, the Service sent me back to college for one year to obtain a master's degree. I took mine in computer science."

"I already know that."

"What you don't know is that my job, when I returned to active duty after I finished the year in school, was to hack in to computer networks operated by our country's enemies."

"You're serious?" Pete said.

"I'm serious. I hacked for the Navy."

"I'm impressed, Dad."

"Don't be. It was my job in the military. I was doing it

to protect our country. I was sanctioned to hack by the government. Doing it that way was not a crime."

"Do you still remember how to do it?"

"Frankly, Pete, I doubt there's anything you can do with a computer I haven't already done," Trace said. "All I'd need now to hack would be to come up to date on current tools to use. The concepts would be the same now as then."

Pete shook his head, stared at Trace, but said nothing. He seemed to shrink into the corner between his seat and the car's door. He narrowed his eyes.

"So now that we know you're being hypocritical in making me stop hacking, can we change the subject?" Pete said.

"We can for now," Trace said, "but that won't change anything we just talked about. And I'm not being hypocritical. I explained why I hacked. That situation was different from what you're doing." Trace paused, then added, "As I said, I expect you to stop hacking and not to do it again. Understand?."

"In that case I want to say something else about it," Pete said.

Trace nodded. "Go on." He slowed the car's speed.

"First off," Pete said, "I won't get caught so you can stop worrying about me. Second, I don't do it very often. And when I do, I use an anonymous proxy server to disguise my ID. I assume you know what that is. They probably even had those years ago when you were hacking in the Navy. My hacks can't be traced back to me."

Trace briefly glanced over at Pete and shook his head. I probably should cut this off now so I can concentrate on driving, he thought.

"That's not the point. Pete. Or, rather, it's only one of the points. I'll say it again. It's wrong to hack. Period. It's against the law, and the penalties are severe when you're caught. Not only that, hacking also is an invasion of privacy."

Trace paused again, then said, "This is the last time I'll say this. I expect you to stop. Today. As of right now. This isn't up for debate."

"Come on, Dad. That's just the tech lawyer in you talking. Just you being Mr. Lawyer. Always so law-abiding and proper. I won't be caught. Believe me."

"Pete . . . ."

"Oh, all right. You made your point." Pete rolled his eyes and looked over at his father. Then he turned back to the door and stared out the window.

"We'll talk about this again later," Trace said. "We're not done with this."

CHAPTER 11

Odessa, Soviet Union
1982

NOTWITHSTANDING VIKTOR RUTKOWSKA'S FRESHLY ACQUIRED positive attitude and his formidable desire to succeed at his new posting, sniper school proved to be so unremittingly demanding and so psychologically isolating that the program would have broken him had he not loved the coupling of skilled shooting with the sniper's survival skills he learned in his training.

The first thing the instruction addressed, even before the trainees received their weapons' instruction, was the shooters' attitudes. They were taught, in sundry ways, not to think of the past and not to think of the future. For a shooter, the instructors drilled into them, there was only the present.

As the shooters' classes proceeded, Viktor quickly became infatuated with the variety of weapons he learned to use, with the endurance skills he acquired, with the competition among himself and his fellow trainees, and with the virtual competition fostered among the trainees and their simulated enemy targets.

Sniper training was rigorous, dangerous, and unforgiving. Mistakes were not merely embarrassing, they often were cause for dismissal from the program, with only occasional second acts allowed. If you survived your mistake, if you were permitted a second chance and did not take a bullet during one of the live shooting exercises you were forced to engage in as punishment, you then might barely make it through the dressing-down you would receive from your instructors. There was no room in the shooter business for errors.

Sniper school was not just about hiding in a tree and locating and taking out a target. It also taught the trainees to move as a group and to confront the enemy as a single unit, with the stealth of a lone sniper, and with the highly choreographed skills of a trained shooter performing as part of a precision, lethal team. This was why the instructors, unlike the trainees, never referred to the recruits as snipers. That designation was too limiting, reflecting merely one of the functions each of the team members would be called upon from time-to-time to perform. Instead, the instructors referred to their trainees as shooters, as a precision team of assassins, the members of which occasionally would fulfill the role of snipers.

As shooters, Viktor and his group first were taught to approach an enemy as a single, cohesive unit, with every member of the team acting as one living organism. They would approach the enemy calmly, moving in one direction, three men covering, the others running, then switch roles. They practiced this maneuver until it was second nature, drilling in mock engagements that were brief, but highly risky.

Viktor and his comrades were taught to live and think as if they always were in a war zone, to never permit their guard to lapse, to sense their environment just as four-legged predators stalking their prey might sense it, and to be wary of and responsive to every sound reaching their ears. In time, those who survived the training would be able to determine the type of weapon an adversary had used, and, in some cases, determine the adversary's location just by hearing the sound of his weapon firing or the sound of the fired round passing by when it missed its target.

The Spetsnaz instructors constantly reminded the trainees that they were special, were the elite, were the most dangerous men in the entire Soviet military apparatus because they were expert marksman who were able to act, move, stalk, and hide with supreme patience. They were the consummate assassins, having received elite Spetsnaz training, having resources others in the military could only dream of if they were even capable of imagining such treasures.

"You will be," the instructors had said, "the most deadly and elite killers in the world, members of that small, honored fraternity who wear the small Spetsnaz tattoo under their arms, the tattoo showing your blood type in Cyrillic."

Once the instructors had weeded out those recruits who did not have the required attitude (since everyone who entered the program had the necessary natural, if yet unformed, shooting skills) and were satisfied that the remaining trainees had achieved the necessary robotic state of mind, the training turned to advanced weaponry.

A shooter's weapons were his lifeblood. Before going on a training mission, Viktor and his comrades would check their weapons, prepare their backpacks, adjust their body armor, and load their firearms, with each man carrying six long magazines, four or five hand grenades, and an automatic pistol.

A Spetsnaz shooter never carried his pistol in his belt, as often was the practice among others in the Soviet military. Instead, a Spetsnaz shooter would put his pistol in a holster which he securely taped to his thigh so he would be free to move around without making noise. Before a mission it was the practice for each man to jump up and down in place to see if anything, including his pistol and ammunition, made any sound that might give his presence and location away.

When the men stalked an enemy as a team, each man carried a Kalashnikov assault rifle as his primary weapon. But when they went off on missions as snipers, with only a single spotter to accompany them, each man carried, instead, a classic, precision Dragunov rifle with its long barrel modified to suppress both sound and muzzle flash.

Each sniper used modified ammunition that contained less gunpowder than was typical for the Army's issued rounds. This assured that the bullets would travel at less than the speed of sound and, in the unlikely event the sniper missed his shot, assured that he would not, by reason of the sound of his bullet, alert the missed target that he had become the sniper's prey and also would not disclose the sniper's location.

The weapons were modified, too, to be as silent as possible

when the shooter moved. All the metal on the sling was removed and replaced with leather strips. The grip and stock were wrapped in black electrical tape.

After his Spetsnaz training, Viktor survived Afghanistan. He left that posting in 1989, two months before the end of Russia's invasion, with eighty-seven confirmed kills as a sniper and untold hundreds of kills as a shooter working with his team. Viktor had out-performed the life expectancy of a sniper in Afghanistan by more than seven years. After a short respite in which he returned to Mother Russia to teach as an instructor of Spetsnaz shooters, Viktor was transferred to Chechnya to engage in the first Russian/Chechen War.

CHAPTER 12

Steubenville, Ohio
1981

I N THE WEEKS AFTER THE incident with his birthday sweater, Anthony nurtured his anger and encouraged it to grow by reminding himself of past slights. Late at night, as he lay awake in bed, Anthony drew upon his vast storehouse of accumulated grievances he held against his schoolmates, and dwelled on those he considered the most egregious. Eventually, he focused his ire on Kenny and Kenny's mother, and contemplated punishments for them.

Anthony believed, as an act of elemental faith, that Kenny had deliberately humiliated him in front of their classmates by disclosing the Goodwill store source of his sweater. He believed, too, that Kenny's mother was complicit in his disappointment and humiliation since she set these events in motion by donating the sweater to Goodwill.

He would teach them to mess with him.

One evening, five weeks after his eleventh birthday, Anthony slipped away from home at approximately 3:15 a.m. He was wearing his birthday sweater.

He walked to Kenny's house, keeping close to the houses along the way to avoid being seen by anyone, even at this dead-of-night hour.

He walked quickly. His heart raced with anticipation as he neared Kenny's house.

As he walked, Anthony patted his pocket and felt the clump made by the two pieces of clothesline he'd cut into ten-inch lengths. He put his hand into his other pocket and gripped the black, laminate Cub Scout penknife his mother had purchased for him at a yard sale when he was eight years old, his mother hoping by this second-hand purchase to lessen Anthony's disappointment because she could not afford to buy him a Cub Scout uniform or to pay the monthly dues required for him to be a scout. Anthony had not been assuaged, but he did love his penknife anyway, even all these years later.

He arrived at the house next door to Kenny's and looked up and down the street. The houses all were dark, the street empty.

He crouched-jogged over to Kenny's front porch, opened the storm door about ten inches, and waited. No lights flashed on to interrupt his mission.

He tied one end of the rope around the inner handle of the storm door and pulled the knot as tight as he could make it. Then he slipped the untied end of the rope through the handle of the inner front door. He pulled the rope taut, again snaked it through the storm door's inner handle, and tied this loose end into a knot around the first knot. He squeezed his hand out from between the tethered doors.

He tested his handiwork.

Anthony tried to open the storm door, but could not pull it out more than a few inches. It held firmly in place, secured by the rope and the closed, tethered inner front door. He knew that Kenny, or someone in Kenny's family, would experience the flip side of this barrier when they hurriedly tried to open the front door from inside the house.

He walked around to the back of the house and repeated this process with the back door and its outer storm door. He assumed there also was an exit door from the house into the attached garage, but decided he'd leave that alone. He had no desire to be arrested for breaking and entering into the garage if he was caught. Besides, with only one more step to perform in this initial family-revenge scenario, Anthony knew Kenny and his family would experience frustration, anger, and, hopefully, fear long before they eventually thought to use the garage exit.

Anthony walked across the street to the bushes and retrieved two rocks he'd previously hidden there. He put on cotton gloves he'd brought with him, and wiped each rock to remove his fingerprints. Then he returned to the edge of the lawn in front of Kenny's house.

He looked up and down the street to make sure he still was alone. Satisfied, he pitched a rock through the dining room plate glass window at Kenny's house. As the glass shattered, he fast-balled the second rock through the living room plate glass window. Then he sprinted back across the street to hide behind the bushes so he could watch the chaos he'd set in motion.

A light flashed on behind a second floor window. Anthony saw Kenny's father leaning against the window sill and looking out. Then lights went on in the living room and dining room. Someone yanked the inner front door open, but it stopped abruptly two inches into its arc. Someone again pulled the door, but it wouldn't budge any further.

Keep it up, Anthony thought, you're only tightening the knot.

The person slammed the inner front door closed. Anthony assumed the same exercise would occur at the back door.

He walked home, satisfied.

For now.

Fifteen days later Anthony completed the next step in his youthful vengeance scenario. This time, although he could not be present to observe Kenny's reaction, he savored the image his recently conceived retribution conjured up for him.

Anthony locked his books in his school hallway locker, only three lockers away from Kenny's, and went to his home room.

Soon after, Kenny hurried from his English class to his locker to drop off his books and grab his gym bag. He routinely did this on Tuesdays when he had 2:00 p.m. Phys Ed.

Kenny put his books under his left arm, supporting them against his hip with pressure from his forearm and elbow, and mindlessly turned the knob of the combination lock securing the locker's door. He slid the latch up, releasing and opening the metal door.

He pushed his books onto the crowded top shelf just above his eye level. Then he reached down and grabbed the handles of his gym bag.

He yanked the bag from the locker and glanced inside as he used his foot to push the locker door closed.

That was when Kenny screamed.

He dropped the bag and screamed again, louder this time.

He pointed at the bag lying on its side on the floor as he back-peddled away. His mouth, now silent, was fully opened in a mimed shriek.

The students who gathered around Kenny laughed at

first, then quieted down as teachers showed up, coming from nearby classrooms.

One teacher, the shop instructor, walked over to the bag to see why Kenny pointed at it. He knelt down and turned the bag over so it now was sitting with its top facing up and open.

The shop teacher retched a dry heave and jumped away.

"Jesus," he said. "Fuck's going on—"

He spun toward Kenny and barreled through the small crowd of curious students, quick-stepping over to him.

"You better have a good explanation for this, Mister," he said to Kenny. "You're in serious trouble."

The shop teacher turned back toward the gym bag just in time to see the school's nurse poking it with the pointed toe of her shoe. She bent over and picked up the bag, cradling it with one arm as she reached into its dark interior.

She suddenly dropped the bag and abruptly plugged the knuckles of one hand into her mouth. Then she turned and hurried away, almost running down the hall.

The dropped bag hit the floor with a thud and rolled over, spilling its contents — the gutted, bloody carcass of a large, gray water rat.

CHAPTER 13

Fort Lauderdale
March 5

T RACE WAS DETERMINED NOT TO let his earlier conversations with Pete spoil their lunch.

During his time as a SEAL, Trace had learned to compartmentalize everything. When he left the SEALs, he carried this trait with him.

Time to compartmentalize, he thought, *to put aside for now my talks with Pete about hacking.*

Trace tipped back his chair, put his feet on the middle iron rail of the fence separating the restaurant from the Intracoastal Waterway, and pulled down the beak of his ball cap, blocking the sun from his eyes. He bit into his crab cake sandwich and washed it down with a mouthful of Bell's ale.

"This is the life," he said, holding his bottle up to Pete in a mock toast.

"It's great, Dad. I could get used to this."

They sat side-by-side facing the Intracoastal, watching yachts motor by not more than twenty feet away from them.

"Do you miss the SEALs?" Pete asked. "I mean, when you're around water like this?"

Where did that come from? This is something I do not want to talk about, Trace thought.

"I always miss the SEALs," Trace answered. "Being a SEAL was a way of life, a mindset, not just a military job you learned to do. You don't let it go easily, if ever." He paused, looked curiously at Pete, then said, "If you're lucky, the friendships you make, the principles you learn, and the trust you place in others, in your team, stay with you all your life."

"I'm curious about something," Pete said. He sat up straight and turned toward his father.

"I once heard Nanna and mom talking when they didn't know I was nearby. Nanna said you quit the SEALs because you let one of your buddies die after a chopper crash. Was that true?"

Trace paused. He wasn't happy this had come up. He'd hoped Pete would never learn about this, or, at least not learn about it until after he'd served in the military himself so he would have some perspective on what had happened.

"I didn't let him die. I couldn't save him," Trace said. "There's a difference." He paused to organize his thoughts. We can talk about it another time."

He looked to see if this satisfied Pete. When Pete said nothing more, Trace said, "Anyway, to go back to your earlier question, sometimes I do miss the SEALs, the camaraderie, the teamwork, and especially the risk, but that was then. This is now. Life moves on."

"So you're not sorry you're not a SEAL anymore?" Pete said. He wouldn't let go of the bone.

"I like my life now just fine," Trace said. "Being a SEAL is a young man's game. Even if I had stayed in, it couldn't have been for more than a few additional years, then I would have been an ex-SEAL any way you look at it."

"Is that when you married mom?"

"Almost. Not quite then. As I said before, after the SEALs, I transferred to the regular Navy and talked them into sending me back to school for one year to get a master's degree. Then, afterward, I met and married your mom."

"How come I didn't know before today your master's degree was in IT?"

"It never came up. It's not a secret. As I said, I used it in the Navy. Now I use it in my technology-based law practice."

"It's ironic, isn't it, Dad, given what we talked about in the car?"

"It's not ironic at all, Pete. It's as I said. The Navy trained me to hack into networks operated by our country's enemies. So when I told you I know what you're up to, I do know. I'm just out-of-date on current tools to use, is all."

Pete shook his head. "Guess then I don't have a chance with this issue, do I?"

"Not if I can help it," Trace said, as he reached over and messed Pete's hair.

CHAPTER 14

Fort Lauderdale
March 5

JANET FULLER LEANED HER HEAD against the top cushion of the rocking chair and pressed her weight back until the rocker reached the apex of its arc. Then she relaxed her pressure and allowed gravity to pull her smoothly forward. She placed one hand on her growing belly, just below her waist, anticipating the occasional light kick from her developing baby.

She stretched out her left leg, lifted it slightly, and looked at her calf.

Those scabs are ugly, she thought. I need to be more careful when I shave my legs.

She put that negative thought out of her mind and thought instead about the baby growing inside her. She patted her stomach and glowed at the touch.

She rocked herself for another twenty minutes, smoothly and slowly, as she hummed a lullaby, her palm flat on her stomach, monitoring the activity within, when suddenly her smile slipped away from her.

Janet blinked back tears and frowned.

Something strange, something menacing was happening to

her. The feeling was subtle, but unmistakable. She could sense its foreboding.

The first describable symptom she noticed was a tingling in her tongue. It felt as if her tongue was waking up, like an arm or leg sometimes did, and was now regaining blood flow after having fallen asleep.

Soon this strange sensation ended, only to be replaced by her lips becoming numb. Janet touched her lips with her finger, then intentionally bit her lower lip. She could not feel her fingers against her lip as she touched it. She did not feel pain as she bit down and drew blood.

She pushed herself up and out of the rocking chair, crossed the bedroom floor, and waddled over to the mirror hanging on the wall above the dresser. She opened her mouth to look at her tongue. It seemed to be a little off-color, a shade of pale blue, but she wasn't sure. Her lips seemed to be thicker, too, puffier than normal. A little swollen, she thought.

"Well," she said aloud to the empty room, "pregnancy does strange things to your body. Everybody knows that."

She turned to go to the kitchen to retrieve her cell phone from the battery charger. She would call her doctor to report her odd symptoms. She'd go see him today if he would permit her to do so.

As she took her first steps toward the kitchen, she realized her neck and throat had closed, had become tight and constricted, almost numb. She tried to swallow saliva to lubricate and open her throat, but she could not swallow at all.

She breathed rapidly now through her nose, taking quick, shallow allotments of air in her panic. Her heart pounded. Her throat continued to close and tighten.

She tried to hurry to the kitchen to retrieve her cell phone, but her legs had become wooden and would not obey her, although her frightened consciousness told her appendages to run. She became dizzy, lost her balance, and dropped to her knees, slamming them onto the hardwood floor. She cried out in pain as she rolled over onto her side. She fought back the urge to vomit.

Janet laboriously pulled herself up onto her knees, keeping both palms flat on the floor, her arms extended and stiff. She rushed short breaths through her mouth as if she had just finished sprinting a 440-meter race, but without the relief that quickly comes afterward to the conditioned runner.

The floor beneath Janet became slippery from tears and sweat.

She tried to stand again, but she was unable to rise up because, as she suddenly realized, she not only was unable to breathe normally, she now was dizzy, off-balance, unusually fatigued, and generally helpless.

She began to sob.

Janet stiffened arms suddenly gave way and she collapsed back to the floor, breaking her fall, first with her chin, then with her chest. She sprawled out on her stomach, lying still, eyes wide open, her arms and legs splayed akimbo.

Her brain was fully functional so she was aware of her situation even as her body refused her attempts to command it. She wallowed helplessly on the floor and stared at the back of her right hand, just inches from her face. A thick, yellow-green substance oozed from the moist scab on her hand, leaking from the abrasion caused when her neighbor's cat had scratched her the week before.

The last thing Janet ever saw was the oozing lesion on the back of her hand.

CHAPTER 15

Fort Dix, NJ
March 5 The present

BRIGADIER GENERAL ANTHONY VISTA PLACED his suitcase on the bed and filled it with underwear, T-shirts, socks, and various travel accessories. He packed everything he'd need with him for the long drive to his new posting in Fort Lauderdale. Everything else he had on station would be shipped to him.

Anthony thought about the years he had spent as the mayor of Margate City, New Jersey, after he had retired from active military service. Those were good years, he thought, but too confining. Running a small resort city had been a challenge at first, until he figured out the existing system and then caused the various parts of government to work together. Having achieved that, now he was bored with being a small-town mayor. This assignment probably would be good for him, whatever it involved.

That said, Anthony admitted to himself in a rare moment of candor that he had mixed feelings about being activated with his Army reserve unit, although he'd always known this was a possibility. These ambivalent feelings arose, he also admitted to himself, from his continued bitterness about the way the Army had mistreated him when he had tried to become a Green Beret. That, he thought, wasn't a good time in my life.

Back then, Anthony's military career, in the heady days after community college ROTC, had moved along the right path leading to rapid promotion. He had been physically fit, highly intelligent, very motivated, a creditable leader, and was sufficiently full of himself to suit the Army's image of its upper-command officers.

After his promotion to lieutenant, Anthony applied to join the Army's Special Forces. He'd met all the physical and intelligence requirements. Because he was a college graduate, Anthony automatically fulfilled the education requirements of the program. Beyond that, he spoke, read and wrote two Romance languages — French and Italian — and was studying both the Mandarin and Pinyin Romanization language systems of Chinese. He told the program's administrative officer he was willing to learn Farsi and other Middle Eastern languages if doing so would aid the Special Forces. He assumed his offer would help assure his entry into the program.

Anthony had relished the thought of becoming a member of the coveted Green Berets. Fortunately, his future as a member of this elite group looked certain and promising until, several weeks into the final Assessment and Selection Course at Camp Mackall, North Carolina, Anthony received an order to report to the commanding colonel's office.

This cannot be good news, he thought, but he couldn't think of anything he'd done wrong.

His stomach knotted as he knocked on the colonel's door.

"But, Sir, I don't understand," he said. "I have all the qualifications. I'm at the top of my class in every category. You know that."

"Not in every category, Lieutenant Vista. Anyway, it doesn't matter. The decision's final. I have no say about it. You don't either."

Anthony's eyes clouded with fury. He couldn't believe they were doing this to him, washing him out, not after all his hard work, his excellent record.

Somebody must have lied about me, he thought. That's the only reason this is happening. It had to be someone who knew he wouldn't make it into the top fifteen cutoff group unless my place above him in the class standings became available.

"I know, Lieutenant," the colonel said, "you have most of the qualifications required, but you also have some problems. Some serious ones." He paused to assess Anthony's state of mind.

"Don't take this personally, Lieutenant. It's for the good of the Service and the Special Forces," the colonel said, his obsequious tone masking his contempt for Anthony.

"But, Sir—"

The colonel cut him off, making it clear by the shake of his head he did not want to hear anything more from Anthony.

"If you handle this right, do your job well, and don't make waves, your career will stay on track. It's up to you, Soldier."

"Sir, with the Colonel's permission, I've dreamed my whole adult life of being a Green Beret. I don't understand"

The colonel turned away and stared out the window.

Anthony continued. "Colonel, I know somebody in my class caused this. If you'll just give me a chance to find out who, I'll—"

The colonel turned back, away from the window, and faced Anthony. His frown sliced through the barrier now separating them.

"Lieutenant Vista, you need to pay attention here. Listen up now." He paused long enough to be sure he had control of the silence. "You need to let it go. Take my advice and either move on or take the hit to your career."

"But, Sir, I—"

"Hear me out, Soldier. I'm trying to make this easier for you. You're in a hole. Stop digging for Christ's sake."

"Sir, I appreciate what you're saying. Believe me, I do. But this wouldn't just happen. Somebody in the program did this to me so they wouldn't be cut in the last round. I think I know who—"

"Enough." The colonel raised his palm to Vista. "Don't say another word. Do you understand me, Lieutenant? Not another word."

The colonel walked over to his desk and spoke into the intercom: "Sergeant, come in here."

Vista and the colonel silently watched one another until the sergeant entered the room and took his place as a witness. Then the colonel turned back to Anthony.

"These are very delicate and difficult matters, Lieutenant Vista. Unfortunately, choices have to be made, even among well-qualified, good men, such as yourself," he said, now making his voice soft in an effort to mask his contempt.

"Your program evaluators concluded you don't meet the requisite profile the Army requires of a Green Beret. Sorry to have to say this to you, Soldier, but that's the way it is."

"With the Colonel's permission to speak, Sir, I don't understand how I don't meet the profile."

"Lieutenant Vista, permission denied. End of discussion. Do you understand me? It's over for you. We're done here."

"But, Sir . . . ." Anthony stiffened. His lower back ached. "Please, Sir. I need to know." He lowered his head. "Please."

The colonel paused, walked around behind his desk, then, still standing and glaring at Vista, said, "All right, Lieutenant, suit yourself. Since you insist, I'll tell you." He looked over at the sergeant to make sure he was paying attention.

"Your evaluators concluded you're not a team player, that's why. You don't have any friends in the unit. Not one."

He paused a beat. "You eat alone, take leave alone, do everything alone. You've made yourself an exile in your own squad."

He paused to let this sink in.

"That won't do for the Special Forces, Lieutenant. We depend on each other. Our lives depend on mutual trust and mutual reliability. Team work." He slowly shook his head.

"How could anyone in your unit feel he could trust you with his life and depend on you to have his back when you don't even talk to anyone in your class?" He pulled the chair out from behind his desk and sat down.

"My advice to you, Lieutenant Vista, is this: Go back to your regular unit. Continue what you were doing before, except also start mingling now. Socialize. Make friends with the men in your unit.

"Keep your nose clean and don't make waves. You're still on the right track for command. Put this Special Forces blip behind you. One day you'll forget all about it."

Anthony dug his fingernails into his palms until his hands stung. His neck turned crimson, but all he said was, "Yes, Sir. Thank you, Sir."

Then he saluted, smartly turned, and left the colonel's office.

CHAPTER 16

Fort Lauderdale March 5

D EREK PETERSON LOOKED INTO THE camera and said, ".
. . the medical situation continues to deteriorate here in
Fort Lauderdale. Doctors have run out of supplies and
have stopped going to their offices. Area hospitals are without
empty beds so they are turning away patients. ERs and clinics
are without medicine, so they are closing.

"The Centers for Disease Control and Prevention reported
this morning that since last Friday eleven more children and
sixteen adults in Fort Lauderdale have been reported as coming
down with the mysterious late-season flu.

"But there is a glimmer of good news. A well-placed source
in the county government told this reporter that the CDC
will soon deliver medicine to Fort Lauderdale. Although we
are told this medication will not cure the disease afflicting our
city, or even prevent people from catching it, the medicine will
alleviate the symptoms for those people who suffer from the
mysterious late-season flu.

"My source assures me, too, that some hospital emergency
rooms, some clinics, and many pharmacies will then reopen.
In the meantime, however, you must remember. Do not go

to hospital emergency rooms unless it is absolutely necessary. For now, for most cases of the illness and otherwise, ERs are officially off limits."

Derek paused and looked briefly at his clipboard. "I have one note of warning to show you how serious the medical situation in Broward County has become." He glanced again at his notes, then looked back to the camera.

"The authorities report that in the past nine days there have been thirty-one reported break-ins at hospital ERs and pharmacies, likely to steal medicines or regulated substances.

"The governor has stated that this lawlessness will not be tolerated and, if necessary, he will call up the state's national guard to protect hospitals and their ERs from unauthorized intrusions."

Derek paused to wipe his forehead with a red paisley handkerchief. "This is Derek Peterson for CNN, signing off for today."

CHAPTER 17

1996/1999

A FTER VIKTOR COMPLETED HIS TOUR of duty in Chechnya in the first Russian-Chechen war, and had returned to Russia as an instructor teaching new recruits to perform as shooters, he found, much to his surprise, that his non-combat time caused him to become philosophical. It was during this lull in his military career, between combat assignments that Viktor, contemplating why he'd shown so little fear, as opposed to much restlessness, during the earlier Afghan and recent Chechnya campaigns, realized that the most frightening times for him during the two wars had been when he was resting and had become aware of all the horrors of the situation he'd previously found himself in. Viktor clearly needed combat and the risk of death or mutilation to maintain his equilibrium. A peacetime-like environment was corrosive for him.

Viktor's second respite as an instructor ended in 1999 when he again was transferred to Chechnya, this time to fight as a sniper/shooter in the second Russian-Chechen war.

———— ✳ ——— ✳ ——— ✳ ——— ✳ ————

Chechnya was Hell on Earth. Perfect for Viktor.

He spent most of his second deployment in Chechnya's

capital city, Grozny, using this urban environment as his base of operations.

His first assignment in the city, much to his dismay, was not as a sniper or shooter. Instead, Viktor and his team were tasked with clearing the city's sewers of mines that had been placed there, first by the enemy, then later by the Russians. The idea was to be able to use the sewers as tunnels for passage from one part of the city to another. Moving about on the surface, even under cover of night, even for men with highly developed stalking and camouflage skills, proved to be too dangerous and costly for the Russian military.

The second Chechen war turned out to be endless. No matter how many people the Russians killed or wounded — civilians, rebels, terrorists, militia, regular military, hybrids, or whatever Viktor and his comrades chose to call them — more appeared to confront the invaders. In time, Viktor came to realize that no matter how many enemy he killed, he could not affect the outcome of the war. He was just marking time until his time was up.

One afternoon during his second tour in Chechnya, Viktor found himself on a personal mission, stalking one of the enemy's snipers who had picked off all of Viktor's comrades, one by one, over three days and nights.

Viktor set out on his own to find the Chechen terrorist.

He set up under cover of night, high on a hill. His position gave him an excellent panoramic view of the countryside. Viktor was camouflaged to blend in with his surroundings.

Viktor knew the general location of his prey, but did not

yet know their precise location. That would come with patience and observation.

On his third day, Viktor noticed a movement among a stand of Cyprus trees, approximately four hundred meters from his hiding place. He pulled out his field glasses and studied the outcropping of rocks and trees. He counted three enemy. Two held weapons; one did not.

Viktor eased his weapon forward and sighted the men through his telescopic site. For his first target, he settled on the soldier who was wearing a pair of binoculars on a strap around his neck. This man, he decided, was currently the most dangerous to him of the three since he likely was the spotter for the other two. Without him, the enemy snipers would be undermined because they would be without their trained set of eyes.

Viktor leveled his sound-suppressed rifle, fixed the man's forehead in the crosshairs of his scope, lowered his aim half a finger, then delicately, slowly, squeezed the trigger. The silent round caught the target just to the left of his nose, blowing half his face away.

Viktor didn't bask in the satisfaction of his kill. He quickly packed up his gear and stealthily moved to another location, one that again offered him a clean sight line to his targets. Then he set up to kill again.

Within minutes Viktor saw the two other targets looking around for something, most likely looking for the sniper who had taken out their colleague. Viktor again focused on the target who now held the binoculars.

He aimed at his target's forehead. He expected the round to make contact just above the man's nose.

This second kill set the third man running.

Viktor felt nothing but contempt for the running enemy. Had the man been properly trained and not been a mere terrorist, an amateur, Viktor thought, he would have gone to ground when his companions were hit, and would later that night slip away under cover of darkness. Instead, he chose to run like a frightened dog. Now he would pay with his life for his cowardice and lack of training.

The running man, at first, was not an easy kill. He ran in a zigzag pattern that caused Viktor to miss two shots. This anomalous result brought Viktor to full fury. He rarely missed a target, let alone twice.

Viktor calmed himself and reverted to his training so that the runner, zigging and zagging like a panicked rabbit, never again stood a chance against him.

Instead of trying to follow his target as he dodged back and forth among the rocks and bushes, Viktor chose a sight line down the middle of the hypothetical path the man ran along, knowing that no matter how much the runner zigged and zagged, he eventually would cross the path's hypothetical middle line, most likely many times, as he dodged back and forth. That was the one constant Viktor could rely on.

Viktor took aim ahead of the runner along the middle line of the man's idiosyncratic running trajectory. When the enemy almost approached the center line and was about to come within his crosshairs, Viktor squeezed the trigger, and the man disappeared from sight. A red blood stain on a rock near where the man had been running was all that was visible to Viktor.

In 2007, with the war in Chechnya still raging, Viktor was deemed too old to continue as a shooter. The military rotated him through various assignments, none of which satisfied his need for risk. After two years of trial and error in various roles, Viktor mustered out of the army and emigrated from Russia to the United States, where he settled near Svetlana, his younger sister, who now lived in Fort Lauderdale.

Viktor, a civilian again, could not become an auto mechanic again because automobile-installed computers had changed cars beyond anything Viktor was familiar with. His youthful training was, all these years later, totally obsolete. He turned, therefore, to weaponry, the only other trade he knew. Viktor opened a licensed gun shop on Route A1A in Fort Lauderdale, not far from the international airport.

CHAPTER 18

Fort Lauderdale
March 5

TRACE PAID THE LUNCH CHECK, then continued to sit with his feet propped up on the fence rail while Pete wandered over to the restaurant's entrance and stood in front of a bulletin board reading messages and notices.

Trace thought about Pete as a wannabe computer hacker. He didn't know how to stop Pete from engaging in this criminal act short of taking away his computer privileges, and he knew that doing this would likely be useless and self-defeating. After all, he thought, Pete needed his computer for his schoolwork. And, if Pete really wanted to go online and hack, in spite of Trace's prohibition, there were easy work-arounds he could use: friends' computers, the public library, and Internet cafés. Trace realized he would have to deal with the underlying problem itself, not just ban it by parental fiat.

Trace recalled a magazine article he'd read a few months before while in his dentist's waiting room. At the time Trace thought the article was foolish, even reckless. Even its title, he'd thought, was questionable: "Parents! Why You Should Hack

Computers With Your Teenager." Trace could not think of any justification for a parent to commit a crime with his child.

Until now.

Today, Trace wasn't so sure. If he could not keep Pete from hacking, perhaps he could keep Pete from hacking recklessly or from hacking into certain computers or from misusing the information his hacks might give him access to. At the very least, he thought, perhaps he could help keep Pete from being apprehended by the authorities, although he wasn't very optimistic about that.

I shouldn't be surprised Pete hacks, Trace thought, not if the magazine article was correct.

The article's author had written that many intelligent teenagers are motivated to hack computer systems for one or more reasons: general curiosity, or the technical challenge to see if they can do it; peer pressure to do it; peer recognition for having done it; or, a teenager's natural proclivity to defy authority, especially parental authority.

If this was so, the author had written, a parent's attempt to stop his teenager from hacking would be futile and would actually fuel the teen's interest in hacking just to defy his parent. But, asked the author, would a teen want to hack networks if his parent joined him in the act?

By participating with his child, the author had written, the parent might be able to steer his teen away from malicious hacking and channel his efforts into white hat hacking. Furthermore, the author argued, the parent's very presence would likely make hacking less appealing to the teen, not cool, not something the teen would want his or her peers to know about. This, in and of itself, might discourage the teen from hacking.

Or, Trace had thought at the time, it might spur him on to do his own, private, malicious hacking. The possibilities made him wonder why he'd ever thought he was fit to be a parent.

Even as he considered this now, even after his failed conversations with Pete, Trace thought that the article and the author's premise were nuts, but he didn't know what else to do about Pete's hacking.

"Pete, we need to talk," Trace said, raising his voice so Pete, who still was reading the postings on the bulletin board, could hear him.

"What's up," Pete said, as he walked back to Trace. "I thought we talked during lunch?"

"Not about hacking, we didn't."

Pete's face flushed. "Come on, Dad, give me a break, will you. We've been all over this. Can't we just drop it and not spoil our time together?"

"No, we can't drop it. I have something to say and I expect you to listen to me. Now sit down," Trace said, pointing to a chair near him. "It doesn't have to spoil our day together unless you let it."

Pete took the seat and crossed his arms over his chest. He stared at the space behind Trace, looking over Trace's shoulder, his head turned slightly away from his father. His eyes narrowed. He seemed to be mentally stomping his foot.

"So, go on, talk," he said. He continued to look beyond Trace.

"You know I don't want you hacking," Trace said.

"You made that clear."

"Because I also know you're not likely to stop," Trace said, "I want to be involved."

Pete's head whipped around so fast to look at his father, he could have suffered whiplash. "What's that mean? Involved? I don't get it." He frowned, suspicious of what he'd just heard.

"It means I want you to show me what you do when you hack. I shouldn't have any problem understanding it, given my Navy experience and my technology law practice. You'll just have to introduce me to state-of-the-art tools."

Pete's jaw dropped. His eyes widened. "This is a joke, right?"

Trace shook his head. "It's no joke."

"What about all the things you said this morning about hacking? Was that just posturing?"

"I meant every word of it," Trace said, "but I also realize I can't be your policeman 24/7. So, if I can't make you stop hacking, and I don't believe I can, maybe I can guide you along into better and safer paths within hacking. To do that, I have to become familiar with the software tools you're using."

Pete stared briefly at Trace, then said, "This is really weird. You're creeping me out, Dad. Picture it: the father and son hacking team busted together. That would make mom real happy. Especially on visiting day at the federal pen. I can't wait to tell her."

"This isn't a joke, Pete. It's an act of desperation by me out of my love for you. You should at least recognize this for what it is and respect why I've made this difficult decision."

Pete nodded, and his grin faded. "All right. Have it your way, Dad. When do you want me to start showing you?"

"On the fishing trip. At night. We'll have lots of time to kill, as well as privacy at night."

"Privacy?" Pete said. "Meaning, as in, mom not knowing? Okay. I get it."

"Make no mistake, Pete, this doesn't change anything I've said concerning how I feel about you hacking. Understand?"

"Sure, Dad. I understand. You just want to bond with me."

As they belted themselves into the car and prepared to drive back to Nanna's, Pete said, "Listen, Dad, this probably isn't the best time to ask this, but I'd like to go to an Internet café for a while. There's one on Sunrise Boulevard. Will you drop me off?"

Trace looked over at Pete, and said, "You're kidding, right? After what we talked about?"

"I'm not going to hack. I promise. I'm just learning a game I don't have on my laptop yet because I haven't played enough to qualify to download it. That's all I want to do, nothing else."

No hacking?"

Pete shook his head. "You made your point, Dad. I gave you my word. You need to trust me."

"All right," Trace said. "Fair enough. I do trust you. I'll drop you off at the café. Call me when you're ready to come home. I'll pick you up."

Pete called two hours later.

"I'm on my way home, Dad, but you don't need to pick me up. We're just around the corner."

"You're walking?" Trace said. "It's too far. What do you mean, 'We're just around the corner?' Who are you with?"

"I caught a ride with my new friend, Karl, a guy I met at the café who was helping me with the game. We'll be outside Nanna's in just a minute. Come downstairs and I'll introduce you to him," Pete said.

CHAPTER 19

Fort Lauderdale
March 13

TRACE AND PETE RETURNED TO Fort Lauderdale after several days and nights fishing in Key West.

Pete dashed into Nanna's kitchen.

"Mom, it was awesome. You should've seen me. I almost caught a huge fish, I mean a marlin, a sword fish, but it got away. I thought my arms would rip off they were so tired trying to land it."

Isabella hugged Pete and kissed the top of his head. "That's wonderful, Honey. Where's your father?"

"My arms hurt so much. I tried to land it for almost an hour, then the line broke. The captain said it would have been a record catch if I had landed it."

"That's nice, Dear. You can tell me all about it at dinner so Nanna can hear it, too. Where's your father?"

"Oh, I forgot. Sorry. I was supposed to tell you right away. Dad's at the rental agency returning the car we used to go to Key West. He said since we're not going anywhere this week, he can save paying for the rest of the week. He'll rent another one if we decide later on we need a car. He should be back soon."

"All right," Isabella said. She hugged him again. "I'm glad you had a good time, but I'm also glad you're home. I missed you both."

"It sounds like you boys had a nice time together," Isabella said. "Pete was so excited describing the one that got away, he could hardly contain himself." She handed Trace a bottle of beer.

"Did you two get along okay with all the time you had on your hands at night?"

"We did fine," Trace said. "He'd become restless, as you'd expect, but we spent a lot of time in the evening working on his laptop. That passed the time quickly. He taught me some useful things about networks, software, and current computer tools I never used before. In fact, I was impressed how much he knows. I also talked to him about some of the lessons I learned during my SEALs' training."

"Really? Why?"

"Because so much of it applies to everyday life. He's old enough now to start thinking about these things," Trace said. "I want him to begin to consider how to deal with the unexpected in life."

"How'd he take to that?"

"Well, I think, because I framed it within a general discussion of what I liked about being a SEAL. This stocked his curiosity. I was careful not to make it seem as if I was passing life-lessons on to him."

"What'd you tell him?"

"I talked about how we learned to make the unfamiliar seem familiar by previsualizing situations and then thinking through our responses in advance."

"Does that really work?"

"Oh, yes, it definitely works. Previsualization fools the brain into believing you've already experienced the situation you are thinking about, even though you haven't. It creates a form of muscle-memory for the brain that will make a situation seem familiar when it actually occurs. In the SEALs we called it making the unfamiliar familiar."

"Interesting," Isabella said. "Actually, fascinating, not just interesting."

"I also pointed out that not every plan works out, so we have to be ready for that in life, too. I explained the SEALs' motto to him: Plan for success, but train for failure."

"Did he understand that?"

"He did. He's mature for his age, Bella. Responsible, too. We have good reason to be proud of Pete," Trace said.

"Maybe so, but I wish he'd pay as much attention to his schoolwork as he does to his computer," Isabella said. "That's going to be a problem."

"I talked to him about that, too," Trace said. "He promised he'd do better after he returns from vacation."

"I hope so. Maybe we made a mistake pulling him out of school so we could come here to see mom."

"I don't think it matters," Trace said. "If he keeps his promise and buckles down when we go back, his time away from classes will have been worth it for that reason alone. If he doesn't buckle down, it won't matter that he lost class time. We'll just have to wait and see."

＊＊＊＊＊

Nanna walked into the kitchen.

"Hi, Trace. Nice to have you home." She stood up on her

toes, kissed him on his cheek, and smiled. "Do you want a coffee after that beer? There's a fresh pot on. How about you, Bella? Coffee?"

"That'll be nice, Nanna," Trace said. "Thanks."

"While you and Pete were in Key West," Isabella said, "the TV news was full of talk about that mysterious late-season flu ravaging the city. It's hitting Fort Lauderdale pretty bad. I don't know more than that, but I'm worried we could catch it. Some people have already died from it."

She paused, then said, "I was thinking, Trace, maybe we should just go back to DC, and take Nanna with us, while we're all still healthy." She tilted her head toward her mother.

Trace thought about this. He'd rather not cut their vacation short if it could be avoided.

"Let me find out more about what's going on before we whack our vacation," he said. "We've counted on this trip for so long, it would be a shame to cancel it if we don't have to. It might just be the news media hyping a story."

"Okay, if you think that's best." Isabella nodded her head in agreement, but her eyes said otherwise. "It's just—"

"Bella, let me find out more, then we can decide." Trace reached over and lightly squeezed her shoulder.

"There's some kind of news conference on TV this afternoon about the flu," Nanna said. "I saw the announcement this morning when I was watching my shows."

"Good," Trace said. "Let's watch it, get some information, then we can make our decision."

CHAPTER 20

Fort Lauderdale
March 13

T HAT AFTERNOON, TRACE, ISABELLA AND Nanna gathered
around the TV to watch the news briefing offered by the
Broward County Health Department. Pete was back at the
Internet café playing computer games with his new friend, Karl.

Randall Boone, the Broward County Administrator,
stepped to the lectern and adjusted the microphone. He tapped
it several times, causing the device to utter a shrill cough.

"Ladies and gentlemen, thank you for coming today. I have
a brief statement I'd like to read. After that, Dr. Tuft — who
as you know is our county medical director — and I will field
questions." He briefly turned part-way around to look at the
man standing behind him, then turned back to the audience.

"Mr. Boone, do you see this unusual late-season flu as a
crises requiring state or federal government intervention?" a
voice in the crowd yelled.

"Dan, please let me read my statement. Then ask me your
question," Boone said. He tightly gripped the edges of the
lectern, whitening his knuckles.

"Ladies and gentlemen, as you know, Fort Lauderdale

has been affected recently by some form of virulent pathogen that has sickened many people in our city. Several people, unfortunately, have died." He paused and glanced briefly at his notes. "I've been in contact with the Centers for Disease Control and Prevention in Atlanta since this problem surfaced."

He reached into his pocket, pulled out a handkerchief and wiped his forehead.

"I've called you here today, ladies and gentlemen of the press, to ask for your help. We need to avoid creating panic in our community. I'm asking you all to remember your responsibility as citizens, first, and as reporters, next."

He tightened his grip on the edges of the lectern and leaned toward his audience.

"Report only the facts as we give them to you," he said. "Avoid rumors. Do this, act responsibly, work with us, and we'll help you do your job."

He did a slow radar-like sweep of the audience with his head.

"On the other hand, if you're not responsible, if you traffic in rumor and innuendo, well . . . I hope we don't get to that point," he said.

He waited a beat.

"Okay, then, let's see what I have here today you might use," he said, as he looked through a stack of papers. He slipped one sheet out from the pile, placed it on top, and referred to it as he spoke.

"Approximately ten to eleven days ago local hospitals began experiencing a marked increase in emergency room admissions. The cause was thought to be late-season influenza, but we now know that this was the wrong diagnosis. We don't know what the disease is yet, but it seems to be some highly-resistant form of flu. The CDS is still running tests to identify it and determine its nature.

"As of this morning," he said, "as far as we can tell, the disease has not peaked. New cases still are being reported in increasing numbers, especially among the elderly and young."

He took a drink of water before he continued.

"As you can imagine, our healthcare resources are strained to their limits. At the present rate of increasing numbers of new cases, we will run out of hospital beds in one more week. And, without some infusion of new medicines, we will run short of meds any day now."

He took another drink of water, turned slightly, and glanced at the man behind him.

"Mr. Boone," a reporter asked, "does that mean, are you implying, there are medicines on the market available right now to treat the illness, but they just aren't available to us to buy right now? Meds that can prevent the disease or cure it?"

"No, Ms. Robinson, I'm afraid it doesn't mean that at all. So far, nothing we've tried seems to prevent or cure this. There are some medicines, however, that can relieve the suffering of patients, affect the symptoms of the disease, but, as far as we know right now, nothing we have cures it or prevents it."

"The CDC has promised to deliver these peripheral medicines and various other supplies to us in the next few days to help us relieve the symptoms of our friends and neighbors who have contracted the illness," he said. "The CDC will also bring in some fresh, rested healthcare workers to relieve our responders who, as you can only imagine, are exhausted and stressed."

The same woman paused, looked at her notepad, then said,

"Doctor, can you tell our listeners if people who took the flu shot this past winter are protected from this disease?"

Boone frowned as he realized he'd just answered this question with his previous response. Was the reporter trying to trap him? Behind the lectern, out of sight of the reporters, Boone shifted his weight, first to one foot, then back again, over and over.

Tuft leaned into the microphone and said, "Good question. As Mr. Boone indicated with his answer a minute ago, the answer to the last question is no. This winter's flu shot doesn't offer any protection against this pathogen."

Boone stepped back to the lectern and pointed to a reporter. He said, "Yes, Mr. Shafer. What's your question?"

"What symptoms should our readers be aware of?"

"I'll take that if you don't mind," Dr. Tuft said, looking at Boone.

"We know that the disease seems to have an incubation period of about one week, maybe a little longer, from the time of first exposure until the first symptoms appears. We hope to soon know more about this from the CDC or the National Institutes of Health.

"As far as symptoms, we've encountered different indications for various people," Tuft said. "Symptoms suggest there are two strains of infection, or maybe one strain attacking its host in two ways. We don't know which it is yet. We're waiting for more information from the CDC, but, in the meantime, here's what we do know.

"There seems to be a pulmonary version and a non-pulmonary version. The pulmonary version attacks the lungs by being breathed in. The non-pulmonary type attacks the blood through open wounds.

"In both cases, the patient starts out with a body rash that spreads. Then the patient develops chills, a severe headache, high fever, and muscle and joint pain. Often, the patient develops a non-productive cough, a dry cough, if you will. The patient will likely incur breathing difficulty, at least with the pulmonary strain of the illness. In all cases the patient will also suffer muscular weakness of the limbs."

Tuft looked out at the reporters. He ignored several who were jumping up, hands raised, vying for his attention.

He continued. "The symptoms are acute. We haven't any reports of mild cases although the symptoms sometimes ebb and flow, with patients seeming to recover, but then lapsing back into an acute state for no reason we can determine. We don't yet know why this occurs in some people and not in others."

He paused, sipped some water, then said, "Finally, some patients do recover from the illness. Others, most, in fact, do not. And sometimes patients are ill for several weeks before they either recover or succumb." He looked at Boone, then turned back to the audience.

"Another thing, I should mention. We think, although we still need more data to determine this for sure, that not everyone exposed to the flu catches it. We don't yet know why that is, but the CDC and NIH are working on this issue, among others. That's all I know for now." He stepped away.

As Boone moved toward the microphone, a woman called out, "Dr. Tuft, Dr. Tuft. May I ask you one more question? It's important."

Boone frowned and did not yield the microphone.

"I'll take this," he said, looking at Tuft, "since I'm here." He looked at the reporter. "Go ahead," he said to her.

"Since this disease seems to be from an unknown source, is

it possible it's caused by a bioweapon set loose by terrorists? Can you tell us if the authorities are considering that possibility?"

Boone, without moving his head at all, glanced over at Tuft and raised his eyebrows. Then he leaned into the microphone and fixed his frown on the questioner. His knuckles whitened again as he tightened his grip on the lectern's edges.

"Madam," he said, drawing out the word and speaking with contrived gravitas, "we have no reason to believe this situation is anything other than Mother Nature at work. For you to suggest otherwise is irresponsible.

"As I said earlier," Boone continued, "we all have to exercise responsibility here. Please remember that." He stared at the reporter until she looked away.

Boone looked over at Tuft, who nodded. Then Boone looked out at the reporters. "We should wrap this up. Any last questions for now?"

"Yes, Sir," a reporter said. "Can you tell us how the infection spreads? What should we tell our listeners and readers?"

"Good question, Sir," Boone said, relaxing his grip on the lectern. "Will you take this, Dr. Tuft, or should I?"

Tuft nodded, said, "I got it," and stepped to the microphone.

"The pulmonary version spreads from person to person through the air. For example, if you breathe in the aerosolized discharge from a patient who coughs or sneezes, then you're at risk. The non-pulmonary type, however, invades the body through open sores, cuts or skin abrasions, then it attacks the blood stream." He looked over at Boone, then back at the reporter. "Does that answer your question?" he said.

Before the reporter responded, Boone moved forward and gripped the microphone.

"Thank you all for coming today," he said. "Please remember

to be responsible. We'll let you know when we have something new for you."

He nodded at Tuft.

They walked off together.

CHAPTER 21

Camp Mackall, North Carolina

A NTHONY VISTA, MORE THAN HE ever would have expected, had enjoyed his brief posting to Camp Mackall. The refresher command courses he'd taken had turned out to be easier than he anticipated so he passed all his courses at or near the top of each class without much effort on his part.

He had also continued to apply the advice given to him years before by the colonel when he washed out of the Special Forces, and he had successfully socialized with his Camp Mackall colleagues. Though this still did not feel natural to him, his effort seemed to have paid off since Anthony gradually, but steadily, rose in command as the years passed.

Yet neither his promotions, his success with the prestigious curriculum at Camp Mackall, nor the imputed honors that flowed to individuals who graduated from the selective and demanding program at Camp Mackall, provided the balm he craved to soothe his long-nurtured wounded pride at having washed out of the Special Forces program. In his view, he now was special only among those who were in the Army's second tier, those who could not cut it as Green Berets or Rangers. Nothing his classmates or instructors now said to compliment his high class standing ameliorated Anthony's felt conviction that he had been unfairly pushed out of the elite corps for one reason, and for one reason only: because he was not and never would be *one of the boys*.

Anthony spent his last days in North Carolina running errands and packing. He had only two days remaining before he drove to Florida and started his new command.

Why Florida? he wondered. And why Fort Lauderdale, of all postings. It wasn't exactly a war zone. Was he now to be charged with protecting the country from unruly college students who flocked to the resort during their spring break?

CHAPTER 22

Fort Lauderdale
March 13

TRACE STOOD UP FROM THE sofa, walked over to the TV, and turned it off. He'd heard enough from the county administrator and the county medical director to set off his internal alarm system. He checked his wristwatch. It was almost 4:30 p.m.

He looked at Isabella. She was staring at him as if he was supposed to know what they should do now. Well, she was right. He did know.

"We can't stay here," Isabella said. "You heard what they said on TV. It's too dangerous."

"I know," Trace said. "I'm convinced. We'll leave."

"We need to take my mother and Pete and go home," Isabella said.

Bella's not focusing, not hearing me at all, Trace thought. "We will, Bella. I'll get us away from here before we become sick," Trace said softly. "I promise."

Twenty minutes later Trace tossed his cell phone a few feet up into the air and watched as it traced an invisible, lazy parabola in the air before dropping down onto the sofa. Seven calls, he thought. Seven walls.

"There's nothing available to fly out on right now," Trace said to Isabella, "not before a week from this Thursday. I reserved seats for that day as a fallback, going into Baltimore though, not DC."

We better not still be here then, he thought.

Trace picked up his cell phone and fingered it, turning it over and over, weaving the small device among his fingers.

"AMTRAK also says it's fully booked and won't sell any more tickets. There aren't any buses either," he said.

"What're we going to do?" Isabella said. Her voice was elevated an octave. "You should have kept the rental car, Trace."

Trace narrowed his eyes and looked at Isabella, but held his thought. She was right, of course, in theory, but how was he to have known at the time? He hated bad decisions that seemed so right when he made them.

"Pete," he said, turning to Pete, who was sitting at the kitchen table reading the hacker magazine, "go online and check Orbitz and Expedia. See

if you can find a flight before a week from Thursday. Any airline, going anywhere on the East Coast. Even the Midwest will do."

Trace looked over at Isabella, then turned back to Pete.

"In fact," he said, "make it going anywhere at all if it just gets us away from here. I don't care where."

"Trace," Isabella said, "what were you possibly thinking when you gave up the car?"

Trace felt his neck and face grow hot. He took a deep breath and swallowed his rising anger.

"Stop it, Isabella. Stop it right now," he said, speaking

barely above a whisper, his modulated tone belying his rising anger. "Think about what you're saying to me. How could I have known this was going to happen?"

Isabella did not reply.

Nanna, who had said nothing during this exchange, looked at Trace, then at Isabella, and said, "I shouldn't have sold my car when my eyes started to go. I probably should have kept it for when you come down here to visit." She stood up from the kitchen table where she'd been sitting with Pete, and shuffled off toward her bedroom.

Trace turned toward Pete. "If you can't find any flights, try looking for a rental car. Even a van or truck. Anything that moves. Even a boat to charter. In the meantime, I'll make more calls."

"Will do, Dad."

Pete looked at his mother and then back at Trace, but said nothing. He picked up his laptop and walked outside to the patio.

Fifteen minutes later, Pete returned.

"There's nothing online, Dad. We're out of luck."

"Oh, Trace," Isabella said, "I'm so worried. What'll we do?"

Trace looked at Isabella, and then walked over and put his arm around her shoulders. He gently hugged her, pulling her into him and holding her close, just briefly, before letting her go.

He turned toward Pete.

"What about nearby towns? Did you try Hallandale, Plantation, Davie?"

"Come on, Dad, give me a break, will you? I tried all around, not just Lauderdale. The story's the same everywhere.

Everything's booked solid. Everybody's trying to get out of town, not just us."

Trace put his hands into his pants pockets and walked over to the window. He stood there, with his back to the room, looking out over the parking lot. He dug his hands deeper into his pockets. Then he turned back to Pete and Isabella.

"I'm going out for a while. See if I can find something for us. I'll be back as soon as I can."

Before they could protest or ask any questions, he turned and walked out the front door.

CHAPTER 23

Fort Lauderdale
March 13

T<small>RACE LEFT</small> N<small>ANNA'S CONDO AND</small> dashed down the stairs, taking the steps two at a time. He smacked his palm against the exit door, slamming it open.

He was angry. Angry at Isabella for giving him a hard time about the rental car; angry at himself for not holding onto the car and having followed the SEALs' mantra about planning for failure; and angry at the general situation in Fort Lauderdale because it made him feel helpless to protect his family. These were not feelings he was used to. Not any of them.

What's more, what was even worse, the situation in Fort Lauderdale made him realize he might actually be helpless to protect his family under these circumstances. This did not sit well with him. It dredged up memories of Panama and the downed chopper.

He hadn't been trained by the SEALs to feel helpless, no matter what the circumstances. He'd been trained to formulate a plan, rehearse and re-rehearse the plan, then act and resolve any problem. That training hadn't left him when he left the SEALs.

Trace stood on the lawn outside Nanna's condo building,

his back to anyone who might be watching him from Nanna's living room windows. He lit a cigarette, drawing the smoke deep into his lungs.

He thought about what to do next. He crushed out his cigarette on the lawn and began walking.

Trace walked east along Federal Highway, certain he would find a cruising taxi along this major thoroughfare. He was wrong. Instead, he found himself confronted with grid-locked, bumper-to-bumper traffic, with horns screeching. All the vehicles headed north in the direction of the I-95 interchange. The southern directed lanes were empty. The northern route provided an escape path that would eventually give these cars the choice, if they ever reached the interchange, to head either north or south on the Interstate.

Trace walked two miles until he came to a 7-ELEVEN convenience store. He was thirsty so he went inside to buy a soda, bought a bottle of cold root beer, and then went back outside to camp with his cell phone near the Yellow Pages book chained to a wall where the empty shell of a former telephone booth still stood.

He avoided calling Enterprise Car Rental, National, Hertz and Budget, the businesses Pete had researched online.

In the end, his calls didn't matter. Each telephone call yielded only a taped message stating either that the car rental office was closed or that it had no inventory available to rent, or both. He decided he would call the last agency named on the list, the only one he hadn't tried yet, one he hadn't even heard of before, then give up and walk home.

Trace placed the call to Wilcox Auto Rental. To his surprise, his call generated a busy signal. He never thought he'd be so happy to hear a busy signal.

He redialed the number once, then twice, then five and six times. He waited a minute or so between redials. The line was busy each time.

He sat on the curb in front of the 7-ELEVEN drinking his root beer and smoking. After his eighth failed attempt to get through to Wilcox, he decided to do something less passive, less reactive. He stood up from the curb, copied out the address from the directory, and asked the 7-ELEVEN clerk for walking directions to Wilcox.

Trace jogged, sometimes walked, and then jogged some more. After half an hour of this, he strode up to Wilcox's front door. What he saw pulled him back into the solemnity of his circumstances.

The office was dark.

It's closed, he thought.

He looked at his watch. It was only 3:20 p.m.

He walked to the front door and flattened his nose against the glass, using his palm to shield his eyes from the reflected sunlight. He squinted as he looked inside.

There was one light turned on.

From the looks of it, he decided, it's an anti-crime light, the kind that lights up an interior just enough to let customers know the business is closed, but bright enough to discourage intruders who could be seen from the outside.

Trace examined the interior of the office, peering through the glass door, looking for some indication of activity. He didn't see any sign of anyone. Instead, he saw a telephone handset suspended just above the floor, dangling at the end of its cord, hanging from the base unit fastened to the wall.

He took out his cell phone and redialed the Wilcox number. The line was busy. He pocketed his cell phone and started walking back to Nanna's condo. He'd try something else when he arrived there.

CHAPTER 24

Fort Lauderdale
March 13

PETE SAT NEAR THE POOL, but far enough away not to be soaked if someone jumped in and splashed. He had his laptop booted up and was connected to the Internet via his wireless modem card. He was downloading pirated music files and updates to the basic tools used by hackers — crack files, key generators, and serial numbers to use with downloaded, pirated software.

———— ✶ ✶ ✶ ✶ ✶ ————

"Hello there, Young Man. Is this seat taken?" the thin, leathery, elderly man said, pointing to the empty chaise lounge next to Pete.

Without waiting for Pete to answer, the man unfurled his long blue, yellow and orange-striped beach towel, spreading it over the chaise.

"No, Sir," Pete said. "My Nanna was sitting there, but she's gone back to the condo for the day."

"Okay," the man said, as he sat down. He dumped the contents of his duffle bag onto the foot of the chaise, sat on the chaise's edge, and began spreading tanning oil over his arms, the front of his chest and shoulders, and up and down his skinny thighs and bird-like legs. He swathed his forehead and cheeks with the gunk. Then he leaned back, closed his eyes, and began marinating under the fierce Florida sun.

Fifteen minutes later the man opened his eyes and turned his head toward Pete.

"My name's Sam Foley, Young Man. I live in Building 5. Are you a snowbird visiting from up north?" He looked Pete over, up and down, then said, "I guess you are. You're as pale as a ghost."

"Yes, Sir," Pete said. "I'm here from Washington, DC, with my parents, visiting my Nanna."

The man nodded, half listening. "Karen, my wife of forty-eight years, bless her, usually comes to the pool with me. We sit in the sun and gossip about our neighbors or talk about old times when we were young and lived in Philly. She didn't want to come today, so she stayed home. She has some kind of a rash on her. Must be from too much sun, I told her."

"I'm sorry," Pete said. "I hope Karen — pardon me, I mean, your wife — will soon feel better."

"She'll be fine. But I feel a little off myself. I'll be okay though. I don't see no rash," he said, as he turned his head and craned his neck to inspect the dark, sagging, wrinkled flesh on the back of his left arm.

Pete turned his head away and rolled his eyes. He looked back and nodded.

After a respectful amount of time passed so it would not seem he was brushing off the man, he said, "Well, Mr.

Foley, I enjoyed talking with you, but I have to go now. My mom expects me back. I hope you and your wife feel better soon." He stood and stepped away before Foley could start another conversation.

CHAPTER 25

Fort Lauderdale
March 14

W HEN HE RETURNED TO NANNA'S condo from Wilcox,
Trace took a seat at the kitchen table. He made small talk
while he ate a snack.

When he finished, Trace took his empty dishes to the sink
and rinsed them. Then he turned back to face his family.

"I suppose you want to know about today."

Pete and Isabella looked at each other, then back at Trace.
Pete shrugged. Isabella nodded. Nanna remained silent.

He walked back to the table, sat down, then described his
afternoon from the time he'd left the condo until he returned.

His story finished, Trace told them that he had formulated
a plan as he'd walked home from Wilcox, but wanted to think it
through a bit more before he offered it to them for their input.

In the meantime, he told them, he would try once more
online to rent a vehicle.

"Pete," Trace said, "go online again and see if you can find
some kind of vehicle to rent."

Pete searched the Web and found six additional, independent car rental sources not listed in the Yellow Pages.

Trace telephoned the rental agencies, but had no luck with the first five. A clerk at the sixth agency said she still had two older model cars available, ones they didn't normally rent, but said she would make one available to him, given the emergency circumstances. She quoted a daily rental fee Trace thought was conveniently inflated, but which he accepted anyway.

The clerk required that Trace place a deposit with her over the telephone using his bank debit card. She then told him she would hold the car for him, but on one condition: Trace had to pick it up within the next hour or he would risk losing it to anyone else who might come along after that time.

"And in that event, she said, "you will also forfeit your deposit as well as lose the car."

Trace reluctantly agreed to the woman's terms.

He gathered his family to explain that he and Pete would go to the car rental agency located on the far west side of Fort Lauderdale. They would rent the car he'd just reserved. Then they would drive back to Nanna's, pick up Isabella and Nanna, and they all would drive away from Fort Lauderdale.

"In the meantime," he said to Isabella, "pack clothing, medicines, bathroom supplies, food, and water for the anticipated drive."

"In fact," he said, "if you're not sure whether or not to pack something, pack it. We can always lose it along the way if we don't want it."

"Mom, charge my laptop and then pack it for me," Pete said. "I can't carry it with me right now when we're trying to move fast."

———————

Trace and Pete set out for the car agency. By his best estimate, Trace figured they should make it there with many of the sixty minutes allotted to them left to spare.

As they walked along Federal Highway, Trace looked at his watch, counting the minutes as they dropped away from the total time allowed them.

"Pete", he said, "try to hitch a ride for us."

Pete walked to the edge of the road and stuck out his thumb. He caught a ride for them within minutes.

———————

Trace checked his watch as he and Pete climbed out of the car that had given them the ride. They rushed up the path to the front door of the Jarrett Car Rental Agency. Trace felt self-satisfied, almost smug.

They were at Jarrett with almost fifteen minutes to spare.

Trace reached out and grabbed the door handle. The door stuck. He pulled again. It was locked. Only then did he notice the closed sign hanging from a thin chain just inside the glass door. It offered no explanation.

"What the . . . ?"

Trace leaned against the door and looked through the glass at the darkened office. The single room appeared deserted.

He stepped away and looked around the front of the free-standing building, hoping to see an employee. He didn't see anyone.

"Come on," he said to Pete. "I want to walk around back, see if anyone's there."

They circled the building and came back to the front

entrance without having seen anyone at all, let alone a Jarrett employee.

"That woman lied to me," Trace said. His face was flushed with anger. "She took my money. It was all a scam." He glared at the front door of the rental agency. "Let's get out of here."

He started to walk back toward Fort Lauderdale. Pete walked quickly, and sometimes almost jogged, to keep up.

They were just into their return walk when Pete pointed to a man leaning against an old Mercedes. He was waving his arm, motioning for them to come over.

"Dad," Pete said, as he pointed across the parking lot, "I think that guy wants us for some reason."

Trace looked at the man and at the car, then at Pete, then again at the man.

"He has a car," Trace said. "Let's go over."

CHAPTER 26

Fort Lauderdale
March 14

A s Trace and Pete walked up to him, the man stepped away from the car, looked Trace up and down, and said, "Thanks for coming over, Friend."

"What's up?" Trace said. His recent experience with Jarrett stoked his defenses.

"Couldn't help seeing you trying to get into Jarrett. It's closed, case you didn't notice. If it's a car you're wanting, I can help you." He leaned against the fender of the Mercedes and placed his meaty palm on its hood.

"What do you have in mind?" Trace said, his voice reflecting his skepticism.

"I have this here Mercedes," the man said, patting the fender. "Had her since '85. Has only 39,000 miles on her. She's like new, hardly broke in."

"How much to rent it?" Trace asked.

"Nothin' at all to rent it, nothin' at all 'cause she's not for rent. She's for sale." The man nodded sharply once to underscore his statement.

Trace tried to process what he'd just heard. He looked at

the car and walked around it twice. For a few seconds, he just stared at it. He had mixed feelings.

Body and paint job look more than thirty-plus years old, he thought, pretty well dented. Probably rusted out underneath.

Trace leaned toward the hood and put his hand on the car. He flicked his finger, launching an imaginary piece of dirt from the hood.

He quashed these thoughts and turned to the man. "How much to buy?"

"Cash. No checks. Don't take no credit cards neither," the man said.

"How much?"

"Five thousand," the man said. "Take it or leave it. No bargaining, no quibbling. Cash on the barrelhead is all I'll take. No checks or credit cards."

"I'll tell you what," Trace said. "Let's the three of us go to the nearest Wells Fargo branch. I'll drive. If I like the way the car handles on the way there, I'll get the money from the bank."

Pete nodded his agreement.

"Let's go then, Partner," the man said.

"I assume you have proof of title with you?" Trace said. The last thing he needed was to buy a hot car.

The man patted his shirt pocket. "It's right here, Friend, right here." He walked around to the other side of the car and climbed into the back seat.

Trace climbed into the driver's seat. Pete rode shotgun.

The car started right up.

Trace drove to a Wells Fargo branch on Federal Highway. It was one he and Pete had passed coming over to Jarrett.

Trace pulled into the customers' parking lot at the side of the building and climbed out of the Mercedes. Pete and the man stepped out, too. Trace stood by the driver's door, waiting for them to join him.

"Any chance you can do something with the price?" Trace said. "It's a lot of cash to come up with on short notice when you're from out-of-town."

"That's the price. I already told you, take it or leave it."

"Okay," Trace said. "I'll take it. Wait here while I go inside and get the money. In the meantime, get out your title. I'll want to look at it when I come back."

Pete looked at the man and then back at Trace.

"Dad, I'll come with you?"

"Sure. Let's go."

They walked across the parking lot and around to the building's front. As they approached the double doors, Trace's throat constricted. He could see that the doors were locked, held in place by a thick chain looped through the two handles. A large printed sign notified the public that this bank branch and all others operated by Wells Fargo in Broward County were closed until further notice by order of the Broward County Department of Health. The sign also stated that all Wells Fargo ATMs (including the one here which would not dispense $5000 in any event) would remain without service or additional cash once they emptied out, until the bank was allowed to reopen.

"Damn it," Trace said to Pete. "Let's go back."

He spun around to return the way they'd just come. They walked back around the building, over to the car.

"That was quick. Here's the title," the man said, extending his hand toward Trace.

"We have a problem," Trace said. "The bank's closed."

"No," the man said, "we don't have no problem. You got the problem. I got the car." He started to climb back into the driver's seat.

"Wait a minute," Trace said, "please," putting his hand on the car's open door. "Don't be so quick. We might be able to get the cash from my mother-in-law. Hold on while I call her."

The man stayed in the Mercedes, his right hand clutching the steering wheel. He put one foot back out onto the macadam.

"I don't have all day," he said. "I'm going to sell this baby to somebody real soon. If you want it to be you, get the money now and let's do it."

"Wait here," Trace said, "while I make the call. I'll be quick."

He walked away and used his cell phone to call Isabella. He learned from her, as he'd expected, that Nanna couldn't come up with that much cash. He then called the Wells Fargo branch office he banked at in Washington.

"Can you wire $5,000 to me today?" Trace said. "I must have it in my hands within an hour. I'm in Fort Lauderdale, Florida, but all your branches here are closed until the flu epidemic ends."

The clerk put Trace on hold, but returned five minutes later.

"That money can be available to you within a few minutes at any one of our branches located in Palm Beach County. Would that be convenient for you, Mr. Austin?"

Trace frowned. He knew what he had to do next. "I'll call you back in a few minutes," he said to the Wells Fargo clerk.

Trace walked back to the man and Pete.

"My mother-in-law doesn't have that much cash," he said, as he approached them.

"I also called the Wells Fargo branch I use in Washington. I'll have the money wired to me at one of their branch offices in Palm Beach County. It can be there a few minutes after I call. All we have to do is ride over to Palm Beach together to pick up the money," Trace said, as he looked at the man.

"Not interested in a wild goose chase," the man said. "Afraid this car's history for you."

"Look—" Trace said, but he never finished his sentence.

"Don't waste my time," the man said to Trace, cutting him off.

"It's only an hour or so we're talking about at the most," Trace said. "Maybe even less. That's all I'll need. I'll pay you an extra $1000 for the extra time . . . Please."

The man shook his head.

"I'll give you a deposit to hold meantime," Trace said. "No strings attached. Here's $210. Take it. It's every cent I have on me."

The man pulled his leg back into the car.

"And here's my vintage fountain pen," Trace said, holding out his cherished Parker Company MANDARIN YELLOW Duofold pen, circa 1927. It's a collector's item. It cost my wife $2,750 to buy it for me for our first wedding anniversary. Take it, too, as a deposit in case the money's not there for some reason. I'll forfeit it all."

The man didn't answer. Instead, he slammed the car door, and in one unbroken motion rolled up the window, punched the door lock button, and started the engine.

He floored the accelerator pedal, let it throttle back to idle, then put the car in gear and floored the pedal again. The Mercedes hesitated, seemed to shudder, briefly spun its rear wheels, and then lumbered away out of the parking lot, shrouding Trace and Pete in a blue-black cloud of diesel smoke.

They didn't speak as they walked back to the condo.

Trace was deep in thought, planning their next move, considering the pros and cons of the plan he'd formulated earlier, but hadn't described to anyone.

Pete kept looking at Trace from the corner of his eyes as if he wanted his father to give him answers to his unasked questions.

As they entered the condominium grounds, Trace put his arm around Pete's shoulders. "This isn't the end," he said. "Not by a long shot. I still have the plan I mentioned before. It's time we all talk about it."

CHAPTER 27

Fort Lauderdale
March 14

T RACE DESCRIBED THE RECENT EVENTS to Isabella and Nanna, covering the time from when he and Pete arrived at Jarrett to the moment the stranger abandoned them in the parking lot. When he finished, he stood, walked across the room, and turned back to face his family.

"I know what I have to do," he said. "I have the plan I mentioned before. Let's talk about it."

Everyone stared at him and waited. After a few seconds, Pete said, "So, what's your plan?"

"I'm falling back on my SEALs' training," Trace said, "on the Rule of Three."

Pete, Bella and Nanna looked at one another and shrugged. They turned back to face Trace in one unified motion.

"What's that mean, Trace?" Isabella said.

"It means that the worst possible decision you can make in a dangerous situation is to make no decision at all. Given that, I've had to come up with something plausible for us to try. That's where the SEALs' Rule of Three comes in."

"Okay, but what's the Rule?" Isabella said.

"The Rule of Three is a decision-making process that requires us to come up with three possible courses of action — just three, no more.

"Did you?" Pete said.

Trace nodded. "I did. Then, applying the rule, I looked at the pros and cons of each of the three, weighed the risks attendant each, and estimated the likelihood that I could achieve each."

"And?" Pete said.

"And then, without debating or re-thinking each of the three possibilities, I chose the one I thought was least risky and most likely to succeed. That one has become my plan. I closed the book on the other two unless the first one fails." He paused and nodded once. "That's the SEALs' Rule of Three."

"That's what you did as a SEAL?" Pete asked.

"Yes. That's what we were taught to do. So, here's my plan based on the Rule of Three.

"The only way I can see us getting away from here is for me to first go out of Fort Lauderdale alone. I'll walk as far as I have to go until I reach some town where I can rent or buy a vehicle to drive. Then I'll come back with it and get you."

"But how far will you go?" Isabella said. "For how long?"

"I don't know. Hopefully not far, but I don't know." He paused, then added, "It doesn't matter, though. I can walk it no matter how far I have to go."

As I walk, Trace thought, I'll remind myself what's at stake for Bella, Pete and Nanna if I don't succeed, if I don't complete my walk and come back with a vehicle. That will be a sufficient trigger to cause me to complete this mission.

Nanna spoke up for the first time since Trace and Pete returned.

"Do it, Trace. If anybody can pull it off, you can. I have faith in you."

Trace walked over to Nanna, leaned down, and kissed her cheek. "Thanks, Nanna."

Once they'd made their decision to follow Trace's plan, Trace, Bella, Pete and Nanna relaxed with one another, feeling at last that they had regained some small measure of control over their lives. At Nanna's suggestion, Trace agreed to wait until morning to begin his walk north. This, she suggested, would enable him to get a good night's sleep and take advantage of the full day's sunlight to walk in.

Trace and Isabella spent the next two hours planning Trace's walk away from Fort Lauderdale.

Isabella filled Pete's backpack for Trace to take with him. She included a home First Aid kit, an old compass that had belonged to her deceased father, and some extra clothing. She also made sandwiches for him to pack in the morning.

Trace called Washington and arranged with his Wells Fargo branch to make $10,000 available to him from the restricted withdrawal money market fund he and Isabella maintained.

"I'll withdraw this money from Wells Fargo's office in Palm Beach when I get there," he told Isabella.

"What if you wind up someplace else?" she said.

"Good point. I'll call the bank back. I'll need some way for the Palm Beach branch to transfer my funds to wherever I end up."

He took his cell phone and made the revised arrangements with the bank in Washington.

To celebrate his plan, and to send Trace off with a good home cooked meal, Nanna and Isabella prepared Linguine Alfredo for lunch, Trace's favorite pasta dish.

After lunch ended, Trace said to Pete, "Want to go over near the beach with me, walk around for a while, spend some time together?"

"Sounds good, Dad. Let's do it." Pete excused himself and said he'd be right back, ready to go in a few minutes.

After Pete left the kitchen, Trace turned to Isabella. "Would you and Nanna like to join us?"

Isabella shook her head. "Go have a good time before you leave," she said. "I'll keep Nanna company here."

As Trace was turning to leave with Pete, Isabella said, "Trace, I almost forgot. The president's going to speak tonight on TV about the flu epidemic. We should watch him."

CHAPTER 28

Fort Lauderdale
March 14

WHEN TRACE AND PETE LEFT the condo and walked over to Ocean Boulevard — the street running for several miles parallel to the beach — they talked about Trace's plan to walk away from Fort Lauderdale and find a car or other vehicle. Pete wanted to go with him, but Trace said no, he needed Pete to stay behind to provide moral support for Isabella and Nanna. Pete reluctantly agreed and dropped the subject.

As they approached Ocean Boulevard and the beach, Trace put his arm around Pete's shoulder. The smell of salt air awakened in Trace some long buried, but very pleasant memories of growing up at the seashore in southern New Jersey.

Trace and Pete fell into a game of tag that started when Pete unexpectedly slapped Trace's shoulder, shouted, "You're it," then ran up the street.

Trace instinctively responded to the challenge and ran hard after Pete, chasing him along the sidewalk. Trace sprinted up behind him, flicked the back of his hand against Pete's shoulder, and said, "Got you."

Trace spun away, leaned forward and started to run. Then,

abruptly, he braked himself and straightened up. He docked his open palm over his eyes, shading them from the sun's glare as he watched a military-style HUMVEE, followed by a flatbed truck, approach from two blocks away.

Pete, running fast, barely avoided crashing into Trace's back. He twisted his body and managed to slip by, lightly bumping Trace's shoulder with his own shoulder before again dashing away.

"You're it, Dad. I shoulder-tagged you."

Then, suddenly aware that his father's attention was elsewhere, Pete stopped running, and turned back to face Trace.

"Why aren't you coming after me?"

Trace ignored Pete's question and continued to look up the street.

Pete turned and followed Trace's gaze with his own eyes.

"What's that?"

Trace turned his head and looked at Pete. "Come here, Son. Right now."

Trace grabbed Pete's wrist and pulled him into the shadows of a storefront entrance. He towed Pete toward the back, out of sight of anyone on the street, deep into the dark.

"Dad, you're scaring me. What's going on?"

"Quiet. I don't want them to know we're here."

"But—"

"I said, be quiet. Please, Pete."

As they watched, the HUMVEE lumbered to a stop almost directly across the street from them. Soldiers jumped from the back of the combat-ready vehicle and deployed along the fuzzy line that separated the sidewalk from the beach sand.

Behind the soldiers, a few feet away on the sidewalk, workmen poured from the back of the flatbed truck and began erecting a seven-foot-high chain-link fence topped with concertina razor wire.

"Dad, what's going on?" Pete stood in the dark entryway behind Trace, and peeked out from around him.

Trace turned and looked at Pete, said, "Hold on a second," and then looked back across the street.

Without taking his eyes from the soldiers and workmen, Trace reached out and put his arm around Pete's shoulder. He gently pulled him in close.

Trace and Pete remained at the back of the storefront entryway for more than forty minutes, until Trace was satisfied they wouldn't be seen by the soldiers or workmen who had moved south along the beach as the fence went up.

Trace stepped over to the edge of the entryway and leaned out to look. The soldiers and workmen were now tiny, dark stick figures. The street was deserted, with no pedestrians in sight. Trace turned back to Pete.

"We can come out now," he said. "They're gone. They can't see us anymore."

Trace walked out of the shadows onto the sidewalk. He squinted — briefly blinded by the bright, late afternoon sunlight reflecting off the white pavement — and shaded his eyes with his palm until his vision adjusted.

He looked up the street one way, and then down the other. He and Pete seemed to be alone.

Trace turned and looked back into the entryway. He could just about see Pete who was sheltering deep in the shadows, staring out at him like an animal in a cave.

"It's okay, Pete. We're alone now. It's all right to come out."

Pete cautiously emerged from the dark, moving toward the sunlight, but not yet stepping into it. He leaned out over the sidewalk and looked up and down the street. Then he stepped out. He riveted his eyes on Trace's eyes, and moved over to him. He stood very close to his father.

After a few minutes, Trace said, "Let's head home, Son. We'll watch the president's TV address with Nanna and mom. Maybe we'll learn something useful."

CHAPTER 29

Camp David, Maryland
March 14

THE PRESIDENT SETTLED INTO THE chair behind his vacation home desk. He ran his hand along the left side of his head, smoothing his well-coiffed hair. He loosened his tie ever so slightly.

Behind him, hanging on the wall, loomed the Great Seal of the United States.

He sat facing the TV cameras, waiting for the producer to signal him to begin.

All the major network television, radio, cable, and online news organizations had crews present. The White House Office of Communications had notified them that the president's address this evening would be a major statement. The networks responded predictably, shipping their crews and equipment pools to the small community of Thurmont, Maryland, deep in the Catochin Mountains near Camp David, where the president was in retreat preparing his address to the nation.

"Please standby, Mr. President."

"Ready, Sir. On "1". Counting down now...5, 4, 3, 2, 1—"

The producer pointed her finger at the announcer who said in his velvety baritone voice, "Ladies and gentlemen, the president of the United States."

"My fellow Americans, I come before you tonight both as your president and as the commander-in-chief of the Armed Forces of the United States.

"It is my sad duty to inform you that approximately three weeks ago foreign terrorists attacked our country at Fort Lauderdale, Florida, using a deadly biological weapon against innocent men, women and children.

"Your government is taking all steps necessary and appropriate to apprehend the terrorist offenders who perpetrated this craven crime. Acting on my orders, the FBI and CIA are vigorously pursuing all leads to identify the terrorists and to learn their country or countries of origin."

He paused to allow this statement to sink in, picked up a glass of water, took a sip, and then looked back at the camera as he replaced the glass on the marked spot.

"The scientists and physicians at the Centers for Disease Control and Prevention have advised us that they have identified the biological weapon used against the people of Fort Lauderdale. It is an extremely contagious and virulent bacteria called Melioidosis, which has been masquerading for several weeks as an undiagnosed, virulent late-season flu."

He paused, took another sip of water, and looked back into the camera. Then he paused again to rivet the audience's attention on his next words.

"As your president, I am taking all necessary steps to prevent the spread of this disease outside Fort Lauderdale, to limit its reach in order to minimize its harm to the rest of our country. Our goal is to prevent a national epidemic while we, at the same time, provide all possible care and comfort to the victims of this attack and to their loved ones who are in Fort Lauderdale."

He shuffled his feet under the desk, even as he maintained unblinking eye contact with the camera's lens.

"I have today directed the CDC and the National Institutes of Health to dedicate research funds on a top priority basis to finding preventative and curative vaccines for this scourge."

The president opened his hands on the desktop, exposing his palms in a plea-like gesture to the ceiling.

He licked his lips.

"Also today, acting to protect our entire country, I have signed an executive order placing Fort Lauderdale under temporary, but mandatory quarantine protection.

"I also have ordered that Fort Lauderdale temporarily be placed under martial law to enforce this quarantine. No one will be permitted to enter or leave the Fort Lauderdale Quarantine Zone for any reason until the danger to our country has passed.

"Accordingly, I have instructed the secretary of defense to activate appropriate Army reserve units from outside the State of Florida to assist in enforcing the quarantine and martial law. To that end, my fellow countrymen, I have today appointed General Anthony Vista, United States Army Reserve, to head the Office of the District Military Commander in Fort Lauderdale. General Vista will have the power and authority to issue enforceable laws within the Quarantine Zone, as he sees fit, to maintain law and order and to protect the health and welfare of our country. General Vista has the full support of this Administration.

"Acting on the recommendations of the joint chiefs of staff

and, in particular, the army chief of staff, I have ordered that the New Jersey National Guard, General Vista's former command, undertake the first steps to implement the quarantine by erecting a chain-link fence around Fort Lauderdale. That process began this afternoon."

He paused again and sipped water.

"My fellow Americans, I know these measures are harsh. I wish I didn't have to apply them, but I do. So I have ordered these steps based on my best judgment, as your president, of what is necessary to protect our entire country and all our citizens and visitors.

"I have acted to limit and contain this contagion to Fort Lauderdale. I have taken these difficult actions, in the full measure of my duties and responsibilities as commander in chief under the Constitution and as your president, to defend our country."

He paused and licked his lips.

"May God in Heaven bless and have pity on the people of Fort Lauderdale. May God also bless the United States of America. Good night, and God bless you all."

When the red light on the camera faded to dark, the president stood. He waved once to the media crews. Then he turned away and walked swiftly from the room.

Day One of the Quarantine had begun.

PART TWO

CHAPTER 30

Quarantine
Day 1

P ETE PULLED ASIDE THE CURTAIN and looked out the window for the source of the noise that had penetrated the barrier established by his iPod, his earbuds, and the loud music he was listening to.

He peeled off his earbuds, left the apartment, and bounded down the steps, arriving at the parking lot in time to see two paramedics rolling a gurney toward a parked EMS vehicle.

"What happened?" Pete said to a women standing near him.

"It's that terrorists' germ the president talked about on TV yesterday. That guy caught it." She pointed to the nearby gurney. "You should've seen him. He's beet red."

"Too bad. Who is he? Do you know?" Pete said.

"Foley something. Never heard his first name."

Pete cautiously walked a few steps closer to the gurney and looked down at its recumbent passenger.

"I know him from the swimming pool," Pete said.

"That's his wife," the woman said, "the one over there crying." She pointed across the parking lot. "She told me he woke up during the night with a headache and fever. Wouldn't let her call a doctor. Said to her that she got well by herself, so he would, too." The woman nodded toward the gurney. "By morning he was delirious so the wife called 911."

The woman suddenly seemed to have experienced an epiphany. She looked hard at Pete as she raised her hand to cover her mouth and quickly stepped back away from him.

"Wait a minute. You said you know him?" she said, as she backed away from Pete. "You were near him at the pool?" Before he could answer, the woman turned and hurriedly walked away.

As Pete watched, the paramedics rolled Sam Foley and his gurney into the EMS vehicle. One paramedic climbed up into the back and closed the doors behind him. The vehicle started up, accelerating as it moved away from the parking area, its siren bleating.

Pete walked back to Nanna's condo.

Trace was at the kitchen table drinking a cup of coffee when Pete returned.

"Hi, Champ. What's going on?"

"Nothing. I was listening to music and heard a siren outside in the parking lot. I went downstairs to see what was happening."

"I heard it, too. What was going on?"

"Not much. An old guy was sick and they took him away."

Pete wondered if he should tell his father that he'd sat and talked with Sam Foley the previous week at the pool.

"About the guy they took away . . . ." Pete said.

"What's that, Pete?"

"Well, you know . . . ." Pete hesitated. He crossed his arms over his chest and looked away. Then he looked back, but avoided eye contact with his father.

"Is there something you want to tell me?"

Pete averted his gaze and looked out the window.

"What's on your mind, Son?"

Pete slipped his hands into his pants pockets, lowered his head slightly, and looked up at his father through heavily-lidded eyes.

"It's nothing. Doesn't matter anyway."

CHAPTER 31

Quarantine Day 5

EREK PETERSON WAS TIRED. HE was ready to wind-up the day's broadcast and get on with trying to adjust himself to life under martial law. He had only to cover the matters given him this afternoon by the Office of the District Military Commander, and he'd be finished for the day.

Derek focused his eyes on the camera and said, ". . . and now, ladies and gentlemen, on to another matter. The Office of the District Military Commander, General Anthony Vista's office, has instructed me to remind you that under Field Order No. 2 everyone must register with the ODMC. The penalties are severe if you fail to register, so take some time and do it today.

"You also must remember that under Field Order No. 2, in order to help prevent the spread of Melioidosis, you are prohibited from congregating in public places in groups of three or more adults.

"Finally, a word of warning and friendly advice from the ODMC: if members of the military should stop you to question you, don't resist, just cooperate. These stops are for your own good."

He paused and wiped perspiration from his neck.

"Routine questioning and ID checks will frequently occur, so be sure you have your official PhotoID with you at all times. You will receive your PhotoID when you register.

"Also, if you are stopped and questioned or if at any time you should yourself initiate contact with the authorities, for any reason other than when you register yourself, keep in mind that your ID information will be entered into the ODMC's central computer database. Don't be alarmed by this. The ODMC maintains this database to help it track the course of the terrorists' disease and to follow the whereabouts of each of us in the Quarantine Zone during these chaotic times.

"Now, having said that to you," he added, "I should point out that it is inadvisable for anyone to be entered into the computer system's database three or more times because upon the third entry your name will be placed on ODMC's watch list. If that happens, should you thereafter again be entered into the database, you might be taken into custody, questioned, and, perhaps, detained."

Derek paused to let this sink in. Then he said, "There's one more thing I need to say before I sign off." He paused.

"To meet my journalist's obligation of full disclosure, I want to tell you that sometimes I will report on news in the Quarantine Zone that I will have learned about in my capacity as a reporter; sometimes I will report on matters told to me by the authorities for the purpose of having me act as their spokesperson; and, sometimes I'll give you my opinion on matters. I assure you that I will always tell you in which capacity I am acting when I address you." He paused to let this sink in. "This is Derek Peterson signing off until tomorrow at 9:00 a.m."

CHAPTER 32

Quarantine Day 7

SEVEN DAYS INTO THE QUARANTINE, Trace found himself watching Pete and thinking about Pete's recent anomalous behavior.

Trace put down the newspaper and again looked at Pete.

Something wasn't right, but he couldn't put his finger on it. Pete didn't seem to be himself. He hadn't been for several days.

Trace sat at the breakfast table, the newspaper spread out in front of him. He started working his way through the front page again. This time he tried to read stories located below the fold, but his concentration was off. Pete occupied his mind.

He stood up and again looked at Pete, who was sitting on the sofa at the far side of the living room.

He looks so forlorn, Trace thought.

Pete sat with his legs pulled up. He had wrapped his arms around them and rested his cheek on one knee.

Trace picked up the newspaper, but then immediately put it down. He stared again at Pete.

Something's wrong.

Trace mentally replayed, as he had several times that morning, Pete's behavior these past few days: Pete had eaten very little at dinner last night and had to be coaxed by Bella to eat at all, even though Nanna had cooked meatloaf with gravy and mashed potatoes, one of Pete's favorite meals. He'd skipped dessert, too. Then he went to bed early, much earlier than usual.

Trace massaged his forehead with his fingertips and squeezed his eyes closed.

This morning at breakfast Pete had turned down Nanna's offer to make blueberry pancakes for him. I never would've predicted that, Trace thought.

As he looked on, Pete squeezed back into a corner of the sofa. He gazed at the television screen, but, it seemed to Trace, he didn't see it. Pete's eyes were unfocused, bloodshot, and seemed to be wandering.

"Son, are you feeling all right?" Trace said. "Pete?"

Pete turned his head in slow motion and looked at Trace, but said nothing.

"What's the matter, Pete? Tell me."

No response.

Trace walked to the sofa and knelt alongside Pete.

"Bella, come here," Trace called. "Something's wrong with Pete.

Isabella, followed closely by Nanna, raced into the living room and went directly to Pete. She dropped down onto the sofa next to him.

"Honey?" Isabella said. "What's wrong? Pete? Honey . . . ."

She sandwiched his hand between both hers.

Trace leaned over and placed two fingers against a pink rash he saw on Pete's cheek. Then he laid his palm on Pete's forehead.

"He's burning up, Bella. Feel him."

Isabella leaned into Pete. She put her fingers on his forehead, but jerked them away as soon as she touched him. She looked up at Trace, then immediately turned back to Pete.

She slid one arm around his shoulders and pulled him in close. Then she put her hand under his head and carefully moved his head from her shoulder to her breast. She hugged him as if he were her newborn.

"Trace. Do something. Get a doctor."

Isabella placed her lips against the top of Pete's head in a lingering kiss and closed her eyes.

Twenty minutes later Trace closed his cell phone and returned to the living room. He sat down on the floor beside Isabella. She still sat on the sofa with Pete, wiping his forehead and face with a damp cloth which she repeatedly moistened using a pan of water placed by her feet.

"I can't get past the answering services," Trace said. "There don't seem to be any doctors at their offices even though we've been told to call them and avoid the hospital. I better take him over to the ER even though we're not supposed to. Help me get him ready."

CHAPTER 33

Quarantine
Day 7

T RACE DRESSED PETE FOR THE trip to the ER. The tropic-
like temperature outside called for a short sleeve shirt and
lightweight slacks or shorts. But guided by Pete's alternate
bouts of sweating and shivering, Trace dressed Pete in the wool
sweater and homeboy baggy jeans Pete had brought with him
to wear on the flight back to DC.

"I'll get a washcloth and bottled water," Isabella said. "Then
I'm ready. I'll take a blanket."

She leaned over and kissed Pete's forehead. She looked at
Trace. "Will we catch this, too? Should we be doing something
to protect ourselves?"

"If we're going to come down with what Pete has," Trace
said, "there's nothing we can do about it now because of the
disease's incubation period. You remember what the county
medical director said on TV about an incubation period. We've
been exposed since long before today."

"What's going to happen, Trace? Pete will be okay, won't
he?" She looked over at him, then back at Trace.

Trace thought for a second about his response, then nodded

twice. "He'll be fine once we get him to the ER and they break his fever."

He picked up Pete and held him in both arms like a sacrificial offering to the gods. Pete lay limp across Trace's parallel arms, his head, arms and legs dangling.

Trace and Isabella walked the four blocks to the hospital. Trace labored under Florida's heat and humidity, the difficulty of his efforts augmented by Pete's dead weight.

He carried Pete to the edge of a parking lot on the hospital grounds and stopped. He could see the ER across the lot, about sixty yards away.

"Hold on a second," he said to Isabella.

He looked across the macadam at two EMS vehicles. Their back doors were flung wide open. They were parked askew near the sloping driveway leading from the parking lot up to the ER.

"Look at those people," Trace said, pointing across the parking lot at a group of twenty or so people who were moving up the driveway from the parking lot toward the ER entrance.

"What are those soldiers doing?" Isabella said.

Trace shook his head. "I don't know. I can't hear the one with the bullhorn this far away."

They watched as the soldier with the bullhorn pantomimed an address to the approaching crowd, his left arm occasionally flailing, his right fist grasping the bullhorn in front of his mouth.

As the group moved toward the ER, Trace and Isabella watched six armed soldiers arrange themselves shoulder-to-shoulder in front of the ER's entrance doors.

Trace instinctively stepped away, walking backwards a few

steps, still watching the ER entrance, creating more distance between the soldiers, himself, and his family.

Trace stopped walking when he reached a copse of chest-high bushes he stepped behind. Isabella followed close behind him, and peeked over the shrubs, looking from Trace to the ER entrance and then back again, several times. Trace continued to hold Pete in his outstretched arms.

As he and Isabella watched from the safety provided by distance and the bushes, the soldier with the bullhorn faced the incoming crowd.

Behind him, standing a few feet away, a female soldier watched. Then she nodded at something the first soldier said to her, and stepped to the side of the entrance.

The soldier with the bullhorn again raised the device to his mouth and spoke to the approaching crowd. Trace still could not hear what the man said.

This soldier moved to the side of the ER entrance, over next to the female soldier. He kept his head turned toward the crowd, even as he stepped off to the side.

Without warning, moving as one, the soldiers in front of the ER's entrance raised their weapons, aimed at the approaching crowd, and fired.

CHAPTER 34

Quarantine
Day 7

Derek Peterson stood on the street corner under the late morning sun gathering his thoughts for his upcoming broadcast.

The bright blue sky and the puffy, cotton clouds contrasted sharply with the squalor on the ground as Fort Lauderdale staggered into the last day of the first week under quarantine and martial law.

Derek looked up and down the street while he waited for his cameraman to finish setting up.

The streets are becoming less crowded every day, he thought. He tried to remember the last time he saw a child outside. He couldn't think when that was.

A humid breeze slapped a yellowed page of newspaper against his leg, wrapping it around his calf and ankle. He bent down and pulled the paper away, crumbled it into a ball, and tossed it back into the street where it was lost among the general detritus of weeks-old, stained fast-food wrappers, cardboard coffee cups, and other trash of a type not generated anymore in the Quarantine Zone.

Derek looked north up the street and then south. As far as he could see in either direction cars, SUVs and other cannibalized or burned-out abandoned vehicles choked Route A1A.

He looked across the street and watched as three young men dressed in T-shirts and jeans — men probably in their late teens or early twenties, Derek thought — walked up to the display window of a men's clothing store, formed a tight huddle, and then looked around. One of the young men reached behind his back under his T-shirt and pulled out a foot-long, souvenir-size baseball bat. He used the small bat to smash the store's plate glass window.

The young men took their time reaching through the broken pane into the window's display area. They seemed unfazed by the wailing burglar alarm they'd triggered.

Derek considered putting the young men on camera and commenting on their brazen lawlessness as a graphic example of the burgeoning crime rate taking hold in the Quarantine Zone. He decided to let it ride and do nothing. Better, he thought, to avoid calling attention to myself and possibly awakening the frustration and anger of the young men and having them direct that anger toward me. Anyway, he thought, looting isn't even news anymore.

He watched as a pack of feral dogs quickly crossed the street, their noses gliding just above the ground, sniffing trash and garbage strewn in their path as they jogged onward. Two dogs jumped up against an over-flowing trash can, knocking it over and spilling its contents. The pack leaped as one fluid unit into the trash pile and rooted around, yelping and barking.

Derek brushed himself off and slicked back his hair with his sweating palms. He faced the camera, but warily watched the dogs from the corner of his eyes. He held his clipboard and notes in one hand and his wrinkled, damp, paisley red bandana in the other.

He looked directly into the lens, squared his shoulders, took a deep breath, and assumed his practiced, self-assured TV reporter-type demeanor. Out of view of the camera his left foot tapped a drum roll.

The camera's red light blinked, Derek's producer said, "Take it, Derek," into Derek's earbud, and the cameraman pointed his finger at Derek. Derek began that day's broadcast.

CHAPTER 35

Quarantine
Day 7

T HE SIX SOLDIERS IN FRONT of the ER's entrance barely completed firing their rounds at the approaching civilians when Trace and Isabella instinctively abandoned the blanket, the water bottle, and Pete's backpack, and rushed away. They didn't say a word as they put as much distance as they could, as fast as they were able, between themselves and the hostile soldiers.

⊁——⊁——⊁——⊁——⊁

Twenty minutes later Trace stood at the foot of the bed looking at Pete and Isabella as he thought about the shooting at the ER entrance.

Pete was lying on his back, shivering, covered to his chin by two light wool blankets. His face was red, his eyes watery slits.

Trace thought Pete seemed to be in that nether state somewhere between sleep and feverish consciousness. The blankets rose and fell like automobile engine pistons, pumping as Pete wheezed air in and out of his lungs.

Isabella sat on the edge of the bed. She had one hand on

Pete's covered chest as if to reassure him he wasn't alone. She wiped his face, neck and forehead with her other hand, using a damp cloth.

Bella looks tired and frail, haggard, Trace thought.

"Bella, can I do anything for you?"

Isabella didn't turn away from Pete to answer. She looked at Trace from the corner of her eyes, then slowly turned her head toward him.

"I'm just tired and worried," she said. "I'll be all right."

Trace walked over and put his hand on her arm. He lightly pressed his thigh against her shoulder, but felt her stiffen under his touch. He opened his mouth to comment, but caught himself and let it pass. He pulled his hand back and moved away.

A few minutes later Trace sat in the living room. He reached over, picked up the Fort Lauderdale YELLOW PAGES and opened the book to the listing of PHYSICIANS AND SURGEONS. He'd already crossed-out more than half the names that morning when he'd tried to find a doctor for Pete before he and Bella had taken him to the ER. Now, he picked up his pencil and cell phone to try the few remaining names on the list.

The results of the morning's telephone calls repeated themselves in Trace's head. The doctors' taped messages were predictably similar: you have reached the medical office of dr. x. we are closed until further notice. there is no medication stored on the premises. if this is an emergency, please visit your local hospital emergency room. Click.

Right, Trace thought. Visit the ER after what they said on TV and after what we just saw.

This time, however, one doctor's message caught Trace's attention with its unique ending: if you are calling because someone you know is or might be suffering from the terrorists' bioagent, Melioidosis, please be aware that the united states food and drug administration has temporarily removed the requirement that a physician's prescription is necessary to obtain related palliative medications.

Trace redialed to be sure he'd heard the tape correctly. He had. This time, however, he focused on the very last part of the message:

such medication currently is not available at this office. we expect it to be available again as soon as the centers for disease control and prevention delivers a promised supply of this medication and others to fort lauderdale. limited supplies of this medication still might be available at local hospital emergency rooms or from your neighborhood pharmacy.

Trace put down the telephone book and plugged his cell phone into the wall charger. Then he went back to Pete's bedroom.

"Any change?" he asked.

Isabella shook her head.

He walked to the bed, kissed Isabella, and put his hand on Pete's forehead. Pete was still burning up. Trace thought the red hue of Pete's rash seemed more intense than before and that the rash now had become crusty and flaking. He wondered if this was significant, but didn't raise the point with Isabella. He also worried about Pete's rapid, shallow breathing and wheezing. He didn't know what it signified, but he figured it couldn't be good.

"He's been shivering," Isabella said, as if she'd read Trace's mind. "He's extremely hot, but he's shivering. His fever won't break."

Trace put his arm around Isabella's shoulders and said, "Bella, I'm going out again to try to find an open drugstore."

Isabella nodded.

"I'll be back before curfew. If not, I'll call."

He started to walk out of the room.

"Trace. . . ."

"What?" he said, turning back.

"Be careful. I can't have anything happen to you, too."

"Trace, is that you?" Isabella called from the back bedroom.

"It's me," he said. He'd made it back just before curfew.

He shook his head in answer to Nanna's inquisitive look as he walked past her through the living room on his way to Pete's bedroom.

It seemed to him that Isabella hadn't moved since earlier in the day. She still sat on the side of the bed holding a damp washrag in one hand and resting her other hand on Pete's chest.

"Did you get medicine?"

Trace slowly shook his head. "Nothing was open. At least no drugstore I could find," he said.

Isabella sighed. She patted Pete's forehead with the washrag.

"What're we going to do?" she said, looking at Trace. "He's no better. Maybe even worse." She turned back to Pete.

"We have to keep him stable," Trace said, "until the CDC delivers the meds it promised." He told her about the recorded message he's heard before he went out. "We need to break his fever and just hold on."

"His rash is spreading to his chest," Isabella said.

"Pete will be all right," Trace said. "We just have to control his fever until the CDC delivers the meds. Any time now."

Trace briefly closed his eyes and thought about the SEALs' Rule of Three. What are the three courses of action he should choose from in this situation? he wondered. What would be the best move to make among them?

CHAPTER 36

Quarantine
Day 9

A LITTLE MORE THAN ONE WEEK after the president addressed
the nation and declared Fort Lauderdale a quarantine zone
subject to martial law, Viktor Rutkowska felt troubled
by the reminders of his Soviet/Russian past that the speech
stirred up for him. If he had closed his eyes and imagined that
the speech had emanated from the Kremlin rather than from
somewhere in Maryland, near Washington, DC, the president's
words would have been clear: The president had turned Fort
Lauderdale into a gulag-style detention camp.

Viktor decided he had to see for himself what this concept
meant in America.

Viktor drove to Route A1A where it bordered the beach.
Sure enough, just as the newsreader had said, the border
between the beach and the highway, as far as the eye could see
in either direction, north and south, was delimited by a steel
hurricane fence topped with coiled razor wire.

Just like at a gulag, Viktor thought.

The images this evoked for Viktor were memories he
thought he'd disposed of for good. Wasn't that why, when he

left the military and opted for a resort to retire in, he'd chosen to move to the United States to be near his younger sister and her worthless American husband in the tropical climate of south Florida, in the so-called land and home of the free? Isn't that why he hadn't settled in the resort town of Novorossiysk on the Black Sea like so many of his retired Spetsnaz comrades?

Viktor turned his jeep away from the beach and headed inland. He would perform two tasks: first he would stop by his gun shop which today, as always, was closed on Sunday, and retrieve some weapons and ammunition to take home just in case he needed them to protect himself. Then he would go to his sister's house and meet with Svetlana to be sure she understood the full ramifications of what was happening in Fort Lauderdale.

Unfortunately, at age forty-one now, Svetlana had been too young when she lived in Mother Russia to understand the import of the gulags. He, her older brother, would have to explain the facts of life to her. Her unworthy husband probably would never understand.

This was not why I came to live in America, Viktor thought.

CHAPTER 37

Quarantine
Day 9

W HEN TRACE RETURNED TO NANNA'S condo from the
condominium association's community swimming pool
where he'd gone twenty minutes earlier to smoke a
cigarette and stretch his legs, he hesitated just inside the door.
The apartment seemed preternaturally quiet.

He looked around.

Nanna was stretched out on the sofa, her eyes open. He
didn't see Isabella, but he expected that. She likely still was
sitting at Pete's bedside. When he looked across the living room
toward their bedroom, he noticed the closed door.

Nanna sat up as Trace started to cross the room. She held
her finger up to her lips in a *shhhh* signal.

Trace nodded.

"Can I get you anything?" she whispered.

Trace shook his head. "How's Pete?"

"The same. Bella's lying down, resting."

Trace walked back to Pete's room. The shades were drawn,
the lights out, and the room dark. As far as he could tell, Pete
was asleep, lying on his side facing the wall. Trace leaned over

the bed, but couldn't get close enough to see Pete's face. He reached across the bed and put his hand on Pete's forehead.

Pete didn't stir.

He seemed cooler than Trace remembered, but not yet normal.

The keening woke them from their deep sleep at 3:20 a.m.

Trace and Isabella launched themselves from bed, tried to rub sleep from their eyes, communicating silently that they must hurry to Pete's room.

Pete moaned. He tossed and turned and shivered. He intermittingly sobbed loudly. Tears ran down his cheeks. His teeth chattered from fever.

He never opened his eyes.

Trace and Isabella spent the rest of the night sitting by his bed, wordless in their worry. They intermittingly dozed in their chairs, but jerked up their heads from time-to-time when they caught sleep trying to reclaim them. Neither acknowledged to the other the felt futility of sitting by Pete's bed in the early morning hours, fighting sleep, helplessly watching their son suffer. They held hands.

At 5:16 a.m., Isabella's hand went limp and became a dead weight in Trace's. He looked over at her. She was napping. Her chin had dropped to her chest. She snored softly.

He looked at Pete. Something in his posture, in the way he was lying on the bed, struck Trace as different. He seemed smaller, more constricted, more frail than before, but Trace couldn't bring the change into recognizable focus, nor could he attribute meaning or significance to it. He just sensed there had been some change.

Trace reached over and touched Pete's forehead. He reflexively pulled his hand back. Pete was noticeably hotter than before.

He sat back in his chair. Tension blossomed in his shoulders and neck bringing with it nascent pain that he knew would develop into a major ache if he didn't quickly get it under control.

He decided to practice the sitting meditation exercise he'd learned when he studied Chinese martial arts. The exercise was similar to the four-count breathing exercise he'd learned as a SEAL, and achieved the same result.

Trace inhaled slowly and deeply to calm himself, counting to four. He held his breath for a few seconds, then let it out, again to a four-count, fully emptying his lungs. He paid attention only to his breathing. He did not feel the stress leach from his body as he'd expected.

CHAPTER 38

Quarantine
Day 9

THE DEPUTY SECRETARY OF DEFENSE looked at his watch and frowned. He made no attempt to be subtle about his impatience. He was ready to end this meeting with his senior staff and with the senior participants attending from the Departments of Health & Human Services and from Homeland Security. He had already spent more time in this meeting today than he'd allocated to discuss Fort Lauderdale's quarantine.

"That leaves only you, Dr. Pryor," he said to the undersecretary for HHS. "What's your report? Please keep it brief."

"Yes, Sir. Thank you," she said, as she stood up and walked to the podium at the front of the small conference room located in the E-ring of the Pentagon.

"We are ready to make air deliveries of antibiotics directly into the Quarantine Zone on behalf of the CDC. We also have some ancillary meds that will give people other relief they might need, meds such as Insulin, heart meds, etc., the usual stuff for chronic ailments.

"The CDC has arranged for the reopening of pharmacies in

the Quarantine Zone as soon as the meds are available there. All we need is for you to give the go-word, Sir," she said, turning toward the deputy secretary. "The national guard is standing by to make the delivery." She nodded and walked back to her seat.

The deputy secretary walked back to the podium. "There won't be any go-word," he said. "There's been a change of plans."

The HHS undersecretary looked confused. "I'm sorry, Sir, but did I hear you right? Did you say—"

"You heard me correctly."

Although the deputy wouldn't tell the undersecretary or anyone else at the meeting, his boss, the secretary of defense, had made the decision to ratchet up the stakes in the Quarantine Zone by posting notices around Fort Lauderdale indicating that meds would soon be delivered by the federal government, then secretly withholding the meds. This would surely put pressure on the control population so the Pentagon could see how they would react.

"But, Sir—" the undersecretary said.

"Madam Undersecretary, listen up," the deputy secretary said, cutting her off. He paused until he was certain he had her full attention. Then he looked hard into her eyes and said, "This is not open for debate. This discussion is over."

The HHS undersecretary was stunned by this revelation.

"But, Sir, if it gets out that we don't have medication to offer, even if it's only to treat symptoms, we'll have a nightmare scenario on our hands. You'll be pitting one group of people against another once the quarantine population realizes meds are unavailable or are being rationed. It will be chaos."

"That's the way it's going to be," the deputy said. He paused and looked around the room. "This meeting is over."

CHAPTER 39

Quarantine
Day 11

T
RACE, STILL CURLED UP IN the chair next to Pete's bed, woke with a start. He looked over and saw Pete sleeping on his side, still facing the wall. He looked at Isabella's wingback chair pulled up alongside Pete's bed. It was empty.

He stood and reached for the ceiling, stretching his arms and back; then he rotated his neck and shoulders. He leaned over and touched Pete's forehead. Still hot.

Trace walked into the living room, looking for Isabella, checking his watch as he did so. It was ten minutes after nine. Nanna was asleep on the sofa. Isabella wasn't anywhere in sight.

He went to their bedroom where he found Isabella sleeping. He leaned over and kissed her forehead, then tiptoed out and quietly closed the door.

Back at the sofa, Trace crouched down until his face was at the same level as Nanna's.

"Nanna," he whispered, "sorry to bother you."

Nanna opened her eyes wide and looked around, disoriented, then looked up at Trace.

"What happened? Is it Pete?" she said, propping herself up on one arm. "Tell me."

Trace gently touched her shoulder and shook his head.

"It's not Pete," he said. "He's the same. Bella is sleeping so I wanted to tell you I'm going out for a while to see what's going on, to try to get a reading on the situation out there. I'll be back before curfew. Ask Bella to call me when she wakes up."

He kissed Nanna's forehead. Then he left.

Trace set off looking for an open drugstore, this time walking south from the condo. As before, all he found were closed pharmacies displaying the notice promising CDC's relief sometime in the future.

After an hour, he decided to head back to the condo. He walked along Commercial Boulevard as he headed home.

He'd walked two blocks when he saw three young people, two males and a young woman, standing on a street corner not far ahead of him. They were passing a lighted cigarette among themselves.

Three people. They better be careful. That's an unlawful assembly under the Field Order, he thought.

He looked around as he approached them, adding a prohibited fourth person to the unlawful assembly.

"Hi. I'm Trace."

They turned and looked at him, but said nothing. The young woman took a step back away from him.

As he spoke, Trace reached into his shirt pocket and pulled out his softpack of CAMEL cigarettes. He held it out to the young woman, stretching out his arm, carefully maintaining his distance.

"It's okay," he said, maintaining eye contact with her. "Help yourself."

The young woman looked over at one of the males, then back at Trace. She hesitated, then stepped forward, took the softpack, and stepped away again. She leaked a soft smile at Trace from behind her companions.

The young woman pulled out three cigarettes, then tossed the softpack back to Trace with an underhand flick of her wrist.

Trace sensed he had to win over the dark complexioned male, who probably was their leader. He was the one the young woman had looked at for implicit permission to step forward and take the CAMELs from Trace.

He turned to face the young man.

"I need help," Trace said. "My son's sick. Do you know if there's an open drugstore anywhere around here?"

The male looked at the young woman, then back at Trace.

"We don't want trouble, Mister," he said. "We're just sharing a smoke."

"No trouble intended from me," Trace said. "Like I said, I just need help."

The other male shook his head. "Everything's closed. Nothing around here's open that I saw."

He looked at the bulge in Trace's shirt pocket.

Trace took the hint and again pulled the open softpack from his shirt pocket. He tossed it over.

"Keep it," Trace said. "My wife's been after me to quit."

Trace and the three youngsters huddled on the corner smoking together, trading such little information as they had, and swapping rumors.

Suddenly, the strident sound of a ponderous, approaching

vehicle interrupted them. They turned as one and looked in the direction of the rapidly accelerating noise.

A HUMVEE rumbled to the curb and stopped just ten yards from them.

Damn, Trace thought, there're four of us.

The three youngsters moved with the precision of a military drill team, bunching together and sliding behind Trace.

Two soldiers, dressed in MOP gear — Mission Oriented Protective suits — jumped to the sidewalk, M-4s in hand. They quickly strode over, positioning themselves, one in front and one in back of Trace and his companions. A third soldier, dressed in a protective suit like the other two, stayed on the vehicle and sat behind a top-mounted M-249 weapon which he aimed in their general direction.

Trace moved his hands into plain sight, with his palms facing outward, so they could see he wasn't holding a weapon.

"Down on the ground," one soldier said, his voice sounding robot-like as it filtered through his MOP suits' speaker system. "Show me your hands. Do it now!"

He pointed his weapon in their general direction and took a short step toward them. He poked the tip of the weapon toward the ground, using puppeteer pantomime to emphasize his shouts, commanding them with his gestures to lie down.

The youngsters dropped to their knees like dead weights, then stretched out face down on the pavement. Trace slowly followed them to the ground, all the while watching the soldier closest to them.

"Don't move until I tell you," the soldier said.

He stepped back from Trace and his companions, and nodded to the other soldier who moved in and patted them down.

"They're clean."

"Get up," the first soldier said. "Keep your hands where I can see them."

Trace and his companions rose to their feet in exaggerated slow motion, not saying anything, and not taking their eyes off the soldier who had spoken to them.

"You can't be four people in public together," the soldier said. "That's an unlawful assembly. There's not more than two allowed together. It's in the Field Order. I could take you in if I had a mind to."

He raised his weapon slightly and took a step toward them. "Give me your IDs."

He took the four drivers' licenses and looked at the photos, comparing each with its live counterpart.

"Watch them," he said to his colleague, nodding toward Trace, "while I check these IDs." He walked back to the HUMVEE.

"Your IDs check out," he said a few minutes later. He hooked his right thumb into his belt.

"I'm going to let you off this time since you're not on the watch list and don't have priors, none until now, that is, since I entered you all into the system."

He turned and faced Trace. "You're not registered," he said to Trace.

He turned to the young people. "You're not registered either."

He paused and looked the four of them over.

"All of you, listen here," the soldier said. "Register before you become violators. There won't be any second chance if you're stopped again and haven't registered. You're now in the computer system.

"And remember," he said, "you can't be three or more people together like you are, so split up." He saluted with two fingers and handed all the drivers' licenses to Trace. Then he and the other soldier walked back to the HUMVEE, climbed on board, and rode away.

Trace and his companions stood mute and watched the vehicle noisily lumber away and disappear around a corner.

Trace faced around and said, "Trace is my name. Trace Austin."

"Ibrahim," the apparent leader said. His skin was dark, his hair coal black with tiny, tight curls, his eyes black, too. He wore a tiny silver hoop in his left earlobe. He had two or three days' growth of beard.

"This is my friend, Jenna Burke," he said, nodding at the young woman. "He's Calvet. Jenna's with me. We're on spring break from college, Jenna and me."

Jenna stepped from behind Ibrahim and said, "My cousin, Alex, comes to Fort Lauderdale every spring break. Said this place is a blast. Guess not this year though. We're looking for him."

The third youngster, Calvet, stared at Trace, but said nothing.

"We've got to go," Ibrahim said.

With that, he turned away from Trace, and began walking.

Trace watched them walk up the street. They turned into an alley and disappeared from sight.

Trace thought, Those kids won't make it here alone. They

better hook-up with someone experienced if they're going to survive martial law.

Trace walked back to the condo. He still didn't know any more about finding an open drugstore than he did when he started out earlier that day. He just knew that Pete had to hang on until the CDC came through with the promised meds. It should be any day now based on the posted notices.

CHAPTER 40

Quarantine
Day 14

T HE WAILING STARTED SOFTLY, MORE as a deep undercurrent
of noise than as an actual lament, more felt by Trace in his
sleep than consciously heard by him.

The sound progressively intensified, elevating its pitch from
basso to tenor, increasing its volume, matching the rhythm of
Pete's now recurring spasms.

Then Pete screamed, and he didn't stop.

His fingers closed into tight, rigid, locked hooks. His
fingernails pierced his palms.

His feet curled and locked themselves into the stiff bound
feet of nineteenth century Mandarin girls.

His torso convulsed.

Trace and Isabella ejected from their chairs, fully roused from
sleep by fear and pumping adrenalin.

Trace put one knee up on the bed and leaned in toward
Pete. He gripped Pete's arms.

Slowly, his own arm muscles straining, Trace tried to

unfold Pete's arms and place them back into a natural position. He couldn't release them from the spasm's grip. He feared fracturing Pete's bones if he tried too hard, so he let up.

Trace lifted Pete's shivering, crunched-up body and pulled him in close. He pressed his forehead against the top of Pete's head and gently rocked him as you would rock a sick toddler to calm him.

Trace lowered himself onto the edge of Pete's bed and sat him on his lap, wrapping his arms around Pete's body, as much to hug him as to keep him from gyrating off his lap onto the floor.

Pete's eyes now were wide open, watery, unseeing.

CHAPTER 41

Quarantine
Day 16

A
T FIRST VIKTOR WAS STUNNED.
Then he was livid.
Finally, he was frightened.

Fear was an emotion Viktor had experienced so infrequently, and had managed to quickly suppress when he did experience it, that its occurrence now, in this land that had been his home for the past six years, unsettled him even more than the events that had given rise to his fright.

Viktor was livid and, by extension, frightened because when he arrived at his gun shop that day to check on it, the gun shop was locked up, sealed tight, with a neon-yellow official notice nailed to the door stating that the business had been declared closed by the Office of the District Military Commander for the duration of martial law. The door was sealed tight by a thick chain and a military-quality lock.

When Viktor walked to the front window to look through it and eyeball the damage the military might have done — if they had even entered the shop — he was shocked by what he saw. As far as he could tell from the little he could see through the dirty window and the weak illumination given off by the crime light he'd left burning, all his inventory was gone. The locked wall racks were open and empty; the glass-top counter-cases were empty; and, the vault door was wide open. So much for my pricey security system, he thought.

Viktor returned to the front door and copied a telephone number from the notice tacked to it. As the notice stated, he could obtain information about the property-taking and about the closure of his business by calling the Office of the District Military Commander. Viktor would call and would find out why they had locked up his shop, closed down his business, and stolen his inventory.

Maybe, if he asked nicely, he thought, they would tell him how the hell he was supposed to earn a living in this so-called land of the brave and the free while his business was closed down.

But the phone call would have to wait. Viktor had one other thing to take care of first.

He walked to the back of the free-standing, former single-family house he rented and used as his retail gun shop. When he reached the backyard, he looked for indications that someone had been there.

Convinced his backyard also had been subject to trespass, Viktor walked to the far end of the property to a small tool shed where he kept a lawn mower and other basic maintenance tools. The padlock he'd placed on its door had been cut off and was lying on the ground in front of the entrance. No surprise there.

He opened the shed door and turned on the light. The interior had been ransacked, but that was all right. He would have done the same thing had he been in the occupying military here. If anything was missing, that would be fine, too. Everything he kept above ground in this shack could be replaced.

Viktor stepped outside and looked around to be sure he was alone. Then he re-entered the shack and closed the door behind him.

The only important question, he thought, was whether the fascists had discovered the cache of weapons and ammunition he'd hidden in the small space below his feet.

CHAPTER 42

Quarantine
Day 16

T RACE SAT IN THE DARKENED bedroom staring at Pete. Isabella had left hours before, returning to their bedroom to try to sleep.

Pete had been sleeping fitfully, reflecting his body's prolonged struggle with his fever and, more recently, his muscle spasms.

Trace had finally stopped fighting his own inclination to sleep, and allowed himself to slip away into a deep slumber. He awoke two hours later, ripped from sleep by Pete's shriek.

Trace bolted upright and looked over at Pete.

As Trace's eyes settled on him, Pete silently jerked his body up off the bed. He arched his back and twisted his torso in a wrenching muscle spasm. Then, just as abruptly, his body released its tension and dropped back onto the mattress.

Pete curled on his side with his chin tucked into his chest, his legs and arms drawn up into a rigid fetal position. He shivered and sweated. Perspiration streamed down his cheeks.

Throughout this contortion, Pete emitted no cry, no moan, absolutely no sound at all.

Pete's anomalous silence in the face of the spasms and contortions unnerved Trace even more than seeing the spasms and contortions themselves.

Pete never opened his eyes.

Trace stared at his contorted body.

Nothing more happened.

Pete lay curled on his side, his eyes closed, sucking his thumb.

CHAPTER 43

Quarantine
Day 16

T HE MANDATORY REGISTRATION PROCESS REQUIRED by Field Order No. 2 was simple: You stood in line to obtain your registration form, filled it out and signed the form, then stood in another line to have it checked for completeness and against your photo identification. If the completed form and your ID passed muster, you then moved to another line which led you to yet another ODMC clerk.

This ODMC clerk took your completed form and scanned the information into a template on the clerk's desktop computer. The clerk then sent your formatted information over the Pentagon's secure, post-9/11 survivable telecommunications network, feeding the information directly into one of the Cray X1E Supercomputers located deep beneath the Pentagon.

The Cray took your information and used its high-speed vector processing powers to mine government and private databases for other information about you. Then, processing with lightning speed, the Cray filtered and sorted this other information according to parameters that had been created as part of OPERATION TESTING GROUND specifically for the Quarantine Zone.

The Cray Supercomputer returned the results of its acquiring and sorting processes back to the ODMC clerk in less time, from start to finish, than it originally took the clerk to scan the completed form into the desktop template.

Trace and Nanna left the condo to register themselves, to register Pete who could not register himself, and to register Isabella who had stayed behind to take care of Pete. Such absentee registrations were permitted under Field Order No. 2, but did cause the people who were registered *in absentia*, as well as the people who registered them, to be entered into ODMC's central database.

After they completed the four registrations, Trace and Nanna returned home without incident.

CHAPTER 44

Quarantine
Day 16

AFTER TRACE RETURNED FROM REGISTERING, Isabella hovered over Trace and Pete, keeping one hand on Pete's shoulder and one hand on Trace's shoulder. Her eyes flicked from Trace to Pete and back again.

Pete's occasional howling had modulated to a soft, continuing moan. Then he suddenly shut down and became silent. A shudder waved through his body.

Trace looked for recognition in Pete's wide-open eyes, but saw none. He looked over at Isabella, then turned back to Pete. He placed two fingers on Pete's neck, pressing Pete's carotid artery, searching for a pulse.

Nothing.

Trace leaned in close to Pete's head to give him mouth-to-mouth resuscitation, but could not get past Pete's knees which remained tucked up above his chin.

He took Pete's head in his hands and tried to turn Pete's face toward him, but Pete's neck was fixed in place.

Isabella stood up slowly and leaned in close, looming over them.

She combed her fingers through Pete's hair. She sobbed and trembled. Tears cascaded down her cheeks.

Trace again searched for Pete's pulse, refusing to remove his fingers from the stilled carotid, waiting for a beat, however faint, to reveal itself.

Nothing.

He looked into Pete's unseeing eyes, then over at Isabella. He shook his head.

Isabella's eyes widened, silently answering her own unasked question.

Trace sucked in his breath and nodded. He leaned forward and rested his lips on Pete's cooled forehead, then reached over and gently closed Pete's eyelids.

Isabella's scream, once it came, surged. It pulsated. It rocketed around the room, echoing off the walls.

Trace leaned over and pulled Isabella into his arms, holding her back as she tried to throw herself onto Pete.

She tried to push Trace away, but he held on.

Then, just as suddenly as she'd screamed and struggled against Trace's restraint, she shut down, became silent, collapsing in complete surrender into Trace's arms.

Trace noticed movement from the corner of his eye, and turned toward it. Nanna stood leaning against the door frame, the knuckles on one hand plugging her mouth.

She looked into Trace's eyes.

Trace slowly nodded, then looked away.

Nanna groaned. Then she stumbled over to Trace and Isabella and put her arms around them, pulling them close into her. She dropped her head down until her cheek rested on the back of Isabella's head, cushioned by Isabella's soft hair.

Nanna cried softly.

Trace and Isabella sat in Pete's room staring at his corpse. No one said anything. Each kept a personal vigil over Pete's body.

Trace glanced at Nanna. Her eyes were closed. Tears ran down her cheeks. He turned to Isabella.

"Bella, we need to talk," he said, nodding his head toward the door. "Let's go into our bedroom."

In the bedroom, Trace sat close to Isabella and took her hand. He told her about the strict, unpleasant burial requirements he'd heard about when listening to one of Derek Peterson's television broadcasts.

Isabella looked at him as if he'd just dropped in from another planet. She shook her head.

"Absolutely not. I won't allow it," she said in a quiet, but resolute tone. "Our son will not be cremated and his remains scattered in a mass, anonymous grave. I *will not* permit it."

She turned her back to Trace.

Twenty minutes later, when they were back in Pete's room, Trace knew that time was making inroads into Isabella's resolve. Her gaze gradually drifted from Pete's body to Trace, from Trace to Nanna, and from Nanna back to Pete.

Still, she said nothing.

After a while Trace said, "Bella, I don't want this either, but we have no choice."

Nanna moved over to her daughter. She took her hand in both hers, and slowly raised them to her heart.

"Bella, Honey," she said. "Trace is right. He told me about this before. We have no choice. It's not just us, it's everyone. Please, Bella, just make the best of this horrible situation. Let Trace make the call to the authorities."

She squeezed Isabella's hand. "Please, Bella."

Isabella didn't say anything. She pulled her hand away from her mother's hands and stood up. She looked at Nanna and then at Trace. She turned back to Pete, bent over him and kissed his waxy forehead. Then she straightened up and turned to Trace.

She nodded once, turned away, and walked out of the room.

Trace watched Isabella walk across the hall and into their bedroom. He watched as she closed the door.

"Nanna, go stay with Bella. I'll make the call."

CHAPTER 45

Quarantine
Day 16

G ENERAL VISTA STARED AT THE stack of seven manila file folders he'd just finished reading, rereading, sorting, and re-sorting.

Each file contained a dossier on an individual who was present in the Quarantine Zone and who, after having registered, had been profiled and flagged by the Pentagon's Cray Supercomputer as a person likely to become a leader of some vigilante movement within the Quarantine Zone. This determination was based on the Cray's profile of the characteristics of such an individual and from other information uncovered by the Cray about each registrant as a result of its data mining efforts.

Of the seven files, two seemed to General Vista to deserve ranking in positions *most likely* and *next most likely*, as positions one and two. Or maybe positions one and one, without having a number two slot, he thought.

He couldn't decide, and the Cray could not help him with this aspect of the process. Instinct, he thought, is what's needed now, not binary numbers.

He pushed the intercom button and called in his major.

"Take these two files," he said, "and pick up these men. Bring them in for questioning."

General Vista thought about the two candidates he'd ordered picked up.

One file described an individual who had led a riot in state prison. The governor later pardoned him because he'd saved many lives, at great personal risk, during a subsequent, unrelated fire following an electrical-caused explosion.

This guy, Vista thought, certainly begs for close scrutiny.

The other file irritated Anthony Vista. It dredged up painful memories of his rejection by the Special Forces.

This file described a man named Trace Austin who had been a member of the elite Navy SEALs, a man who had been decorated for courage demonstrated during OPERATION JUST CAUSE in Panama when his chopper had been shot down and he saved two of his three trapped teammates by pulling them from the burning helicopter. The file also indicated that Austin had unexpectedly quit the SEALs soon after.

Austin, Vista thought, was a man who had abandoned his teammates, his brothers, and his country by quitting the SEALs for some reason not disclosed in his file. This ingrate doesn't have a clue what he gave up. He isn't a hero, no matter he was decorated. He's a quitter. He abandoned his men, his service, and his country.

Vista made a mental note assigning Austin to undisputed first place in the likely vigilante-leader threat assessment pile. He smirked as he thought about meeting this Trace Austin person when the major picked him up and brought him in.

CHAPTER 46

Quarantine
Day 16

THE AUTHORITIES CAME TO NANNA'S condo that afternoon and took away Pete's body.

The next day a team of ODMC medical technicians showed up unannounced and drew blood from Trace, Nanna and Isabella, ordering them to remain inside the condo until the laboratory results came back and indicated that they did not show evidence of having contracted the illness.

One day later, Trace, Isabella and Nanna received notice they were disease free.

The next morning, Isabella rushed into the bedroom, ran past Trace who was stretched-out asleep on his stomach on the bed, and went directly to the bank of windows. She raised the shades and let the bright early morning sunlight flood in.

She rushed back to the bed and grabbed Trace's shoulder. She shook him. "Trace, wake up."

Trace bolted upright into a sitting position, blinking his way out of a dream.

He turned toward Isabella. "What's wrong?" he said. He blinked hard and shook his head in short, quick lateral sweeps, trying to whisk away the sleep.

"It's my mother. She's yelling in her sleep. She's hot like Pete was."

Adrenaline kicked in, bringing Trace fully awake. He stood up and breathed deeply.

"Let's go see," he said.

Ten minutes later Isabella quietly closed the door to Nanna's bedroom and stepped out into the hallway. She walked to the living room and sat down on the sofa next to Trace.

"Why's this happening, Trace? First Pete, now my mother. I can't take this anymore." She buried her face in her hands and sobbed.

"I don't understand it," she said. "The tests said we didn't have the disease. How can this be?"

Trace put his arm around Isabella's shoulder and pulled her in close. He stroked her hair, gently, moving the palm of his hand down toward her shoulder, stroking her over and over. Isabella always found this soothing.

"All I can think of," he said, "is that for some reason it didn't show up yet in the blood work. Maybe Nanna was still in the incubation period when they tested us. For all I know, we might all be infected, still incubating the disease, and will come down with it in the next few days."

Isabella cried silently now, her head on Trace's shoulder. Trace could feel her sobs pulsating against him as her chest heaved. He pulled her in closer, leaned back on the sofa, then stretched out holding Isabella against his chest and side, partly

on him, partly on the sofa. They fell asleep stretched out
this way.

Trace woke fifteen minutes later. Isabella, still sound asleep,
had pinned him to the sofa with her body weight.

He eased himself out from under her until he could sit up
part way. Isabella opened her eyes.

"What's the matter?" she said. "Is it my mother?" She
started to stand up when Trace took her by her wrist and eased
her back down onto the sofa beside him.

"You've been sleeping, stretched-out on me. I woke up for
some reason. I didn't hear Nanna or anything. I just woke up,"
he said. "Let's check on her."

A few minutes later they tiptoed out from Nanna's bedroom
and eased the door closed. Isabella returned to the sofa. Trace
sat on the floor facing her.

"What should we do?" she said.

Trace took a deep breath. "You stay with Nanna. I know
I've done it before, but I'm going to call some drugstores. If
that doesn't work, and it probably won't, I'll go out again to
find one that's open."

It was too early to call drugstores so Trace shaved, showered and
ate breakfast. When he finished, he rinsed his dishes, filled his
coffee mug, and went into the living room.

He picked up the YELLOW PAGES. The book still was
open to the pharmacy section, just as he'd left it on the table.

Trace looked at the listings and saw three drugstores he hadn't yet crossed-out. He picked up his cell phone and dialed.

The first two responded with familiar recorded messages informing him that the pharmacies were closed until they received the promised shipment of medicine from the CDC — any day now, the recorded messages said.

The last call, however, the one to Horvath & Sons Drugstore, arrested Trace's attention.

At first, Horvath's recorded message merely reprised the information Trace had just heard on the recorded messages for the other two drugstores he'd just called. But there was one significant difference.

As Trace was about to hang up, the recording stated that although the pharmacy did not yet have the CDC's promised medicines, the pharmacy was well-stocked with non-prescription OTC medicines that could be used to relieve the discomfort caused by the terrorists' disease.

Trace listened to the message all the way through. Then he dialed the number again and listened one more time.

Maybe I can learn something about when the CDC's delivery will be coming, he thought. He decided to visit the drugstore.

Trace wrote down the store's address and telephone number, put the paper into his shirt pocket, kissed the sleeping Isabella goodbye, and walked to Horvath & Sons Drugstore.

CHAPTER 47

Quarantine
Day 19

THE INSIDE OF HORVATH'S LOOKED like a COSTCO big-box store, but on a smaller scale. It was organized in row after row of metal shelving stretching along parallel aisles. The aisles that Trace could see were each wide enough for three supermarket shopping carts to pass through at the same time without any one of them having to yield to the others.

Trace stood inside the entrance and looked around for the prescription counter. He saw an overhead sign indicating it was across the store, near the back.

That figures, he thought. About as far away as it could be, so you have to pass other items to get your medicine. Good for motivating impulse buying.

Trace walked along the mostly empty shelves, stepping over debris on the floor. He soon reached the prescription counter.

The pharmacist was a thirties-something Hispanic woman with coal black hair pulled back in a bun. She had beige skin, almost creamy almond. She was tall, about 5' 9", and was long-distance runner thin.

The woman stood behind the counter, her arms folded

across her chest, doing nothing, just staring into space as if she were waiting for the store to open and for customers to arrive with their prescription forms.

Trace stopped about ten feet from the counter so he wouldn't startle her when he interrupted her musings.

"Good morning," he said. He smiled to allay any fear she might have of being alone with a male stranger in the empty store's remote back corner.

In spite of Trace's good intentions, the woman seemed startled by the sound of his voice.

"I was wondering," Trace said, "if you've received any of the CDC's promised medicine? My wife's mother is ill."

The woman slowly turned her head toward Trace and frowned. She didn't say anything. She just stared at him, at first, then slowly shook her head.

After a long pause, she said, "There is none and there won't be any."

Trace thought she looked angry. He also thought she looked sad.

He took a tentative step toward the counter.

"When do you think you'll get some, if you know? I understand I won't need a doctor's prescription, will I, given what's going on?"

"You won't need a prescription because there won't be any medicine to buy. I just told you that."

Trace stiffened. He could feel a tension knot beginning to form at the back of his left shoulder.

"What're you talking about?" he said, keeping his tone friendly and inquisitive, not accusatory, although he felt accusatory, as if the woman's statement was tantamount to a declaration that the situation she described was her fault.

"There are printed notices all over town. We've been counting on it—" he said.

"It's not coming," the woman interrupted. "I know what I'm talking about," she said, speaking quietly, but resolutely.

Trace forced himself to slow down his breathing.

"That's not possible. Why would the government post signs around town stating that the CDC is going to deliver meds, then not deliver them? It makes no sense."

"I don't know why," the woman said. "I just know that's the way it is. I checked. You can believe it or not, whatever you want."

Trace inhaled deeply, held his breath, then slowly let it out. "What do you mean you checked?" He worked to keep his voice friendly.

The woman seemed annoyed that this conversation was still going on, but she answered him, her voice truculent now.

"When our last delivery was late, extremely late, I tried to contact our supplier. They told me to contact the CDC for information. I tried, but got nowhere.

"My phone calls weren't taken and weren't returned," she said, "so I called a friend in Atlanta — he's also a pharmacist — and asked him to check with his contacts at the CDC. He tried, too, but he also got nowhere. Well, almost nowhere."

She unfastened her collar button, opening the neck of her white jacket.

"My friend learned that the CDC had rescinded the delivery order to Fort Lauderdale. There was no reason given for it, at least no reason he could find out."

She stared down a nearby aisle, looking away from Trace. Then she turned back to him.

"Then", she said, "someone from the Department of

Homeland Security visited him at work and interrogated him about why he was asking questions about the meds. They warned my friend to back off and drop his questions or the next visit would be from the FBI to arrest him for interfering in a matter of national security."

She seemed to lose herself in some thought for a moment. Then she looked back at Trace, but said no more. She shrugged. "That's how I know."

"You're sure?" Trace said. "You're absolutely sure?"

She nodded and raised her eyebrows. "I'm sure."

Trace walked back toward the condo thinking about the import of what he'd just learned. None of this made sense.

Why would the government post signs about making deliveries, then block the deliveries? Maybe the woman didn't know what she's talking about in spite of what her friend had told her. Maybe her friend wasn't reliable or he had an ax to grind against the government, he thought. He couldn't see the authorities actually doing anything like that.

He was frustrated.

But if the woman was correct — and the evidence he was familiar with suggested she might be — then there seemed to be nothing he could do to help Nanna, just as he had been unable to help Pete and to help his SEAL team member in Panama.

That wouldn't do. He hadn't been trained to accept inaction and consequent failure. He'd been trained to face a problem, apply the Rule of Three, then resolve the problem or, at least, fail trying. He had not been trained to become passive in the face of obstacles.

I'll fall back on my training, he thought. I'll see if there is some way to put together a team of people so we can help one another as we deal with the quarantine and martial law.

All he had to do now was find these people and quickly train them to think and act like SEALs.

———— ✳ —— ✳ —— ✳ —— ✳ —— ✳

He was five minutes into his walk away from Horvath's, heading back to Nanna's condo, when he heard someone call his name.

He spun around and faced the caller.

"Hey, Trace."

He nodded. "I don't remember your name," Trace said, "what with the reception we received from those soldiers the other day."

"No problem. My name's Ibrahim."

The young man looked around, scoping out the street in both directions. Then he turned back to Trace.

"A lot's happened since I saw you before."

"Like what?"

"Like soldiers stopped us when we were out walking and arrested Jenna. She was taken away."

CHAPTER 48

Quarantine
Day 20

VIKTOR RUTKOWSKA, FOUR DAYS AFTER the day he removed his cache of weapons and ammunition from beneath his tool shed floor, again dialed the telephone number he'd copied from the notice posted on the front door of his gun shop. He wanted to ask about the closing of his business and how he would be paid for his guns and loss of business. This was the first time anyone in half a week had picked up the phone and answered his three calls.

Just like the bureaucrats in Mother Russia. Useless fools.

"How am I to earn a living if I cannot sell my guns?" he said. "You tell me. You're the government."

"Sorry, Sir, the woman's voice on the other end of the telephone call said, "but that is not our problem. We are here to protect everyone. You must make do on your own."

"But this is America," Viktor said. "I am citizen now, have rights like all American citizens. You cannot take my guns from me and not pay me. I read the American Constitution when I studied to be citizen. I have rights. Not like in Russia."

"We have emergency powers, Sir, as it states in the notice

put on your premises where you found this telephone number. You are welcome to come to our headquarters, examine the inventory of your property we created, and then file a claim for compensation.

"Be sure to bring purchase receipts and proof of ownership with you if you come here. That's all we can do for now to help you. Thank you, and call again if we can be of service" The young woman ended the call without further word.

Viktor stewed. This was outrageous. This is what he expected from his former homeland, not from America. He hadn't relocated all these kilometers from Mother Russia, learned what was necessary to become an American citizen, only to have the so-called American dream stripped away from him, just to be told by some fool of a bureaucrat he was out of luck.

Well, he thought, I will show them who they're dealing with. I will make the authorities regret they stole my guns and destroyed my business.

CHAPTER 49

Quarantine
Day 20

TRACE LOOKED SKEPTICALLY AT IBRAHIM, paused, then said again, "Jenna, arrested? Why?"

"I don't know. They didn't say why."

Trace nodded.

Ibrahim described how he and Jenna had been out walking when soldiers drove up and surrounded them. After some questions they took Jenna away.

"They made me lie face down on the sidewalk. One of the soldiers kept his boot on my back. They let Jenna stand. I was left face down when they took her away. I don't think ten words were said the whole time."

"Did they check your IDs?"

Ibrahim shook his head. "Never asked for them."

That's strange. "Look, Ibrahim, I'm sorry to do this, but I've got to get back to my family. I was on my way there when you stopped me. There's a problem with my wife's mother I need to deal with.

"Let's meet later today. We'll figure out some way to find out about your friend."

Ibrahim frowned, but nodded. He seemed disappointed.

"How about on this corner at 3:00?" Trace said, as he checked his watch.

Ten minutes later Trace sat on the floor in front of the sofa, facing Isabella, his legs crossed Buddha-style. Isabella sobbed. She buried her face in her hands.

Trace reached out to touch her, hesitated, and then pulled back. She needs to cry this out, he decided.

At 2:40, Trace looked in on Nanna. She was sleeping. He came back to the living room and explained to Isabella that he was going out to meet Ibrahim.

Trace arrived late. Ibrahim was already there, smoking and pacing. When he saw Trace, he flicked his cigarette into the street.

"Sorry I'm late," Trace said.

"No problem."

"Anything go on while you were waiting for me?"

"Some army-types in their protective suits walked by and gave me the eye. Guess they wondered why I was standing here alone doing nothing but smoking. Fortunately, they left me alone, didn't stop and ask."

"Have you come up with any reason Jenna might've been arrested?"

Ibrahim put his hands into his pockets. "No," he said, "I've been with her most of the time since we arrived here. If she did something wrong, I'd know, and I would have done it, too, and also been arrested."

Trace thought about this. He decided not to say what he was thinking, that it probably was something in Jenna's past, something picked-up by the ODMC's computer when she registered. Instead he said, "We need to find where they've taken her, then find out why. Did the soldiers say anything at all that might help?"

Ibrahim shook his head. "Nothing."

Trace stared into space, thinking. I should be keeping a low profile. That's always best in conflict. It increases your options to act.

He looked at Ibrahim. I shouldn't let this kid bumble his way into trouble. I need to watch out for him.

Trace looked back at Ibrahim, shook his head slowly, then said, "We'll go to ODMC's headquarters, ask about her. You okay with that?"

Fifteen minutes later, Trace and Ibrahim sat in a reception room at The Pillars Hotel — a room that once had been used for banquets in this renovated hotel-turned-military headquarters building. Movable accordion dividing walls ran from the floor to the ceiling along metal tracks.

After stating their business to the corporal sitting behind a dark-green metal desk, Trace and Ibrahim sat side-by-side at a long wooden table filling-in security questionnaires.

Trace quickly navigated his copy of the form, inserting his name, his pre-quarantine residence and business addresses, and his social security number. He checked the No boxes alongside the questions whether he ever was known by any other name or if he had ever been convicted of a felony. He checked the box for military service, and explained his SEAL career in one line.

He filled in Isabella's married and maiden names, and, reflexively, inserted Pete's name in the blank for children. When this last action registered in his consciousness, his momentary lapse brought his form-completion to an abrupt halt.

Jesus, did I just do that?

Trace took his fountain pen and carefully drew a thin line through Pete's name, which still was legible, but now clearly no longer applicable. Then Trace wrote, just above Pete's excised name, *Recently deceased.*

The form completed, Trace carried it and his photoID to the corporal. Ibrahim trailed closely behind. The soldier looked over both forms, then said, "Take a seat. The colonel will see you when he's ready."

He stood up from his desk and walked the forms out of the room.

CHAPTER 50

Quarantine
Day 20

Approximately fifty minutes after Trace and Ibrahim arrived at the hotel, the corporal answered the ringing telephone sitting on his desk and then walked over to them.

"Follow me," the corporal said. "The general will see you now." He turned to lead them down a corridor.

"General?" Trace said. "I thought we were waiting for a colonel?"

The corporal ignored the question. He led them to an office and knocked on the door.

After he saluted and exchanged some words with the person inside, the corporal led them over to chairs in front of a large desk.

An officer — a general, as Trace could tell from his uniform insignia — faced them from the other side of the desk. The nameplate on the desk read, General Anthony Vista.

Armed sentries stood at parade rest, one on each side of the desk, facing Trace and Ibrahim.

———⊁——⊁——⊁——⊁——⊁———

"What can I do for you gentlemen?" General Vista said.

"We're here to—" Trace started to say.

"Mr. Austin," Vista interrupted," as he focused his attention fully on Trace, "I've been looking forward to meeting you. Tell me, why did you abandon your brothers in the SEALs?"

Trace jerked up his head, suddenly extra-alert. "I didn't abandon anyone. It wasn't like that. Anyway, what's that have to do with anything?" How does he know about Panama? And why does he care?

"I have an order out to pick you up, Mr. Austin. I guess I can kill it now that you're here."

Trace was confused. He said, "Why would you want to pick me up?"

"I'm asking you again, Mr. Austin," Vista said, as he stood up behind his desk and faced Trace directly. "I know you received a decoration after the Blackhawk crash, but that was political. Doesn't mean crap. You're a disgrace to this country's uniform. You better have had a good reason to have deserted the SEALs. There are men who would give anything to have the opportunity you abandoned, the opportunity to be a member of our military's Special Forces."

Trace frowned, but decided to answer Vista's anomalous statement in vague terms. "It's ancient history. It has nothing to do with anything now." Nothing, perhaps, except there's a pattern there for me, he thought. First my SEAL teammate, then Pete, now Nanna. None helped by me.

"That's a matter of opinion, Mr. Austin." Vista stared at Trace and narrowed his eyes, but said nothing more. He looked over at Ibrahim, then immediately back at Trace.

"You're both in our computer database," Vista said, looking first at Ibrahim, then at Trace. "Let's see why." He tapped some keys on the desktop's keyboard and watched the computer's monitor.

"Here we go," he said. "First, a warning against unlawful assembly for you both. That's one entry. Then your report, Austin, of your son's death. That's two entries for you. Your presence here today is another entry for you both." He paused, looked hard at Ibrahim, then said, "Why are you here today, Young Man?"

Trace answered for Ibrahim. "Your soldiers took away a young woman named Jenna Burke, his friend," Trace said, nodding at Ibrahim. "We want to know why she was arrested and where she's being held."

"That's classified."

"Let us see her," Trace said.

"Not possible. As I just said, it's classified."

"With all due respect, General, you can't just pick up some kid and hold her—"

Vista slammed his fist on the desktop.

"Yes, I can, Mr. Austin. I can pick up and hold anyone I want, for any reason I want, or for no reason at all if I want, including holding you," he said. "That's what martial law is all about."

Trace felt his neck and shoulder tighten. He forced himself to concentrate on his breathing. He stared hard at Vista.

"In fact, Austin, if you're entered into the database again, for your fourth time, for any reason at all, we'll hold you, too, for as long as I want. Consider yourself warned."

Trace, from the corner of his eyes, saw Ibrahim shrink back against his chair.

"Now, if there's nothing else you gentlemen need, I have

work to do," Vista said. He looked at Trace, smiled a crooked smile, and said, "I'm glad we finally met."

He nodded toward the corporal who took a step toward Trace and Ibrahim. They left with the corporal.

They were five minutes into their walk away from General Vista's office when Ibrahim finally spoke.

"Were you really one of those crazies, those SEALs?"

Trace's eyes narrowed. He looked at Ibrahim, started to snap his reply back at him, but hesitated and held his thought. He nodded his answer, then added, "I was. Not anymore. I'm retired." He picked up his pace.

After another ten minutes of walking, Trace and Ibrahim arrived back at the corner they'd met at earlier.

"I have to get back," Trace said. "Call me if anything comes up."

CHAPTER 51

Quarantine
Day 20

VISTA CALLED HIS MAJOR INTO his office.

"Have this person followed," he said, as he handed Trace's file to the officer. "I want close attention, daily reports on all his activity, but no engagement. Not yet.

"I don't care if he's aware he's being followed."

"Yes, Sir."

"I want the names of everyone he associates with, not just generalities about him meeting some unknown male or meeting an unidentified female."

CHAPTER 52

Quarantine
Day 22

THREE DAYS AFTER BEING SNATCHED by the roving military patrol while she was out walking with Ibrahim, Jenna jumped from a HUMVEE as it slowed down and pulled over to the curb. She looked up and down the street. Satisfied no one was watching her, she nodded to the soldier who was manning the vehicle's automatic weapon, threw him a kiss with the flick of her wrist and hand, then pranced off.

She headed for the hotel, silently rehearsing what she would say to Ibrahim about her absence, although she hoped he wouldn't be there. That would be the easiest situation to deal with for now.

Jenna picked her way across the hotel lobby to the place where she and Ibrahim had been squatting. He was there, stretched out against the wall, sleeping. She stood above him and looked down, smiling. Now that she actually saw him, she was glad he was there.

Jenna lowered herself to the floor, keeping her back against the wall. She stretched her legs out in front of her. Once settled, she carefully lifted Ibrahim's head, holding it in both hands, and placed it on her lap. Ibrahim didn't wake up. Jenna fell asleep sitting in that position.

Later, when the noise of the lobby had substantially subsided, when the rheostat had been turned down bringing dusk to the room, Ibrahim awoke. Finding himself with Jenna, with his head on her lap when he opened his eyes, he hugged her waist as she slept.

Ibrahim never noticed that Jenna was feigning sleep, her eyes not quite closed, watching and listening.

Jenna remained quiet as Ibrahim settled back into sleep. She closed her eyes and remained still.

When she was sure Ibrahim was again in a deep sleep, she eased herself away from him, stopping her movements every few inches to see if he stirred.

When finally she was satisfied she could stand without waking him, she stood up and then threaded her way through the lobby, out onto the front steps, into the night's curfew.

Outside now, Jenna reached into her back pocket for her cell phone. She punched in a number and pushed the SEND button.

When someone answered her call, she said, "I'm back in. I'll call again tomorrow."

She pressed the END button and walked back into the hotel. On the way she opened the phone, removed the SIM card and broke the chip in half. She placed one part of the SIM Card in her pocket to dispose of later and the other half in the trash can just inside the hotel's entrance. She stopped walking briefly, inserted a new SIM card, and pocketed the phone.

CHAPTER 53

Quarantine
Day 22

THE DEPUTY SECRETARY OF DEFENSE waited until the door locked, sealing him and the senior members of his staff into the Pentagon's Level 4, ultra-secure Sensitive Compartmented Information Facility — known as a SCIF — meeting room.

"We've received the first comprehensive reports from Fort Lauderdale," he said. "The data are consistent with the information generated by the CRAY computer models and data mining efforts."

He paused and looked at his notes.

"There is one anomaly, however. The rise and apparent success of several vigilante groups supporting the population far exceed the model's predictions."

"What do we know about this, Sir?"

"Not enough. Actually, not much, at the moment. The most active vigilante group, called Friday's Progeny — after Robinson Crusoe's island mate, I suppose — has been penetrated by one of our assets. We'll soon know more about Friday's Progeny than they know about themselves," he said.

"Now, let's move on and get a short status report from each of you . . . ."

CHAPTER 54

Quarantine
Days 22 and 23

TRACE TOSSED AND TURNED ALL night, debated getting up and going to the living room to read, but each time surrendered to reason and tried again to sleep. Finally, about an hour after dawn, he gave in to his restlessness and sat up.

He looked over at Isabella. She was sleeping, lying on her stomach.

He knew she'd gotten up during the night, probably to look in on Nanna, because he had rolled over several times and reached for her, but she wasn't in bed.

Trace tiptoed around the room gathering his clothes, took them into the bathroom, and showered and dressed. When he finished and was ready to leave, he went back over to the bed and kissed Isabella as she slept. He left the bedroom, closing the door softly behind him. He wrote a brief note telling Isabella he was going out for a few hours to reconnoiter the Quarantine Zone. He wanted to think about how he would create a SEAL-like team from amateurs he hadn't even met yet. He let himself out the front door and walked toward the beach.

When Jenna woke that morning, Ibrahim still was sleeping, but his head was no longer on her lap. He was curled on his side with his back to her. She sat up, stretched, and then stood and walked across the lobby, stepping over and around sleeping bodies. She went outside and began walking toward the beach in search of something to eat.

Trace was about to cross the street when he realized the young woman walking in front of him was Ibrahim's missing friend, Jenna.

He picked up his pace until he was almost by her side, but decided to move away a few feet so he wouldn't startle her.

"Hello, Jenna," he said. "Hello."

Jenna stopped walking and turned her head around at the sound of her name. She looked at Trace, staring at him without any sign of recognition, then turned away, again facing the direction of her walk. She resumed her former pace.

"Jenna," Trace said, "it's Trace Austin. We met on the street corner the other day with Ibrahim and that other guy. I gave you my pack of cigarettes."

She slowed her step, stopped, and turned back to face him. She squinted as she examined his face.

"Oh, right." She nodded, but did not smile. "It's you," she said dismissively. She turned away to resume her walk.

"You're supposed to be missing, arrested," Trace said. "Ibrahim's worried about you. How'd you get here?"

"I'm okay," she said. "I've already seen Ibrahim. Everything's fine."

"Where've you been?" Trace said.

"I was arrested, nothing else. They asked me some questions, kept me for three days — at least I think it was three days — then let me go."

Trace narrowed his eyes. Why did the authorities go through that exercise with her just to let her go?

Jenna said, "Ibrahim's fine."

"Where is he?"

"At the hotel, still sleeping. At least he was sleeping when I left. I'm looking for something to eat," she said.

"Let's go get Ibrahim," Trace said.

Jenna paused, contemplating Trace's suggestion. "Okay, for now," she said, "but at some point soon I need to eat."

They walked silently, each warily watching the other from the corner of their eyes, but trying not to show it. They started across Royal Palm Drive when Jenna pointed and said, "Look over there. It's Calvet."

Trace followed Jenna's pointing hand. He saw three soldiers, dressed in MOP gear, grouped around a young man. Trace recognized him.

"It's your friend," Trace said.

"He's not our friend," Jenna said. "We met him just before we met you. He tagged along with us. We don't know him at all." She paused, looked briefly at her wristwatch, then continued. "Let's go over and see what's going on."

Not waiting for Trace to agree or disagree, she started across the street.

"Wait a second," Trace said. "We shouldn't get involved."

He was too late. Jenna was almost crossed the street and reached Calvet and the soldiers.

He decided not to follow her. He already had too many entries into the ODMC's computer system to risk another. He wouldn't ignore General Vista's warning about what would happen to him if he again was entered into ODMC's computer system.

CHAPTER 55

Quarantine
Day 23

"Ladies and gentlemen, this is Derek Peterson, CNN, coming to you live from the Quarantine Zone.

"Before I begin our regular daily broadcast, I've been instructed by the Office of the District Military Commander to bring you this news alert."

He paused briefly to let his audience ready itself to listen.

"This past week a roving gang of vigilantes, calling themselves Friday's Progeny, broke into and looted several private businesses and stores as well as government warehouses. Their calling card is a homemade printed broadside they leave behind in which they castigate the ODMC. This, of course, violates Field Order No. 3, and cannot be tolerated.

"Although these gang members reputedly distribute food and other necessities to the Quarantine Zone population, make no mistake about it. Their real motive is to profit on the illegal black market, which harms all of us who obey the law and who ask for no more than our fair share under the circumstances.

"I have been instructed by the Office of the District Military Commander to tell you that anyone who aids or cooperates with Friday's Progeny or with any other vigilante gang will be severely punished. This also applies to anyone who participates in any manner in the black market.

"Ladies and gentlemen, here's a word of advice from this reporter: Don't be foolish and risk your freedom, however tempting a transaction might be. Do not participate, directly or indirectly, in the black market.

"To the gang members of Friday's Progeny, and to other gang members, the commander of the Quarantine Zone, General Vista, says: If you're caught looting, you'll be shot on sight. There won't be any warnings. There won't be any second chances. Consider yourself notified.

"Now," Derek said, "let's get on with today's regular Quarantine Zone news report . . . ."

CHAPTER 56

Quarantine
Day 23

"Hey," Calvet said, looking at Jenna, "Where've you been?"

Before Jenna could answer, a soldier said to Calvet, "You know them?" The soldier looked at Jenna, then across the street at Trace. He did not wait for Calvet's answer. He raised his arm, pointed his finger at Trace, and motioned to him to cross the street to join them.

"Come here," the soldier yelled.

Trace warily walked across the street and stopped next to Jenna.

The soldier turned back to Calvet, and said, "I asked you, do you know them?"

Trace jumped in to head off Calvet's answer, and said, "Not really. We briefly met the other day. We don't really know each other at all." He didn't want to be associated with Calvet, an unknown quantity, if Calvet had done something wrong.

Calvet glared at Trace.

"Move along then," the soldier said to Calvet, "before we

start over with you after we finish with your friends here." He nodded his weapon at Jenna and Trace.

Calvet walked away without saying another word. He looked back over his shoulder once, then turned a corner and was gone.

The soldier turned his attention back to Trace and Jenna.

"Give me your IDs," he said, holding out his hand.

Trace and Jenna handed over their registration photoID cards.

"Down on your stomachs", the soldier said. "Keep your hands where we can see them."

He turned to one of his companions. "Check them for weapons."

A few minutes later the soldier returned from the HUMVEE. Trace assumed he had checked their identities, any priors, and any entries into the computer system. This worried him. He remained mindful of General Vista's warning.

"Get up," the soldier said.

Trace and Jenna started to stand, but the soldier poked the tip of his weapon into the small of Trace's back, and said, "Not you. Just her." Trace lowered himself back down to the sidewalk.

The soldier handed Jenna her ID.

"We haven't entered you into the system as a courtesy," he said to her. "I'm letting you go with a warning. Watch your step."

Trace could see Jenna from the corner of his eyes. She was looking down at him. She opened her mouth as if to say something, but apparently thought better of it because she remained silent.

Trace turned his head slightly and craned his neck to face her. He said, "Jenna, call my wife. Her name's Isabella. He recited Nanna's landline telephone number. Tell her what happened. Please, call her."

Jenna looked at the soldier and then back at Trace. She seemed to hesitate.

"I will," she said.

The soldier looked at Jenna, and said, "Go before I change my mind."

"Yes, Sir," she said, and walked away.

The soldier turned his attention to Trace who still was prone on the sidewalk. He poked him with his M-4.

"Stay down," he said. "Put your hands behind you."

Trace obeyed.

A soldier yelled from the HUMVEE, "This guy's been flagged on the watch list. Restrain his wrists and legs. We're taking him in."

CHAPTER 57

Quarantine
Day 23

T HE SOLDIERS DROVE TRACE FROM the street corner where they'd grabbed him to the Broward County Detention Center, now under the control of ODMC. They handed him off to two intake soldiers.

After he was processed, two other soldiers escorted Trace to a room, told him to sit in one of the two available chairs, and then chained his leg shackles to an iron ring protruding from the floor near the chairs. They checked his wrist restraints, left them in place, then left him alone.

The room was windowless, illuminated only by a single light bulb hanging from the ceiling. The two chairs and a small medical gurney comprised the room's furniture. There was a waste basket with a lid, marked on its side and top, Caution. Hazardous Medical Waste. A skull and cross-bones decal dominated the lid.

Trace sat quietly and waited.

After what seemed to Trace to be an interminable wait, the door opened. An armed guard and another person walked in, both dressed in MOP gear. Neither spoke.

The guard took a position near the door, facing Trace. The other person walked over to the gurney, retrieved some apparatus from it, walked back to Trace, then sat in the other chair next to him.

"I'm going to draw blood to test if you've been infected. Then we'll know if we have to wear these protective suits when we're with you."

Trace nodded at the face mask.

"We'll have the results in about an hour." The voice was that of a woman.

"That fast?"

The woman nodded. "New technique. Getting faster every day."

Almost two hours later, two soldiers, not wearing protective gear this time, entered the room. They said nothing, but Trace inferred from the absence of their MOP suits that he wasn't infected.

They unhooked his leg shackles from the ring in the floor, but did not remove the shackles from his legs. They motioned for Trace to follow them. Trace shuffled out into the hallway. They led him down another long, windowless corridor.

They entered a room that was similar to the room Trace had just left, except this room contained a raised platform, like a small stage, at one end. An officer sat behind a desk up on the platform, facing out toward the rest of the room. The table seemed to Trace to be bare except for an open laptop.

A folding chair, down in front of the stage, faced the platform. The limited light in the room emanated from a single bare bulb which dangled over the officer, hanging from the ceiling at the end of a long cord.

The guard ordered Trace to sit.

Trace shuffled over to the chair and lowered himself onto it. He placed his cuffed wrists and hands on his lap and fixed his eyes on the officer up on the platform.

The guard walked over to the platform, went up the four steps, and walked over to the table. He saluted the officer, placed the envelope containing Trace's personal effects on the table, saluted again, and walked back down and off to the far side of the room, somewhere behind Trace, out of his sight.

The officer sitting on the platform stared at Trace, but said nothing. After several minutes passed, he lifted a pen from the table, glanced at it and then set it back down, sorted through some papers, and looked back at Trace.

"Tell me your name, age, home, and work addresses. Tell me the names of your immediate family members."

He entered Trace's answers into a computer form.

"While you're here you'll have no contact with any other detainee. Should you inadvertently see someone else while you're here, you will not communicate with that person. Do you understand?"

Trace nodded.

The officer looked at his papers and entered some information. Then he looked at the two soldiers standing at the far end of the room.

"We're finished for now. Remove him."

Trace was hungry and thirsty. No one had offered him anything to eat or drink. He had a headache. When he looked up at the window, dim light no longer stole into the room. It's nighttime, he thought. He worried that Bella probably was worrying about him. He was thankful he had asked Jenna to call her and explain what had happened.

"I've seen enough. I'm ready for him," the officer said, as he turned off the monitor he'd been watching.

The officer turned from the monitor to the corporal. "Bring Austin to Interrogation Room Two."

While he waited in the room to see what would happen next, Trace practiced *T'ai chi*'s standing meditation, clearing his mind, pouring out his stress. After approximately twenty minutes into his practice, the door opened. A corporal and two guards walked in.

The corporal said, "Follow us."

One guard stepped in front of Trace. The second moved behind him. The corporal followed the three of them.

They left the room and turned left, walking along the same poorly lighted corridor Trace had walked before, but in the opposite direction. When they almost reached the end, the lead soldier stopped, pulled open a door, and stepped away.

Trace and the corporal entered the room.

This room, like the others, was almost bare except that an officer sat behind a large, government-issue, dark green metal desk. A folding chair stood open in front of the desk.

The seated officer told Trace to move forward and stand in front of the desk.

Trace's arm remained cuffed and his ankles shackled.

196

The officer stared at Trace as if he was contemplating something unfathomable about him. Then he smiled, but it was not the smile of a friend.

"Sit," the officer said.

Trace lowered himself onto the chair.

"I have questions. I advise you to consider your answers carefully. By the time we're through with you, we'll know whether you are a misguided patriot or an enemy of the people."

Why would he call me that? Trace wondered.

CHAPTER 58

Quarantine
Day 23

"IDENTIFY YOURSELF," THE OFFICER SAID.

"Trace Austin—."

"Speak up. I can't hear you."

"I said, Trace Austin." His eyes swept the major and then noticed the darkened two-way window or mirror set flush into the wall behind the officer. He could not tell which it was, but he had no doubt about its function. Someone was watching the interrogation.

"Why did you abandon the SEALs, abandon your warrior brothers?"

Trace did a mental double-take. That again? What's that have to do with anything?

"I can't hear you. Answer the question."

"Personal reasons. It's not important anymore."

"What's your address?"

"Do you mean here in Florida or when I'm not in the Quarantine Zone?"

The interrogator remained silent, not clarifying his

question. Then he said, "I am asking you again: Why did you abandon your privileged position with the SEALs?"

Trace's stomach tightened. He didn't answer.

"I can't hear you."

"Why am I here?" Trace said. "I haven't done anything wrong."

"Answer the question."

"I'm not saying anything until you tell me why I'm here."

"Very well." The major paused and gathered his papers into a pile. "You're here because you are a potential troublemaker. The computer model says so. Now, answer the question."

"That's ridiculous."

"Answer the question. I'm losing patience with you."

"Why am I being held?"

"You've been entered into the watch list. That's a serious offense. Only terrorists and enemies of the people are entered into the watch list."

"That's nonsense. I haven't done anything wrong. The only thing I'm guilty of is bad timing, being in Fort Lauderdale when the terrorists attacked."

"You must answer my questions and confess what you've done or plan to do that caused you to be placed on the watch list."

The officer turned to his right as if he was about to address some invisible person standing there. He glanced up at the wall, then turned back to face Trace.

"Listen," Trace said. "I'm telling you there's been a mistake. I'm not what you seem to think I am."

"We don't make mistakes where homeland security and terrorism are concerned. You're in the computer system, on the watch list for a reason. Confess your offenses."

"Think about what you just said to me," Trace said. "It's

right out of Kafka." Trace paused to take a deep breath. "I haven't done anything wrong, I tell you."

"No, it is not out of Kafka. This is America, not Czechoslovakia in the 1930s. Kafka isn't relevant here. Now answer my questions."

"This is absurd," Trace said again, his voice becoming louder. "I haven't done anything wrong." His tone grew more insistent.

"Of course you have," the major said, "otherwise you wouldn't be here and you wouldn't be on the watch list. We don't make mistakes."

Trace took a deep breath. He deliberately slowed down his breathing. He paused a beat, then addressed the major again.

"Let's start over," Trace said. "We can clear this up." He paused. "What exactly am I accused of doing wrong?"

"You are accused of being an enemy of the people or, to be more precise, accused of being a person who's likely to become an enemy of America. You might as well confess what you intend to do. We're on to you."

Trace expelled his breath with a rush. He shook his head.

"This is bullshit. Your argument's circular. I'm a loyal, law abiding, patriotic American citizen. I love my country. I haven't done anything to harm it and wouldn't."

"Then why'd you quit the SEALs, abandon your comrades?"

"That again?" Trace paused, slowly shook his head, then said, quietly this time, "I demand to be released."

"You won't be released unless you confess your crimes."

"I haven't committed any crimes," Trace said. "You said so yourself. I'm being held because of what you think I might do, not for what I've done. There's nothing for me to confess."

"You must confess," said the officer, "otherwise we won't let you go. We have the evidence against you."

"If you have the evidence against me, why do you need my confession?"

"It's the procedure. You're in the system. Four times. You're on the watch list. So now you must follow the procedure and confess."

Trace sighed.

"This is an endless loop. You're talking in riddles. Your argument is bootstrap. I haven't committed any crimes, any offenses against America, and I don't intend to."

"If that's so, Mr. Austin, why are you locked up here?" the major said, smiling smugly. "The mere fact that you haven't committed any crimes, but are here anyway, proves you are likely to commit an offense in the future."

Trace was appalled by the man's density. He shook his head, then shut down, at a loss what else to say to get through to the officer. He stood mute, staring at the major.

The major broke the silence. "I'm asking you again, one last time. I suggest you answer me. Why did you quit the SEALs?"

"Let me try this again, very slowly," Trace said. "Maybe, just maybe, if you pay real close attention, Major, this time you'll get it. Are you ready?" He paused. "Here goes: It was personal. That's all I'll say about it. Personal. Nobody's business. Just mine and my wife's."

He paused again, but then added, "It had nothing to do with my loyalty. I haven't done anything wrong, and, again, I don't intend doing anything wrong. You're making a mistake holding me. Now, do whatever you want to me, I have no more to say. I'm done here."

"So," the major said, "you still think we made a mistake?" He glanced at the back wall. "Many traitors say that when they're brought here, but that's a narrow, foolish attitude." He looked down at a file, then spoke again.

"Think about it. There are almost two hundred thousand people in the Quarantine Zone. Of all of them, why would *you* be brought here rather than one of them if you weren't the one who's guilty?"

Trace stood mute, stared, and thought once again of Franz Kafka.

The major nodded at Trace. "It's clear to me," he said, "even if you don't admit it's clear to you. You were entered into the system and placed on the watch list because you either committed an offense or are likely to commit one. Maybe even more than one. That remains to be seen. The mere fact that you're in the system four times is, itself, a crime. You can't deny you're guilty of that, can you."

He grinned and nodded again. "So, there you are, Mr. Austin. Now, I've answered your question, you answer mine."

Trace sighed again. It was pointless to argue.

"Which question? I've lost track."

"Why did you leave the SEALs when you did?"

Trace said nothing. He didn't know what else to do in the face of the man's absurd reasoning. He shook his head in disgust and remained quiet.

When it became clear that Trace wasn't going to say anything else, the major walked out of the room, leaving Trace alone with his thoughts, one armed guard, and his unseen observer behind the one-way window.

Trace couldn't begin to guess how long the major was gone. He lost all track of time as he paced the perimeter of the room under the watchful eyes of the guard.

Eventually the door opened and the major walked back in.

He took his time settling himself behind the desk, then looking through a file he carried in with him. He made a conspicuous show of writing notes.

Trace waited for him to ask his favorite question again: Why'd you quit the SEALs?

Instead, when he finally spoke, he said to Trace, "You're free to go. Pick up your belongings at the property clerk's window on your way out."

Behind the window, unseen by Trace, General Vista turned off the videotaping machine. He wrote a note in a small spiral-bound notebook and put it into his jacket pocket. Then he stood and left the observation room.

CHAPTER 59

Quarantine
Day 24

T HE DAY HIS INTERROGATION ENDED, as Trace slipped his key into Nanna's front door, he wondered what sort of reception he would receive from Isabella. He'd been away almost thirty hours.

Even though it now was late afternoon, he considered the possibility that Isabella might have been awake during the night with Nanna, so she'd be napping now. He pushed the door open slowly with his left hand and looked inside before stepping in. What he saw pulled him up short. The living room had been ransacked.

Isabella sat on the floor in front of the sofa. She had her knees pulled up to her chin, her arms around her legs, and her head resting on her kneecaps. She looked up at Trace as he pushed open the door.

One glance told Trace that Isabella was crying.

Trace ran over to her and, dropping to his knees, took her in his arms. "Bella, are you all right? What happened?" He looked around the disheveled room.

Isabella looked at Trace through clouded, wet eyes. She

pushed him away. When he reached out to her, she held up her palm and shook her head.

"Where've you been?" she said. "I've been frantic."

She got up and walked to the far end of the sofa, sat down, but then immediately stood again. She turned back to face Trace.

"Why didn't you call? I've been going out of my mind with worry. I can't stand it when I don't know what's going on. You know that."

She walked back and forth as she reprimanded him, going first to one side of the room and then to the other.

"The authorities picked me up and were holding me, Bella. Didn't Jenna call you? She said she would." He walked over to her.

"Who's this Jenna person you're talking about? How do you know her? Why did she know what happened to you, but I didn't?" She stopped pacing and faced Trace. "What do you mean they picked you up? Who did?"

"She's the young woman I met the other day with the two young men. I told you about them," he said.

Isabella reluctantly nodded. "Why were you with her now?"

"I ran into her on the street when I left to see what was going on outside. I wrote you a note. Didn't you see it?" Trace said. "We were on our way to see her friend, Ibrahim, but were stopped by soldiers. They let her go, but held me. I gave her this phone number and asked her to call you so you'd know what had happened to me. She said she'd call."

"Well she didn't. I've been worried sick."

"Bella, what happened here?" He made a sweeping motion with his arm. "Where's Nanna?"

His questions provoked a new round of crying. Isabella sank down onto the sofa and buried her face in her hands.

"Damn it, Trace, why weren't you here when I needed you?"

She stood up and walked across the room, then turned back to face him.

"What happened here?" she said, using a tone of voice that mimicked Trace's voice. "Do you really want to know?" She paused, then said, before Trace could answer her question, "Okay, I'll tell you what happened here, Trace. I'll tell you exactly what happened."

She walked back to the sofa and sat.

Trace was bewildered by the intensity of her anger.

"Bella—"

"Be quiet, Trace. Just be quiet and listen."

Trace nodded and walked across the room. He lowered himself to the floor, his back against the wall, to give her the physical and mental space she seemed to need.

"My mother is gone," she said.

Trace's jaw slackened. "Oh, Bella, I'm so sorry. Oh, God. I hope, at least, she died peacefully."

Isabella stiffened. "No, Trace. She's gone. Not here," Isabella said, "not dead."

"What're you talking about, Bella? Start at the beginning."

"I don't know where she is," Isabella said. "This afternoon some county health people came with soldiers. They said we were in violation of some Field Order for not reporting mom's illness. They said she had to be tested again. We all do." She wiped her eyes.

She stood up and paced two steps away, then turned back.

"They took my mother away, wouldn't say where. I wanted to go with her, but they wouldn't let me."

Trace frowned and looked around the room. "Did they say anything that might help us figure out where she's at?"

"I don't know," Isabella said. "It all happened so fast. I was screaming at them. They wouldn't let me talk to her before they took her. She was so frightened."

Trace thought about this. "Let's start over," he said, deliberately speaking softly, nodding his head as he spoke.

"Tell me everything that happened since I went out the other morning. Try not to leave out anything even if it doesn't seem important."

Trace walked over to Isabella, and hugged and kissed her. He moved to the other end of the sofa, sitting with his legs tucked under him, facing her.

". . . and then," Isabella said, "there was banging on the door. It frightened me. When I opened the door there were soldiers in the hall. One had a battering ram. I guess he was about to knock down the door." She shook her head slowly. Her eyes filled with tears.

"You're doing fine," Trace said. "Take your time."

"The soldiers rushed in wearing some kind of biohazard suits, pointing their guns, racing around like madmen. They kept shouting, 'Who's here? Tell us who else is here.'"

She sniffled and wiped her nose on her sleeve. "It was so confusing. There was so much happening so fast. And so much screaming by the soldiers. I was terrified."

Trace nodded, but didn't say anything. He didn't want to break her mood by telling her this was standard, by-the-book penetration protocol intended to cower the occupants of the place invaded. Let her keep unloading information now, he thought, tell it all to me while she has momentum.

"The men looked in at my mother, asked about her, and then left her alone, closing her door. They looked through everything, every drawer, every shelf, every closet in every room. They tossed away things as they finished with them." She looked over at the chaos in the living room. "They made me feel like a criminal."

Trace nodded. "You're doing fine," he said.

"Trace, what's going on? Where've you been? I don't want to lose you, too. First Pete. Now my mother . . . ."

Trace stood and went to Isabella. He sat alongside her, pulled her in close to him, and held her. She put her head on his shoulder and began to cry.

After a few minutes she pulled away, sat upright and said, "Where was I? Oh, yes . . . ."

She shuddered briefly. "The soldiers ordered me to sit at the breakfast table while they tore the place apart. They copied the hard drive from Pete's laptop and took all his CDs. They asked me if we had any other computers or smartphones, iPods, iPads or other smart devices."

Trace nodded, but kept quiet.

"They asked me mom's name, to spell it. They wouldn't tell me why. Then they left except for one soldier who stood guard in front of my mother's bedroom door. He wouldn't even let me go in to check on her."

Isabella turned her head and looked over at the closed door leading into her mother's bedroom. She turned back to Trace.

"They must have reported my mother to someone because this afternoon other people came with soldiers and took her with them. Now I don't know where she is. They gave me a telephone number to call later, after eighteen hours, they said. What should we do?"

"We can't do anything yet, Bella, not today, not with the curfew in an hour or so. We need to think this through."

Isabella nodded. She looked at the debris scattered around the living room. She sniffled, wiped her eyes and nose with a tissue, and said, "I'll pick up in here. You get some rest, Trace. Then tell me what you've been through while you were gone. I'm sorry I was angry before. It's just—"

"No problem, Bella. No problem at all," Trace said.

With that, Isabella bent over, picked up some placemats from the carpet and carried them to the buffet's top drawer which was sitting empty on the floor.

Trace grabbed some scattered cloth napkins from the floor, refolded them, and placed them in the same drawer.

As he gathered up the buffet's scattered contents, Trace wondered why Jenna hadn't called Isabella.

CHAPTER 60

Quarantine
Day 24

"Let's get started," the deputy secretary of defense said, so we can wrap this up and get back to our offices." He glanced briefly at his notes. "As we've discussed at our other meetings, we are continuing to study the control population in Fort Lauderdale. As part of that, we recently made a small amount of meds available to ameliorate symptoms of the terrorists' disease. Now we'll take it to the next step and see what happens."

"Aren't we going to send in more meds?" the undersecretary of Health and Human Services asked?

"We're going to implement a secret triage program," the deputy said, ignoring the woman from HHS. "Under this new program, meds will be withheld from everyone under age four or over age seventy. Physicians who have these groups of patients in their care will also see to it that they will be given only the minimum amount of food necessary to sustain their lives, no more."

"You can't do that," the undersecretary of HHS blurted out. "That's criminal."

"This is wartime, Madam," the deputy said, as he glared at her.

"But you don't need to do that," the woman said. "There are sufficient stores of medicine and food elsewhere in the country that can be brought to Fort Lauderdale. Think what you're doing," she said.

"That's not the issue," the deputy said, spiking his voice with maximum sarcasm. "Of course we have sufficient stores of meds and food to bring in, and we'll make them available in due course.

"In the meantime, this is our rare chance to see how a population might react in circumstances where we are unable to deliver food and meds to it. We are fortunate the terrorists afforded us this opportunity, and we have no intention of wasting it."

CHAPTER 61

Quarantine
Day 25

TRACE AND ISABELLA, EXHAUSTED FROM their separate but shared ordeals, slept well that night. Isabella backed up against Trace's body, pressing into his stomach and chest, curving her body to fit snuggly into his. Trace slept with his arm draped over Isabella, holding her firmly in his sleep as if he was afraid she would float away if he let go. He fell asleep with his lips pressed against the back of her neck.

They woke a little after 10:00 a.m., first Isabella, then Trace, both surprised how late they'd slept. After showers and some basic primping, they rendezvoused at the kitchen table.

Trace picked up the box of cereal and emptied the last of its contents into Isabella's bowl. He took both hands and pretended to strangle the inverted box, trying to squeeze out some unseen cereal from its dark, empty interior. Nothing came out. He crumbled the empty box into a rough, cardboard ball and tossed it in a lazy arc across the room into the sink. He walked across the room to the refrigerator and looked inside.

"The fridge looks like when we were first married and

broke," he said. He reached deep into the refrigerator, took out a mostly empty carton of orange juice and handed it to Isabella.

She checked the *sell-by* date, looked at Trace, then nodded her head. She poured the juice over her cereal. "Not quite my idea of the breakfast of champions," she said.

"Beats dry cereal, I guess."

Isabella shrugged and pushed the bowl over to Trace. "Have some," she said. "We'll share. I'm not eating this stuff alone."

Trace put up his palm to stop her. "I'll pass for now. I'll have something later. What's left in the cabinets? Anything edible?"

"Half-empty jar of peanut butter. Not even the kind you're crazy about," she said. "It's chunky. A tin of unbaked dinner rolls, a few cans of soup. A box of raisins. Stale crackers. Plus a few things in the freezer."

"A half-full jar of peanut butter and other stuff," Trace said. "Not enough to carry us for long. I'll go out, look for more. Want to come?"

"Yes, I do," Bella said, "but I can't. I want to be here in case my mother comes home while you're out."

"Okay," Trace said. "I'll call those kids I told you about, Ibrahim and Jenna. I want to talk to them about possibly teaming-up with me to get through the quarantine."

"A SEAL team?" Bella said.

"A SEAL-like team," Trace said. "If they're trainable, that is."

Trace called Ibrahim. He and Jenna agreed to meet Trace someplace where their presence would not violate Field Order No. 2.

Food was scarce in the Quarantine Zone. Existing stocks had become depleted soon after the quarantine began. Fresh vegetables, fruits and meat disappeared from general circulation once farmers realized that the return they made under ODMC price controls did little to offset the cost of producing and harvesting their crops, then bringing them to town. The choices among farmers came down to letting their crops ripen and rot in the fields, feeding it to their ever-diminishing herds of livestock, or selling the crops on the black market.

It took Trace a little more than thirty minutes to walk to the Palm Court Hotel at 3rd and Las Olas, the hotel where Ibrahim and Jenna currently were living as squatters.

From the outside this 1930s hotel looked just as Trace remembered it. He had stayed there three years before on the recommendation of Harlan Crockett, one of his law partners, when Trace had come to Fort Lauderdale to find a condominium apartment to buy for Nanna after Isabella's father died.

He particularly liked the hotel's European ambiance with its terra-cotta floors, fireplaces in abundance, lush tropical gardens, a view of the New River, and rooms furnished with period furniture. Much to his surprise, he even enjoyed the traditional tea and scones offered in the lobby every weekday afternoon from 3:00 – 5:00.

Trace walked up the faux marble steps, across the broad patio, and into the entrance hall. He did not notice the soldier watching him from a dark entryway across the street.

The first thing he sensed upon entering the vestibule was the foul odor that enveloped him like an intense morning fog.

He looked around. Trash cluttered the floor.

He stepped over and around human flotsam as he carefully walked across the vestibule to the lobby. He paused at the lobby's entrance and looked inside.

The lights were turned down. Most of the open space was cluttered with debris.

He looked around hoping to see Ibrahim or Jenna.

He studied the room systematically from where he stood at the entrance, following a mentally constructed grid system. He didn't see Ibrahim and Jenna.

As he turned to leave, his cell phone rang.

"Don't leave," Ibrahim said. "We'll be with you in a minute."

Trace looked around again trying to find them.

"Where are you?" he said. "I just looked for you and Jenna. I don't see you."

"Look up. No, look more to your right," Ibrahim said. "We're up here on the mezzanine level."

Trace saw Jenna slowly waving her arm back and forth in a slow arc. He raised his hand and tentatively waved back. Then he put the phone to his ear.

"I'm going outside," he said. "Meet me on the patio,"

Jenna gave him the thumbs-up signal.

As he made his way from the hotel into fresh air, Trace took a long breath and held it. Then he let it out slowly. He thought about the fact that Jenna hadn't called Isabella as she'd said she would. He thought about how her failure to place the call had caused Bella so much anguish. He decided to file this information away for now, not raise it, but not forget it either.

Trace sat off to the side of the building, on the patio, hidden behind a high, well-trimmed boxwood hedge that blocked his view of the street and sidewalk and, in turn, protected him from being seen. Ibrahim and Jenna joined him there.

They made small talk at first, chewing on events that had affected them. They avoided the subject of Jenna's arrest and subsequent release. Jenna did not mention that she hadn't called Bella.

The talk soon veered to food, or, specifically, to the lack of it, and their shared persistent hunger.

"There's nothing to eat at the hotel," Ibrahim said. "Not even a candy bar or crackers. I know because I looked."

"That's what we do today then," Trace said. "We find food." He looked at Jenna. "We can't all go out together. We'll be stopped again if we do. I'll go with one of you, either one. Your call. "

"Ibrahim should go," Jenna said. "I'll be okay. I have you both in my cell phone directory if I need you."

That decided, Ibrahim hugged and kissed Jenna. Then he and Trace left.

As they left, Trace thought, I'll hold-off saying anything about teaming-up until I see how this kid thinks and acts while we're out. I need to see, at the very least, that I can rely on him. Part of being a successful SEAL, Trace knew, meant that you accurately tracked the psychological mind-set of your comrades.

Jenna waited for half a minute to pass after Ibrahim and Trace left, then she walked away from the patio and out onto the sidewalk. She watched as Trace and Ibrahim turned a distant corner and walked out of sight. Then she pulled out her cell phone and pressed a speed dial button.

The phone at the other end of the call rang twice before someone answered it.

Jenna said, "They just left the hotel. What do you want me to do?"

CHAPTER 62

Quarantine
Day 25

Trace and Ibrahim walked away from the beach side of Fort Lauderdale, crossing in quick succession Isle of Palms Avenue, Royal Plaza, Coral Way, and San Marco Drive, as they headed toward Fort Lauderdale's downtown business district.

"What'd you have in mind when you said we'd try to find food?"

"I meant we'd first see if there's some government source we can tap into that we don't know about," Trace said. He paused to consider what it was he thought they should do. Then he said, "As much as I hate to say it, we should go to the ODMC headquarters to find out. If that doesn't pan out, we'll figure out something else to try."

They walked almost three-quarters of a mile when Trace said, *"Ibrahim?* Is that a Middle Eastern name? It sounds Biblical, Old Testament-like."

"It's Middle Eastern. Syrian. Abraham in English."

"Syrian?" Trace said. "How long have you been in the United States?"

"Since 1994," Ibrahim said. "I came with my parents and sister from Israel."

"Wait a minute," Trace said. "Israel? I'm confused. Are you Syrian, Muslim, or an Israeli Jew? Or, what?"

"A Syrian Jew with U.S. citizenship now. My family and I were members of a small Sephardic Jewish community in Syria, in Aleppo to be exact, where my ancestors lived for almost three thousand years."

"I didn't know there were Jews in Syria," Trace said.

"There aren't many, not anymore."

"How'd you get to Israel?"

"In the early 1990s after the Madrid peace conference, President Clinton pressured Syria to allow its Jews to emigrate or, at least, travel. The government acquiesced about travel, but not emigration. But to travel, we Jews each had to post four thousand dollars as a bond for our return, and we were required to leave a family member behind as a hostage."

"What'd you do?" Trace could see that this discussion troubled Ibrahim, but he wanted to know this person better, so he'd keep asking questions.

"My mother, father, younger sister, and I posted our cash bonds and received travel visas, provided we returned within twenty days. Obviously, we didn't care about the money and planned to forfeit it as the price of leaving Syria behind us once and for all."

"Who stayed behind as the hostage?"

"That part is very sad," Ibrahim said. He frowned. "My grandmother — my nanna — stayed behind as our human bond. She insisted we go without her, and not return. She said she wanted to die in her village, nowhere else, not even in Israel. We've never heard from her again. We assume the worst."

Trace considered this. Ibrahim could be an important ally here. *I need to know more about him.*

"Were you in the Israeli army?"

"Of course," Ibrahim said. "All able-bodied men and women serve. I did my duty."

"Were you a combat soldier, special ops? Did you train in some specialty?" Trace asked.

Ibrahim stiffened. "Why do you want to know?"

"I'm hoping you have some special skill that will be helpful while we're in the Quarantine Zone. As you know, I was a SEAL. I have certain SEAL-taught skills that can be useful. I was thinking maybe we can team-up and support one another until the quarantine ends."

"I was a nerd computer specialist. I attacked enemy computer network systems for the military," Ibrahim said. "I never saw actual combat, I'm happy to say."

"A hacker. . . Well, it's not too likely we'll need that skill to survive here, but who knows."

They walked in silence for a few minutes when Trace said, "How well do you know Jenna?"

"Pretty well, I guess," Ibrahim said. After a brief pause, he added, "Probably not all that well. It depends. Why?"

Trace didn't answer.

Ibrahim said, "Probably as well as you can know someone from school. We met in the U. S. Army ROTC after I came to America, became a citizen, and entered college. Jenna was my ROTC squad leader. I never did get used to calling her *Sir.*"

Trace chuckled. "You two are pretty close, then?"

"Close enough. We were lovers for a time at school, but

not anymore. Now we're friends. Nothing physical. Well, sometimes physical, but not usually. Why?"

"She's in ROTC?"

Ibrahim rolled his eyes. "Oh, yeah. She's in it big time. Unlike me. I did it for the money for a while, then got out. Jenna went on to the advanced program. She'll have a two year Army commitment after she graduates. She'll be a second lieutenant."

"Interesting," said Trace. "And you trust her?"

"Of course. Why?"

"No reason," Trace said. "Just curious."

Trace paused at the steps leading to the entrance of ODMC's headquarters.

"Are you okay?" Ibrahim said. "You look upset."

Trace looked up at the row of windows on the floor where he'd been held and questioned. He turned to Ibrahim. "I'm fine. It's nothing."

A guard at the entrance required that they state their business before he would admit them to the building. Then he told them they were at the wrong place for food information, that they needed to visit any post office or Army recruiting office to obtain the food rationing regulations.

"We're not asking about rationing," Trace said to the guard. "We want to ask about sources of food. Rationing is irrelevant if you can't first locate the food."

The guard frowned at Trace, and said, "Move along. I've answered your question, Sir."

Trace turned to Ibrahim as they walked away. "There's a post office four or five blocks from here, at 12th and Federal Highway. Let's go there, see if we can get an answer."

As they walked away from ODMC headquarters, Trace's cell phone sounded. Trace pulled the phone from his pocket and looked at the screen.

"It's my wife," he said. "I need to take this."

Trace turned his back on Ibrahim and walked a few steps away, listening to Isabella as he walked. When he ended the call he turned back to Ibrahim.

"I need to go," Trace said. "It's my mother-in-law. I'll explain later. Keep your phone turned on. I'll call you."

CHAPTER 63

Quarantine
Day 25

A s Trace turned away, anxious to return home to Isabella, Ibrahim called him back.

"But, Trace—"

Trace hesitated, then turned around to face Ibrahim.

"What, Ibrahim? I'm sorry, but I have to go. Can't it wait?"

"I was just wondering. Should I try to find out about food while you're gone? I mean, when will we hook up again?"

"Sure, that's good. You do that. We can talk or meet later. As I said, I'll call you."

"I'm sorry," Ibrahim said. He scuffed the sidewalk with the sole of his shoe. "I just wanted to know what to do, that's all. I'll wait for your call."

Trace stepped back over and put his hand on Ibrahim's shoulder. He gave the boy a light squeeze.

"No problem, Ibrahim. I'll call as soon as I can. Then we'll get together again. All right?"

Ibrahim nodded.

———※——※——※——※——※———

Trace slipped his key into the front door lock as if he were a burglar afraid of waking occupants. He turned the key and then the door knob, and slowly eased the door open, inch by inch, not knowing what to expect inside.

As the door glided open, Trace saw Isabella on the sofa, stretched out, resting on one elbow with her head on her upturned palm, looking expectantly toward the door.

She lifted her head and made a *be quiet* signal with her finger and lips.

Trace nodded. He went directly to Isabella, lowered himself onto the edge of the sofa, and kissed her. He lifted her partly up into his arms and pulled her in close to him. He buried his face in her hair, inhaled her familiar, comforting fragrance, then kissed her again.

"I missed you," he said. "Where's Nanna?"

"Sleeping. I had to leave her door open. She's afraid to have me close it."

"I guess Nanna doesn't have Melioidosis," Trace said, "else they wouldn't have let her come home."

"She won't eat or drink anything," Isabella said. "I tried to give her tea, but she vomited it back up.

"Do we have anything to feed her?" Trace said.

"Only those stale crackers from this morning, but mom wouldn't even try them. She doesn't talk, doesn't say anything at all. I don't know what to do."

Trace held Isabella in his arms. He felt as if they were reliving their moments together during Pete's illness.

After an hour with Isabella, Trace said, "I should go back out.

I'm meeting that young fellow I told you about, Ibrahim. We're still trying to find food."

"What should I do while you're gone, Trace?"

"Give Nanna ice chips. They'll melt in her mouth. The fluid will be good for her if she can hold it down."

Isabella nodded, but said nothing. She pulled away and went back to the sofa, dropped into the corner, and tucked her legs up under her.

"I really do have to go, Bella. I have no choice. We need food. You know that."

She nodded.

"Be careful, Trace."

Trace nodded, checked the battery read-out on his cell phone, and left. He called Ibrahim as he walked down the stairs.

CHAPTER 64

Quarantine
Day 25

ISABELLA, LEFT ALONE BY TRACE in the condo, decided she had to pull herself together and administer to her mother's needs. She started by following Trace's advice. She would give Nanna ice chips to offset possible dehydration.

She went to the refrigerator, removed some ice cubes from the tray, wrapped them in a dish towel and crushed them using the flat end of the jar of peanut butter as a makeshift mallet. She put the ice chips in a bowl and, with a spoon in hand, went into Nanna's bedroom.

Nanna was lying on her back, her eyes closed. She was breathing through her open mouth in short, wheezing breaths.

Isabella pulled up a chair and settled in alongside the bed. She was troubled by what she saw as she looked carefully at her sleeping parent. Nanna's condition seems like Pete's, she thought.

Nanna's skin was pale yellow, dry looking, and seemed to be stretched drumhead tight across her boney frame. Her skin seemed almost translucent.

Isabella had washed her mother early that afternoon

after Nanna had relieved her bowels in bed. Isabella avoided considering the implications of the blood she's seen in her mother's stool.

She took Nanna's hand and held it between both hers.

Nanna opened her eyes and turned her head toward Isabella.

"Mom, I have ice chips for you to suck on. The water will make you feel better."

Nanna shook her head, barely moving it.

"Please, Mamma. You need liquids. Just try a little for me. Please."

Nanna opened her mouth. Isabella spooned some ice chips into her mother's mouth. Nanna closed her mouth, melted the chips, and swallowed. Then, like a baby bird, she again opened wide.

Isabella repeated this until all the ice chips were gone.

"I'll get some more, Mamma."

Isabella didn't wait for an answer. She hurried to the kitchen and repeated the process of creating a bowl of ice chips. Then she hurried back to her mother.

When she returned to the darkened bedroom, she knew something was wrong. She smelled Nanna's fresh vomit and voided bowels.

She dropped the bowl and ran across the room to her mother.

Nanna was on her back, her eyes wide open, with one hand on her stomach, and the other, claw-like at her open mouth as if she had been surprised and terrified by something she'd seen. A brown stain migrated from beneath her.

Isabella put her palm on Nanna's forehead.

Nanna's eyes and mouth remained open, unmoving.

Isabella collapsed onto her chair and cried.

Isabella took her time washing Nanna. Then she sprinkled Nanna with toilet water. She fixed her mother's hair and put some rouge on her cheeks and lipstick on her lips. She dressed Nanna in clean underwear, Nanna's favorite print dress, and slippers.

She sat alongside the bed in the darkened room, her hands clasped on her lap, staring at her mother. After two hours, Isabella left her mother's body, now freshly adorned and clean, lying on top of the remade bed, her arms crossed at her chest, her eyelids closed by Isabella's loving touch. She walked out to the living room to wait for Trace to return.

CHAPTER 65

Quarantine
Day 25

W HEN THEY GOT BACK TOGETHER again, Ibrahim briefed Trace on what little he'd learned at the post office about the food rationing system. "I didn't learn a thing about food sources, just rationing."

"Here, take this," he said. He handed Trace the printed rationing regulations he'd picked up at the post office.

Trace glanced at the printed sheet, folded it, and put it in his pocket.

"Let's see what's going on with this," Trace said. "We still have some daylight left before curfew. Let's go back to the post office and ask some questions."

They walked along Riverwalk, a wooden promenade parallel to the north bank of the New River, until the walkway came to an end near the Museum of Discovery and Science. Then they cut over toward Fort Lauderdale Hospital at Las Olas Boulevard and SW 16th Street.

Trace didn't like what he saw downtown. He'd seen this same situation before, during OPERATION JUST CAUSE, when his SEAL team had gone into Panama to arrest Noriega.

He expected the New Jersey National Guard — the Fort Lauderdale occupying force — to be more diligent and caring on U.S. turf. Clearly, he decided, he was being naive.

Everywhere Trace looked he saw debris. Garbage was piled up along the sidewalk and curbs. Trash cans overflowed. He recoiled from the stench.

Trace's cell phone rang. He looked at the CallerID.

"I have to take this," he said to Ibrahim, looking at the readout dial. "It's my wife."

He walked away a few paces, but this time did not turn his back to shield his conversation. He watched Ibrahim while he spoke softly to Isabella. When he finished, he walked back, shaking his head and, as he spoke, opened both his palms as if to say, *What can I do? It's out of my hands.*

"Sorry to do this to you again," he said, "but I've got to leave you. Isabella's mother just died."

The living room was dark, the blinds drawn. Bella was nowhere in sight. Trace walked into their bedroom, hoping to find her. She wasn't there. He went to Nanna's room. She was sitting in the dark staring at Nanna.

He walked over and put his arm around Isabella to hug her. Then he took one of her hands and slowly pulled her up from the chair. He led her to the living room, over to the sofa, where they sat together. He held her while she slumped onto his chest, her head on his shoulder. He kissed her head and neck and held her close to him.

After a few minutes, she pulled away and stood up.

"Trace, I don't know what happened. I mean, Mamma was resting so peacefully. I went to get more ice chips, then when

I came back she was gone. I don't understand it." She wiped her eyes.

"I don't know what to tell you," Trace said. "I'm so sorry. I loved Nanna."

CHAPTER 66

Quarantine
Day 25

AFTER TRACE LEFT ISABELLA, HE and Ibrahim hooked-up again in front of the Palm Court Hotel. They skipped exchanging pleasantries.

Before they did anything else, Trace went into the hotel and convinced the hotel's manager to allow him to leave Pete's laptop, which he'd brought with him, in one of the large safe deposit boxes used by guests to store valuables. He had decided that leaving the computer at this hotel would be prudent because the authorities would be returning again to Nanna's condo. He did not want the laptop confiscated by the authorities. He might need it sometime.

Trace paid the hotel's manager one hundred dollars to ease the man's decision. Then he and Ibrahim left for downtown.

Trace and Ibrahim walked for ten minutes when Ibrahim grabbed Trace's arm to stop him. He pointed to a park bench off to their right, about forty feet away. A woman sat on the bench holding an infant in her arms. She cried as she rocked the baby.

Trace and Ibrahim looked at one another, then at the woman. They glanced around to make sure no soldiers were in sight.

Trace nodded to Ibrahim, who nodded back. They walked over, stopping about twenty feet away from the woman.

Trace said, speaking warmly, "Excuse me, can we help you?"

The woman looked up and pulled her baby in closer to her chest.

Trace said, still speaking softly, "We didn't mean to frighten you. We just want to know if we can help you or your baby?"

The woman said nothing. She kept her eyes on them and clasped her infant close to her breast.

"Okay, then," Trace said, "sorry to bother you." He made a *let's go* motion with his head, directed at Ibrahim, and said softly, "Let's move on. We're frightening her." He turned away from the woman and started to walk.

Ibrahim followed, turning his head to look back at the woman as they stepped away.

"Please help me. My baby's hungry and sick," the woman said from behind them.

Trace and Ibrahim stopped walking and turned back, but didn't approach the woman.

"May we come over to you?" Trace said. "Or we can talk from here. It's up to you."

The woman nodded. "Come over."

Trace and Ibrahim listened as the woman described her uncertain existence with her infant. She told them her husband had become ill and died. She said she couldn't find much food, and that she had no money to buy the little she did find. Her baby had been crying for days, she told them, because he's hungry.

"Now he doesn't cry hardly at all. He doesn't do anything except stare. He barely sleeps. He doesn't even mess his diapers anymore," she said.

"Listen, Miss—" Trace started to say, when Ibrahim tugged at his arm.

Trace turned his head and looked at Ibrahim, who pointed up the street. Trace turned in the direction of Ibrahim's pointing finger.

A HUMVEE was speeding directly toward them.

CHAPTER 67

Quarantine
Day 25

T HE HUMVEE BOUNCED ITS FRONT wheels up over the curb onto the sidewalk and stopped.

Two soldiers, dressed in MOP gear, jumped from the vehicle and lumbered over.

"Hand over your IDs," one of the soldiers said, canting his head from Trace to Ibrahim, then to the young woman. He extended his hand to them.

Trace and Ibrahim pulled out their registration photoIDs. The woman looked at her baby, then let go with one hand and slipped her pocketbook's strap off her shoulder. She handed the pocketbook to Trace.

"Mine's in my wallet. Please get it out. I don't want to put my baby down."

Trace reached into the woman's pocketbook looking for her wallet, but his mind was on General Vista's warning to him that if he was again entered into ODMC's database, he'd be arrested and possibly held indefinitely. He realized he had to buy time while he thought of some way to avoid having his ID logged in to the computer system.

"We weren't doing anything wrong, Sir," Trace said to the soldier who seemed to have the highest rank between the two.

"The two of us," he said, pointing first to Ibrahim and then back at himself, "were walking into town when we saw this woman clutching her baby and crying. We stopped to help her. That's all. We were with her less than a few minutes when you arrived."

"You're an unlawful gathering of three people," the soldier said. "Four with the kid. There aren't exceptions in the Field Order."

"No, Sir," Trace said, "not in the Field Order itself, but maybe in its interpretation or enforcement by you." Time now for some serious social engineering, he thought. Trace took a deep breath.

"Please use your discretion, Sir. Let us go with a warning. We really were just trying to help this poor woman and her baby."

"Got any priors?" the soldier said.

Trace's shoulder and neck tightened. He didn't answer.

"Yes, Sir, I have one prior," Ibrahim said.

The soldier looked at the mother and baby. He paused. Then he said to the other soldier, "Take these IDs and run them."

He reached out to hand the ID cards to the other soldier.

Trace's SEALs' training and his nine years of *T'ai chi juan* martial arts practice instinctively took hold. Time thickened and slowed down for him. Nothing extraneous registered in his consciousness. He was immersed entirely in the moment, suffused with present mind intent. All he saw, the only thing he was aware of, was the one soldier standing close to him — his present adversary — holding out the IDs to hand to the other soldier, who had placed his weapon by his side at parade rest.

Trace's mind became independent of Ibrahim, the woman, her infant, the HUMVEE, and its crew.

Without taking his eyes from the nearest soldier, and without making any noticeable bodily movement, Trace emptied his left leg of its weight, pouring its energy, power and *chi* into his right leg. He rooted his full right leg and foot to the ground, and sank into his leg.

Trace's left leg and foot now rested on the sidewalk, completely empty of all energy and power, weightless, but to all external appearances when viewed by anyone not well versed in *Tai chi juan*, unchanged.

Still maintaining eye contact with the soldier who was handing off their IDs, he tucked-in his coccyx and slightly bent his knees so that now he crouched, almost imperceptibly.

Without warning, he rotated his waist to the right, away from the soldier. In the same movement he pushed off with his right foot sending his coiled energy force, his *chi*, from his right leg into his empty left leg.

He whipped his left foot up and around, using the arch of his left foot to kick the soldier, who was holding the IDs, in the side of his kneecap. he aimed his kick through and beyond the soldier's knee, continuing his motion, sweeping the man's leg out from under him.

The soldier shrieked in pain and dropped to the ground. He grabbed his knee with both hands and rolled around on the pavement, yelling, "Jesus, Jesus. . . ."

Trace followed through by kicking the weapon that was resting at the side of the other soldier's thigh up and away from him, leaving the standing soldier unarmed. Trace yelled at Ibrahim, "Come on, let's go."

Trace started to run, then stopped and turned back toward

the fallen soldier. He wanted to find his photoID and scoop it up, hoping to avoid being identified. He saw it on the ground near the soldier he'd assaulted, but also saw two soldiers emerge from inside the HUMVEE.

The soldier he'd assaulted, now beyond his own shock at the attack, screamed for help and pointed at Trace. He turned toward Trace and Ibrahim, but had no weapon to raise against them.

Trace gave up the thought of retrieving his ID, and ran as fast as he could, heading across the street.

Ibrahim, as surprised by Trace's attack as were the soldiers, looked first at Trace, then back at the soldiers. He hesitated, bent over the fallen soldier and picked up his ID, then ran toward Trace. He kept his head down and leaned forward, trying to turn himself into as small a target as possible.

One of the soldiers who emerged from the interior of the HUMVEE fired at Trace and Ibrahim. His rounds chipped the edge of the building bordering an alley as they fled into its depths.

Ibrahim followed Trace across the street, then around the corner and down another alley, then back up another street. His lungs burned from too little oxygen. He slowed his pace as his initial fear waned and his adrenalin rush ebbed.

When they'd covered four or five blocks, Ibrahim, panting hard and wheezing, said, "Trace, wait. I have to stop. Wait, I can't breathe."

Ibrahim stopped running.

Trace slowed, turned his head back toward Ibrahim, then looped around and jogged back to him.

Trace, too, breathed hard, short of breath. Damn cigarettes! Without saying a word, Trace took Ibrahim by the arm and steered him behind an asparagus fern hedge, away from the street, hidden from the view of anyone at ground level looking for them.

They stood without speaking, each bending forward from his waist, each resting his hands on his knees with his head dropped forward, breathing fast, short, desperate gulps of air.

Ibrahim straightened up first. "Are you out of your mind," he said. "Are you stone crazy? We're dead meat now because of you."

He started to pace in a small, tight circle, shaking his head from side to side as he walked.

"I don't believe this is happening."

Trace watched him, not saying anything.

"What possessed you to do that?" Ibrahim said. He shook his head, slowly, sadly. "Now what'll we do?"

When Trace finally answered, he didn't raise his voice. He issued an order to Ibrahim, using his best command tone and posture. He stood tall and looked directly into Ibrahim's eyes as he spoke.

"Be quiet, Ibrahim," he said gently, but firmly. "Get hold of yourself and be quiet. I don't want to hear another word from you until you've gotten yourself under control."

He stared at Ibrahim with an uncompromising glare. Then, when Ibrahim settled down, he again spoke to him, this time using inviting tones.

"I had no choice," Trace said. "I'm in the ODMC's system too many times. I was warned. If they had checked my ID I would've been arrested and detained until the quarantine ends. I had no other option. I'm sorry you had to be there for that, but that's the way it is."

He said no more, letting his words sink in.

Ibrahim relaxed his posture and looked at Trace, then looked away, then back again. He pulled himself together and stood erect. He walked away a few feet, stopped, seemed to be brooding over some thought, then turned back to Trace.

"I'm okay now. No, that's not right, I'm not okay. I'm in control now, but I'm definitely not okay." Ibrahim took a deep breath and slowly let it out.

"What're we going to do? Where'll we go?" he said. He wiped his forehead with the back of his hand.

"Slow down, Ibrahim," Trace said. "Take it slow. We'll be fine. Just pay attention to what I do and what I say."

Trace waited a beat, then said, "That's better. You'll be all right." He nodded at Ibrahim.

"First," Trace said, "before we do anything else, we need to make brief phone calls to our ladies."

CHAPTER 68

Quarantine
Day 25

"ISABELLA, IT'S ME. I CAN'T talk for long. There's a problem. Just listen to me. I'm all right, but I can't explain it right now and I can't come back home yet. I'll call you soon. I love you."

He powered down, ending the call before Isabella could raise questions. He handed the phone to Ibrahim.

"Your turn," he said to Ibrahim. "Make it quick. We have only two or three minutes of phone time before they can ping our location. Then give me back the phone. I'll remove the battery and SIM card until we're ready to use the cell again."

It took Trace and Ibrahim forty-five minutes to walk to the hotel. They used all the evasive tradecraft Trace had learned as a SEAL, including executing a Surveillance Detection Route, called an SDR, crossing some streets and doubling back on others, to make sure that hadn't been followed.

When they finally approached the hotel, they circled around

it looking for soldiers or anyone else surveilling the structure. Before they entered the hotel, Ibrahim called Jenna again.

"Look around, Jenna," he said. "Does anything seem unusual? Are there soldiers inside? Or anyone who doesn't seem to belong?"

Jenna said all was as usual, "...if," she added, "you want to consider the chaos at the hotel usual."

Trace and Ibrahim hurried across the street, up the steps and over the patio. Trace entered the hotel with a mixed sense of relief and apprehension.

Once inside, Trace looked up and down the hallway as they walked from the large vestibule toward the lobby's entrance. Nothing seemed out of place to him, at least no more so than the last time he was there stowing Pete's laptop in the safe deposit box.

"There's Jenna, waving from across the room," Ibrahim said. He raised up on his toes and waved back at her.

Trace and Ibrahim threaded their way to the far corner of the room where Jenna stood waiting for them.

Ibrahim took Jenna in his arms and kissed her. "I missed you," he said. "You won't believe what happened to us. We're in serious trouble."

Ibrahim told Jenna about the close call he and Trace had experienced with the soldiers. She listened without comment or asking any questions.

Trace listened carefully, too, trying to gauge Ibrahim's state of mind from his perception of the events as he related them to Jenna. Trace decided he couldn't read Ibrahim yet or, for that matter, read Jenna either. He'd have to pay more attention to them.

When Ibrahim finished, Jenna looked at Trace, and said, her sarcasm palpable, "Nice going."

She looked at Ibrahim again and raised her eyebrows. Then she turned back to Trace, and said, "Now what?"

"I don't know," Trace said. "I can't go back to the condo, although my wife's alone there."

"Were you followed?" Jenna said.

"I doubt it. We were careful," Trace said.

"You both wait here," Jenna said. "I'll go outside and light a cigarette. I'll look around. When I come back in, if I take out this green bandana and wipe my forehead with it, there's trouble. I won't come over to you. If I don't take it out, then we're okay, and I'll walk back over."

Jenna stepped into the sunlight and walked across the patio, around the side of the building. She pulled out her cell phone, punched in a speed-dial number, and waited while it rang.

When she heard her call answered, she said, "It's me. They're back at the hotel in the lobby. I don't know how long I can keep them here. Hurry."

CHAPTER 69

Quarantine
Day 25

"YOU HAD THREE MEN WITH you, an armed HUMVEE, and the resources of this office, yet Austin still got away?"

"Yes, Sir."

Vista stood up and walked around his desk until he was in front of the major.

"Put out an order to find Austin. I want him arrested. He's not to be harmed. I want him alive to interrogate. I'll get to the bottom of what he's up to or he won't leave here."

He returned to his desk and sat down.

"Major, listen up."

"Sir?"

"Make this grab your top priority. I want Austin, and I want him soon."

CHAPTER 70

Quarantine
Day 25

TRACE, IBRAHIM AND JENNA SAT on the floor at the rear of the lobby, their backs against the wall. Jenna and Ibrahim stared at their cell phone chargers, watching the red lights blink as their phones sucked in energy.

Trace stood and stretched.

"I'll be back. I'm going to walk out the kinks in my legs," he said.

Jenna looked at him, narrowing her eyes, then glanced at the lobby's entranceway, but said nothing. Ibrahim looked up at Trace, nodded once, and then went back to watching the red light flashing on his charger.

Trace walked to the side wall that faced the patio.

Floor to ceiling drapes, hanging at ten foot intervals, lined the wall. Trace hoped these drapes hid the French doors he'd noticed when he and Ibrahim had walked across the outdoor patio.

He approached the first curtain and took its edge in his hand as if this action was an afterthought. He pulled the edge out and turned it over to inspect it. His subterfuge rewarded him. He saw French doors behind the drapes.

He looked around to see if anyone was watching him. He didn't see anyone. He quickly stepped behind the drapes.

Trace turned to the French doors.

The doors were locked, as he expected they would be. He turned the latch, unlocked them, and opened one door a crack.

Trace reached into his pocket and took out the food rationing regulations Ibrahim had given him. He tore off a corner, crushed it into a tiny, compact ball, and forced the wad into the metal opening where the door latch would ordinarily fit when the door closed. The door now would not lock when it closed, even if someone were to take the trouble to reset the lock button.

He stepped out from behind the drapes and repeated this process three times along the curtained wall before returning to Ibrahim and Jenna.

"What were you doing behind the curtains?" Ibrahim asked when Trace sat down.

"Jamming the locks on the French doors in case we have to go out that way in a hurry."

"Cool," Ibrahim said.

Trace looked over at Jenna.

She's watching the lobby's entrance pretty intently, he thought.

He walked over and sat down beside her.

"You seem to have something on your mind," Trace said.

"I'm fine," Jenna said.

She stood up and walked a few feet away, then started to pace. She looked again, furtively this time, toward the lobby's entrance.

Trace watched her. He narrowed his eyes. There are three kinds of people who pace, he thought. Those who are thinking through a problem, those who are nervous, and those who have something to hide. He decided in Jenna's case, she had something to hide and was nervous about it.

"Want to talk about what's bothering you?"

"I said I'm fine. Nothing's bothering me. I told you."

Jenna walked over to the other side of Ibrahim, and sat down beside him.

Trace stood up and followed her.

"Mind if I join you?" he said.

Without waiting for her answer, he cork-screwed his legs down and sat in a Bodhisattva-like posture, his legs crossed at the ankles. He faced Jenna and looked at her straight in her eyes. He held her gaze until she looked away.

Then she turned back to face him.

"Why do you keep looking at me like that?" she said. "What's wrong with you? You're creeping me out."

"Why do you keep looking at the entryway?" Trace said. "Expecting someone?"

"I don't keep looking at it. Anyway, it doesn't mean anything. Why are you picking on me?"

"You've been sneaking looks at the entrance since Ibrahim and I got back here," Trace said. "Who're you expecting?"

She shook her head. "I don't know what you're talking about. Just leave me alone." She glanced at Ibrahim, then back at Trace.

Trace opened his mouth to answer, but a deep voice cut him off.

"Is there a problem here, Jenna?"

Trace's alarm system kicked into high gear. He looked in the direction of the voice, even as he instinctively started to stand to reduce his vulnerability. What he saw stopped him cold.

A young man in his middle or late twenties stood four or five feet away facing him and Jenna. He was fairly big, at least 6'2", and two hundred-plus pounds. From the looks of his arms, chest and shoulders, Trace decided, that's muscle, not flab.

He wore his hair cut close, Marines' boot camp style. His neck seemed to be an extension of his head and broad shoulders rather than a defined and functioning body part of its own. Mr. No Neck, Trace thought. A jock. Probably a weight lifter or wrestler. Strong, powerful, and muscle bound, not quick and limber, not agile and able to cope with *T'ai chi's* speed and dexterity in hand-to-hand combat. At least, I hope.

Trace started to straighten up, alert to act if necessary. He looked at No Neck, then at Jenna, then back at No Neck.

"Sit down," No Neck said to Trace. His tone brooked no opposition.

Trace didn't move. He remained suspended in his half-standing, half-kneeling *T'ai chi juan* attack posture, his upward motion stopped *in situ*. He was fully alert to any threatening movement by No Neck.

"Sit down," No Neck said again, looking hard into Trace's eyes. "Please," he added after a brief pause.

As he said "please," No Neck stepped away from Trace, lessening Trace's perceived threat.

Then No Neck melted to the floor, drilling down into an Indian-style sitting position.

Trace relaxed and nodded to No Neck as he, too, dropped to the floor. He settled in next to Jenna.

Trace watched as No Neck looked at Jenna, then at Ibrahim,

whose eyes were like silver dollar pancakes. Then No Neck looked back at Trace.

"It's time for us to talk," he said.

He turned slightly and pointed across the room, through the vestibule, directly at the entrance door.

"Let's go outside to the patio," he said. It was not a request.

No Neck stood up and walked away without saying another word.

CHAPTER 71

Quarantine
Day 25

TRACE PULLED UP A PATIO chair and narrowed his eyes as he faced No Neck. He remained alert to any physical threat.

"Why's it time for us to talk?" he said, reprising No Neck's last statement. "I don't have a clue who you are or what you're talking about."

"I know some things about you though," No Neck said. "Enough to know we've some common interests." He paused, then continued, "I'm Alex."

"Skip the introductions," Trace said. "I don't care about your name. What do you think you know about me?" His eyes scanned the patio as he spoke.

"I know your son died while you and your wife were visiting here."

Trace's stomach tightened.

"I know your mother-in-law also died in the Quarantine Zone. You tried to get medicine to help them both, but couldn't."

"Who are you, besides your name?" Trace said.

"I also know the government is deliberately withholding food and medicine from the Quarantine Zone," No Neck said.

Trace tapped his foot and clenched and unclenched his fist.

"There're other things you should know," No Neck said. "Just hear me out. You won't be sorry."

Trace looked at No Neck, held his gaze, then nodded.

"Do you remember when you met Jenna?" No Neck said. "On the street corner."

"I remember."

"She told you she came here for spring break, that her cousin was here." He paused. "I'm the cousin."

Trace now understood No Neck's source of information about him and his family.

"What's your point?" Trace said.

"We can help each other. We can share skills to make our lives better while we're stuck here, help us survive until the quarantine's over."

"What skills do you think I have that would be useful to you? I'm a middle-aged technology lawyer. Unless you need a computer manufacturing license or a software development contract, I won't be much help."

"You underrate yourself. I know you're an ex-SEAL. You have team-building skills and survival skills that can be useful for all of us. I also know you have serious computer skills. You'd have to have them for your kind of law practice."

"The key term concerning my time with the SEALs is *ex*. What you call my SEALs' skills, they're history. Too rusty to rely on."

"Maybe," Alex said, but I doubt you've lost your trained instinct for survival, your trained state-of-mind, the mind-set that makes a SEAL a SEAL."

"For the sake of argument, suppose you're right. So what?" Trace said. "Let's flip this around. What do you bring to the table. You're a college kid playing at being a warrior?"

Alex laughed. "Not quite. I also have a history, a life before college. I'm older than my current college level would suggest."

Trace was curious, but said nothing, waiting. He wanted to see where the kid would go with this.

"Before college I was in the Pembroke Avenue Crew, a Brooklyn street gang. I specialized in organizing limited resources into useful tools and weapons. I was good at what I did."

"Nice résumé," Trace said. "What're you proposing, that we form a street gang?" Trace shook his head. "If so, count me out. I won't do that. Not even under these circumstances. I'm law abiding by nature and by training."

"Since I've been trapped here," Alex said, ignoring Trace's objection, "I've been reactive, even passive at times, responding to decisions made by other people who don't give a damn about me. You've probably been the same way."

Trace nodded.

"I don't know why it is," Alex said, "but the government's not looking out for any of us. Otherwise there would be enough food, medicine and other necessities brought into the Quarantine Zone. It's not like they can't fly this stuff in from the rest of the country if they want to. They were able to do that after Hurricane Katrina, weren't they?"

Trace again nodded, but again held his tongue.

"If the authorities aren't going to help us, we need to take care of ourselves. There are plenty of people around the Quarantine Zone who feel the same way."

Trace said, "Suppose I agree, then what?"

"For starters," Alex said, "we should get Ibrahim, Jenna and me over to your condo. We should stay together in one place, a private place. It'll be safer than squatting in hotel lobbies like we've been doing."

"We can't stay at my place." Trace described his recent run-in with the soldiers, then added, "They'll be watching for me at the condo. We would need some other place."

Trace paused and thought for a moment.

"We also need to get my wife away from the condo, but I can't be the one who does it. Any ideas on that front?" he said, curious to test Alex's wiliness to help and his creativity.

"I'll do it tonight, in the middle of the night," Alex said. "I'll bring your wife out tomorrow morning after curfew ends. We'll walk out together like we don't have a care in the world. But she needs to know I'm coming."

Trace and Alex talked this over and decided to try it.

"I'll call Isabella," Trace said, "but not with my cell phone. I don't want to be pinged and traced from its GPS chip."

Alex handed over his phone.

"Tell her to keep her phone open. If I get through surveillance, I'll call her. I'll let the cell ring twice, then hang up. I'll call her right back, let it ring three times, and hang up again. She's not to answer either time. Then I'll come to her door and knock the same way. Two knocks, then three."

"What if there's a problem?"

"Then it won't be her problem, it'll be mine. In that case, she should stay put until you come up with a different plan. If that happens I won't be in the picture anymore."

Trace dialed Pete's cell phone number. Isabella picked up on the second ring.

"Bella. It's me. Just listen to me. I have to keep this short."

He told her the plan.

PART THREE

CHAPTER 72

Quarantine
Days 25 and 26

T RACE AND ALEX LEFT THE patio and rejoined Jenna and
Ibrahim in the hotel's lobby. Alex whispered the new
arrangement to them. Ibrahim suggested they shouldn't
continue to stay at the Palm Court Hotel since he and Jenna
probably were familiar faces there by now. They all agreed
they'd move to the nearby Hotel Carlota where none of them
had been before.

* * *

At 2:10 a.m. Alex propped himself up on his elbows. He was
lying on a small berm overlooking the entrance to Nanna's
condominium building. He'd been on the hill for almost forty
minutes, watching and listening for some sign of surveillance.

The night was quiet except for the chirping of crickets,
the occasional hoot or screech of an owl, and the constant,
undulating whine of cicadas.

Although Alex eventually satisfied himself there were no
human watchers around, he worried there might be cameras in

place of human assets, but he didn't see any. It still was too dark for the drones to be out. He decided to make his move.

Alex entered the building and stepped behind the stairs leading to the second floor. He dialed Isabella's cell phone and performed the prearranged signals. Then he hurried up the stairs and, using his knuckles, knocked the same prearranged signal pattern on the condo's door.

Isabella opened the door for Alex, stepped out of the way to let him in, then leaned her head out into the hallway. She looked up and down the hall, but didn't see anyone. She quickly closed the door.

She and Alex quietly introduced themselves, whispering into each other's ear.

The next morning Isabella stood by the sofa in the living room and whispered, "Alex, it's 6:00 a.m. You wanted me to wake you. It's time to leave."

Alex opened his eyes, rubbed them, and looked up from the sofa at the voice that had just pulled him away from a dream.

He bolted upright.

"Is that you?" he whispered. "You look great."

He smiled and complimented Isabella on her overnight transformation from an attractive, fit, middle-aged woman into a frumpy, elderly woman.

Isabella was wearing one of Nanna's wigs, a blue-grey hairpiece with tight curls. She also wore one of Nanna's house dresses which she'd stuffed with rolled shirts and small towels to fill-in the vast hollows it now contained. She held Nanna's cane in her hand.

"I'm ready when you are, Young Man," she whispered in Alex's ear, using a simulated, high-pitched elderly voice.

"Perfect. Just perfect," he whispered back. "Let's hit the road. I'll take you to the hotel."

CHAPTER 73

Quarantine
Day 26

"So that's the situation, Sir," the major said.

"What do you mean she disappeared?" Vista slammed his fist on the desk. "How could she disappear? You were surveilling her, weren't you?"

"Sir, I don't know what to say."

The major stood at attention, his back straight and rigid. Beads of sweat formed on his forehead.

"We proceeded last night just like every other night since we started the surveillance, Sir."

"Then where is she, Major?"

"We don't know, Sir." He stared, unblinking, at the wall behind the general.

The major remained at attention, his eyes staring straight ahead, intentionally unfocused so he could not see the general in his peripheral vision.

"You screwed up my chance to take the ex-SEAL, you fool. His wife was going to be our bait."

The major remained silent, resolved not to speak unless asked a specific question, lost in his own unpleasant thoughts.

"When did you last log her in?"

"At 2345 hours, Sir. We monitored the female subject using the parabolic mike with the Super Ear. We heard her prepare herself for sleep, sing to herself, then settle down. We heard her turn off the radio and click off the light. After approximately thirty minutes, when we heard nothing more, we assumed she was asleep, so we relaxed contact until morning."

"But she wasn't sleeping, was she, Major? She was playing you."

"No, Sir. I mean, yes, Sir, she was. I mean . . . ."

Vista shook his head in disgust, turned away, and went behind his desk and sat. He stared down at the desk-wide blotter.

The major continued. "We resumed full monitoring at 0700 hours, Sir. At 0900 hours, because we still hadn't heard any activity, but thought she might still be asleep, we sent in a decoy disguised as a civilian looking for his wife. The apartment was empty." He imperceptibly rolled his shoulders to release tension.

"We've flagged her and her husband in the system, Sir. It's just a matter of time before they tip their hands and we have them."

Vista shook his head slowly and then stood up and walked out from behind his desk.

The major watched Vista approach from the corner of his eyes. The general loomed as a large, dark shape, becoming larger and larger in his peripheral vision. Vista stopped in front of him, just eight inches away.

The major remained at attention, unblinking and unflinching in the face of the general's proximity, staring straight ahead. Perspiration pooled on his chest and back. His shirt pasted itself against his back.

"You lost my ex-SEAL, you sonofabitch." Vista leaned in closer.

"I want him, Major. Do you hear me? I want him now. Today. Not tomorrow. Not next week. Today."

He paused to wipe away spittle leaking from one corner of his mouth. "I order you to find the ex-SEAL and bring him to me. Do you understand me, Major? Do I make myself clear?"

"Yes, Sir."

The major ignored the spray that pelted his face and looked over the general's shoulder at the wall. His lower back throbbed.

"What are you going to bring me, Major?

"I am going to bring you the ex-SEAL, Sir."

"When are you going to bring him to me?"

"With all deliberate speed, Sir."

"No, damn you. You're going to bring him to me today, Major, or, by God, I will bust you down to sergeant before this night's over. Do you understand me?"

"Yes, Sir. I understand you, Sir."

"Get out of here, Major, out of my sight. The next time I see you, you better be dragging the ex-SEAL to me, chained. Do I make myself clear?"

"Yes, Sir."

"Yes, Sir, what, Major?"

"Yes, Sir, you've made yourself clear. The next time you see me, Sir, I will deliver the ex-SEAL to you. That will be today, Sir. In chains."

CHAPTER 74

Quarantine
Day 27

T RACE AND ISABELLA LEFT THE Palm Court Hotel first.
Twenty minutes later Ibrahim and Jenna left. Fifteen
minutes after Ibrahim and Jenna, Alex left. One by one
they infiltrated themselves into the nearby Hotel Carlota's
crowded lobby.

Trace, Isabella, Ibrahim and Jenna, but not Alex, set
themselves up as squatters in a small meeting room. Alex did
not move in although he spent the morning with them. When
asked why by Trace, Alex remained vague about where he
planned to spend the night. This aroused Trace's curiosity, but
he decided not to press the issue. For now.

———— ✳ ——— ✳ —— ✳ —— ✳ —— ✳

They were hungry. None had eaten a full meal in days. The
common sound heard among them when they weren't talking
was the growling of their complaining stomachs.

"We need to eat," Alex said. "I have my ration coupons.
Does everyone else?" he asked, looking at the others.

"Mine are at the condo," Trace said. "I can't risk getting them now."

"I don't have mine either," Isabella said. "I never got out to get them. I can still go do it though." She looked at Trace.

Trace raised his eyebrows and shook his head. "I don't think that'd be a good idea."

"Trace is right," Alex said. "I'll share my coupons with you both."

"I'll pool mine, too," Jenna said.

"And me," Ibrahim said.

That evening after curfew, Alex and Trace sat in the back of the main lobby talking. They decided to avoid the room where Trace and the others would sleep in an attempt to be less familiar to anyone already in that room. Ibrahim, Jenna and Isabella were off exploring the hotel.

"Something's bothering me," Trace said.

"What's that?"

"When I was looking for medicine for my mother-in-law, a pharmacist told me the authorities had blocked shipments into the Quarantine Zone. She said the posted notices from the CDC were lies. That's about the same thing you told me. Do you really believe it?"

"Afraid I do."

"It doesn't make sense. Maybe it was unintentional, another FEMA screw-up," Trace said, "like during Katrina."

"I don't know why," Alex said. "Anyway, this problem's with the CDC, not FEMA."

"Whatever. I don't get it," Trace said. "It goes against

common sense and everything I believe. We're missing something here, something key."

Two hours later, Trace and Ibrahim left the hotel. They were looking for other individuals out on the street, with a view to possibly forming a team with them.

"Tell me again," Ibrahim said, "why you want to meet people?"

"To see if we can put together a small team of people having different, useful skills we can share to help us all survive the quarantine. I'll train us all in the SEALs' methods of teamwork."

After an hour, Trace and Ibrahim headed back to the hotel. They hadn't come across anyone Trace wanted to recruit for the ad hoc team.

CHAPTER 75

Quarantine
Day 28

"WE'VE SEARCHED EVERYWHERE, SIR, BUT we can't find Austin or his wife."

Vista stared into the major's eyes.

A charged silence hovered over the junior officer.

The major desperately wanted to look away from the general and loosen his shirt collar, but he remained at attention, his back rigid, his neck and shoulders sore, resolutely staring back into the general's slitted eyes. He willed himself not to be the first to blink.

He lost.

"What are you doing to find them, Major?" the general said in a voice so soft, so non-threatening that it inherently carried an implied threat with it.

"We have a fugitive warrant out, Sir. If they show anywhere our facial recognition software will tag them. Or, in the unlikely event they use their cell phones or credit cards, we'll have them then."

"You better hope so, Major. You just better hope so. I haven't forgotten you failed me the other day."

Twenty minutes later a knock on General Vista's office door interrupted him. He unlocked the door, left it closed, and returned to his desk.

Seated again behind his desk, he said, "Come in."

The major walked in, snapped to attention, and saluted.

"We've spotted him, Sir. The male subject, but not the wife. He's with another male subject, identity unknown, an Arab-type from his looks. They are walking along Royal Palm Drive."

General Vista nodded and smiled. Then his smile twisted.

"Keep Austin in sight, Major. Block-off all escape routes. When the area is secure, take him."

He thought for a few seconds, then added, "Bring him directly to me. Process him later. I want him with me as soon as he's here."

CHAPTER 76

Quarantine
Day 28

T RACE STOPPED ABRUPTLY AS HE and Ibrahim walked back
to the hotel. He put up his palm to signal Ibrahim to wait.
He looked around.

"Something's odd," he said. "I can feel it."

Ibrahim looked at him, frowned, then looked around.

"I don't see anything. What's the problem?"

Trace looked up and down the street. He, too, saw nothing.
Then it came to him.

He saw nothing.

That's strange, he thought. No pedestrians. Not in any
direction. Not even a few scattered along the sidewalks. No
vehicular traffic either.

"We have to get out of here," Trace said. "It's too quiet.
Come on, Ibrahim." He started running.

Trace, with Ibrahim tagging close behind, ran across Royal
Palm Drive directly into an alley located between George's
Greek Restaurant and Kingston Hardware. As they entered the
alley two HUMVEEs rumbled around the corner and headed
toward the last place Trace and Ibrahim had been standing.

At the same time, another HUMVEE approached from the opposite end of Royal Palm Drive.

A KIOWA WARRIOR helicopter suddenly swooped into view, the whump, whump, whump of its rotor blades drowning out all sounds below. The KIOWA swung low over the neighborhood, back and forth like a pendulum.

Trace and Ibrahim stopped running once they were in the alley out of sight. Their lungs strained for air, sucking in breath in short, desperate pulls. Ibrahim bent over from his waist, his hands on his knees, gulping air.

Trace watched both ends of the alley, swiveling his head back and forth. The last thing he wanted was to be trapped there.

Trace's breathing gradually returned to normal. Ibrahim now stood erect, still breathing hard, but more slowly and evenly than before.

"We can't stay here," Trace said. "Eventually they'll find us."

"What'll we do?"

"We need to get inside, out of sight, somewhere we can stay until dark. Then we'll see. Right now we have to get away from here."

Trace walked to the far end of the alley and peeked out, looking up and down the street. He didn't see anyone out there.

"Get ready to run," he said, turning toward Ibrahim. "When I give the signal, bend low and go as fast as you can into that alley over there," he said, pointing across the street.

"Right," Ibrahim said. He took a deep breath and bent slightly forward at the waist, his hands on his hips as if he was a long distance runner at the starting line of a 10K race.

"Keep running no matter what happens. When you get into the alley, stop," Trace said, "Don't go out the other end."

Ibrahim nodded.

"Wait for my signal. I'll be right behind you."

Trace walked to the edge of the alley where it intersected with a small patch of grass. He looked out, surveilling the area again in both directions. He didn't see any soldiers or, when he looked up, any helicopters or drones. He knew, however, that many drones flew too high to be seen from the ground, so he also knew that he and Ibrahim were at risk of being spotted from above even when he thought no one was watching.

Trace held up his hand, signaling Ibrahim with his palm to wait. Then he put up three fingers. He closed one finger and looked back to see if Ibrahim was following his signals.

Ibrahim crouched now as if ready to sprint, on signal, and nodded.

Trace looked back at the street. He held up one finger. Then he gave his signal, using a throwing motion with his arm.

"Go! Go!," he said. "Go!"

Ibrahim dashed from the alley, followed by Trace just behind him. They crossed the sidewalk, the street, and another sidewalk on the other side of the street, and ran into the alley. There were no shouts or shots. As far as Trace knew, they remained undetected.

They skidded to a stop in the alley, making Trace think of Wile E. Coyote in the Roadrunner cartoons.

Trace turned around and hurried back to the alley's entrance. He looked up and down the street. He didn't see any soldiers, but now he saw a small drone hovering above.

He walked to the other end of the alley and performed

the same surveillance with the same result, except he didn't see any drones.

Trace and Ibrahim repeated their escape ritual seven more times over the next hour until they were almost three miles from the original alley. They huddled in their most recent refuge as Trace considered their next move.

His protocol in a situation like this — the protocol that had been drilled into him when he trained as a SEAL — was clear. The first thing he and Ibrahim had to do was find someplace safe in which to take refuge. Then he could plan their next move.

"We have to get inside," Trace said. "We're vulnerable as long as we're outside. Drones will eventually tag us."

"Where to? The hotel?"

Trace shook his head. "No, not yet. Not until we have a better understanding of our situation. We need to find a place, some empty house or building, where we can spend a few hours until after curfew."

CHAPTER 77

Quarantine
Day 28

T HE MAJOR RAISED HIS FIST to knock on the door, then
hesitated. Instead, he pulled out his handkerchief and
wiped his forehead. He jiggled his necktie knot to loosen
it, inhaled deeply, and tentatively let out his breath. He sucked
in his stomach. Then he rapped his knuckles against the wood
in two quick bursts, just the way the general liked.

He waited at attention.

After almost one minute, he heard the door lock disengage,
but the general did not open the door.

More silence.

I wonder what he does behind the locked door? he thought.
Actually, I probably don't want to know. He squirmed at the
range of possibilities.

He lost his smile and his stomach knotted at the sound of
the general's voice coming from the far side of his office.

"Enter."

"Austin got away again, Sir. And still no leads on his wife.

"That won't do," General Vista said, sotto voce, more to himself than to the major.

Vista turned away and faced the window. When he turned back, he narrowed his eyes, looked at the wall beyond the major, and smiled.

The major had never before seen the general smile. It didn't look natural. That's really creepy, he thought. Seeing the general's smile made him even more uneasy than he already was.

Vista looked back at the major, still smiling.

"Put out an order against the ex-SEAL. Arrest him. This is not to be a stop and question intervention. He's to be stopped and taken into custody. If he resists, act accordingly." He rubbed his palms together and nodded several times.

CHAPTER 78

Quarantine
Day 28

TRACE AND IBRAHIM MADE THEIR way along more streets and alleys until they came to Fort Lauderdale's only historic residential district, Sailboat Bend, an eclectic, mixed-use neighborhood with narrow streets that follow the course of the New River. The district is known for having million dollar riverfront mansions sitting across the street from, or next door to, run-down apartment buildings, seedy tourists' homes and squalid guest houses.

Trace looked for a house that was closed-up for the off-season. He scouted several homes, but rejected them all because they were too close to their occupied neighbors. Then he found one that seemed right.

He and Ibrahim hid behind a crop of bushes and watched the house for almost one hour, looking for any sign of life inside. They didn't see any.

"Follow me," Trace said. "Stay low, move fast."

They crept along the perimeter hedge, keeping their profiles low, staying close to the hedgerow until they came to the backyard.

"Wait here," Trace said. "I'm going to test the door's lock. Watch for my signal to come over, then come in low and fast. Get right inside. Don't stop until you're inside."

Trace straightened up and, for the edification of any passerby who might see him, sauntered over to the back door as if he didn't have a care in the world. He carried, tucked under his arm, a yellowed, folded newspaper he'd taken from a partially full recycle basket near the garage.

When he arrived at the back door, Trace gently rattled the handle to see if he could determine how many locks bolted it.

Good, he thought. Just one latch lock. No deadbolt.

He knocked loudly, waited a beat, then knocked twice more. He put his ear to the door and waited. There was no sound inside. He knocked again, listened and waited. Still nothing. No person and, even better, no dog.

So far.

He looked around. Satisfied that he and Ibrahim were alone, at least as far as he could tell, he slipped a credit card into the crack between the door lock and the door jam, and jiggled the card up and down as he simultaneously turned the knob. The stock lock popped open.

He looked back at Ibrahim, and held up his palm, signaling him to wait. He knocked again and listened. Still just silence from within. He slowly turned the knob and opened the door just wide enough to put his head inside. He leaned into the kitchen.

"Hello. Is anyone here?" he called loudly for the benefit of anyone who might be inside.

No response. No sound at all. Especially no sound of paws and paw nails running across the floor somewhere in the house.

He listened and absorbed the house's emptiness, not quite convinced yet.

Trace turned back toward Ibrahim and held up his palm again. Then he stepped into the kitchen. He yelled again, louder this time.

"Hello. Anyone home? Gas company here to check for a reported gas leak." He paused, listened a second, then said, "We need your permission to enter to check for the leak."

Again no response.

Trace looked around the kitchen, ready to bolt if necessary.

He was cautious as he walked across the kitchen to the archway leading to the dining room. He knew that even though he had not evoked a response by knocking on the door and calling out, someone still might be there, deliberately refusing to answer him, also waiting and listening, either angry or frightened, or both, hiding and armed with a weapon. All he was reasonably sure about was that there was no dog in the house. He was not at all certain there was no armed man or woman waiting for him to appear before them, ready to invoke Florida's *Stand Your Ground* law.

He stood at the entryway between the kitchen and dining room, and listened.

He wiped the perspiration from his forehead using his shirt sleeve.

And waited.

He returned to the kitchen and walked over to the sink, opened the two doors below the basin, and looked into the storage area. He found what he was looking for in a box under the sink.

Now, as satisfied as he could be that no one was home, without making a visual inspection of the entire house, Trace stepped back to the door and waved his arm, signaling Ibrahim to come in.

Ibrahim dashed over the threshold into the kitchen, and stopped short. Trace put his hand on Ibrahim's shoulder and held a finger of his other hand to his lips to indicate he wanted Ibrahim to be quiet.

Ibrahim nodded.

Trace put his lips close to Ibrahim's ear. "I think we're okay, we're alone, but I need to make sure."

Ibrahim nodded again.

Trace whispered, "We'll check every room. I'll inspect while you keep watch." He reached over to Ibrahim. "Take these and put them on," he said, handing Ibrahim a pair of latex gloves he'd taken from under the sink.

Then Trace stretched gloves over his own hands.

Trace and Ibrahim methodically worked their way through the house, room by room, closet by closet, looking under every bed and behind every upholstered chair. At last satisfied they were alone, Trace, with Ibrahim trailing close behind, returned to the living room and sat down on the floor. Ibrahim dropped down onto the sofa.

"Now what?" Ibrahim said. "What if the owners come back while we're here?"

"They won't," Trace said. "This place is closed up until October or November."

"How do you know? It looks lived-in to me."

"The hot water heater's turned off. The air conditioning's set to 95º. The house is closed for the summer until late fall or early winter. The owners probably are snowbirds from up north."

"Then we can stay as long as we want," Ibrahim said. He swung his legs up onto the sofa, clasped his hands behind his head, and laid back against the armrest.

"We'll leave in a few hours, after curfew starts," Trace said.

"Why should we leave if no one's going to be here? Anyway, where will we go? The hotel?"

"Not the hotel. Not yet. I don't know where, but we need to keep moving. No telling if a neighbor or a drone saw us come in here."

They spent the next forty-five minutes looking through the walk-in pantry, various cabinets, and drawers. They methodically worked their way through the attic and the attached garage, opening boxes and inspecting everything they found. They carried their discovered loot back to the kitchen and set it all on the Formica-covered table.

Trace ate the uncooked contents of a can of spaghetti he found. Ibrahim ate pickled beets. They shared a box of stale Ritz crackers. This was all the food they found. Then they each took a turn napping while the other kept watch.

At 9:30 p.m. Trace eased open the back door and listened. There was no sound save the rubbing solicitations of male crickets. He crouched and eased himself through the doorway onto the back porch, still watching and listening for any indication of human presence. Ibrahim followed him, gently closing and latching the door behind him.

They crept down the three steps to the backyard and walked close to the house, trying to blend into its bulk and darkness, then moved along its side toward the front yard.

Trace leaned around the corner of the structure, sticking his head out only as far as necessary for his eyes to clear the building and sweep the street in both directions. He didn't see any sign of life so he pulled back in and put his lips close to Ibrahim's ear.

"Let's go. Stay behind me, keep low."

Ibrahim whispered, "Right."

Crouching, Trace took a step away from the side yard.

He'd barely moved when, from the corner of his eyes, he saw a slight movement in the bushes. He abruptly stopped walking, even as his adrenalin began to pump.

Trace reflexively assumed the *T'ai chi juan* fighting posture, and waited. He prepared to defend himself or, if appropriate, to attack.

The bushes moved again.

Trace peered into the dark, squinting to sharpen his visual penetration of the gloom.

What he saw froze him in place.

CHAPTER 79

Quarantine
Day 28

"Good evening, ladies and gentlemen," Derek Peterson said. "Here's this afternoon's news from the Quarantine Zone." He glanced at his clipboard.

"The Centers for Disease Control and Prevention reported today that the number of new cases of the terrorists' disease remained level this week for the first time since the terrorists' attack.

"The CDC cautions, however, that this good news should not be interpreted as an indication that the quarantine is about to end. It is too soon to draw any such inference."

He paused and wiped his neck with his red paisley bandana.

"The CDC also stated that the decreasing number of new cases reported might only be an anomaly. The CDC will continue to monitor the situation and report back to us.

"Now, on a less positive note," he said, "the CDC has advised us that the number of deaths resulting from the terrorists' disease and from secondary causes such as malnutrition and dehydration increased during the same period. Overall, the number of such deaths in the Quarantine Zone continues to rise. The CDC stated that this is not unexpected because there is always a lag time between an actual decrease in the number of new cases reported and the resulting decrease in deaths from those cases previously reported. We'll have more on this as we receive more information."

He lowered his clipboard and nodded at the camera.

"This is Derek Peterson, CNN, signing off."

CHAPTER 80

Quarantine
Day 28

As TRACE STARED, FIVE SHAPES, each at least six feet tall and linebacker-wide, each dressed in black from head to toe, stepped from behind the bushes alongside the house and approached Trace and Ibrahim, blocking their way out of the side yard.

Trace's adrenalin level continued to spike. He spun around to see the possibilities behind them, and to look for an escape route for him and Ibrahim.

Four other, similarly large and identically clad figures, one of whom carried an assault-style automatic weapon with a sound suppressor attached, approached them from behind, blocking this potential escape route.

Trace straightened up and slowly raised his hands in surrender, to show submission, to reduce the tension inherent in the situation. He had not been trained by the SEALs to commit suicide. Nor could he recall anything from his study of the *Tao te Ching* that argued in favor of suicide in a situation such as this.

He looked over at Ibrahim and nodded. Ibrahim raised his

hands, too. Trace winked at Ibrahim to calm him, suggesting by this gesture that this would likely be no big deal once it was sorted out.

One dark figure stepped forward and patted them down.

To Trace's surprise, since he hadn't known they were there, two more large, human shapes emerged from the darkness near the house.

That makes eleven in all, Trace thought. So far.

One of the shapes carried a large black canvas gym bag. He tossed it to the ground, then leaned over, unzipped the bag, and reached inside. He removed two black overalls, two black T-shirts, two black wool watch caps, and two pairs of black gloves.

The shape tossed one set of clothing to Trace and lobbed the other at Ibrahim who, crippled by the situation he and Trace found themselves in, watched the garments soar through the air, bounce off his chest, and fall to the grass.

Ibrahim said, "Sorry," and hurriedly scooped them up, looking furtively at the large shape with the automatic weapon.

"Dress yourselves," the figure said, making it clear to Trace and Ibrahim that they, too, should blend into the night.

CHAPTER 81

Quarantine
Day 28

VIKTOR RUTKOWSKA THREW HIS EMPTY vodka bottle to the floor and watched it smash into a shower of shards. He was in a foul mood. He had drained his last bottle of vodka and had no hopes of replacing it.

Twelve days had passed since Viktor's gun shop had been padlocked and his inventory taken by the ODMC. Meanwhile, Viktor hadn't seen a dime of income and had not received any government compensation for the forced taking. He angrily watched as his modest savings (which he secreted at home, not in a bank) drained away as he was forced to raid his savings to purchase increasingly expensive black market food, vodka, and other necessities for survival.

Viktor rummaged around his home searching for a wayward bottle of vodka, one he might have stashed in more affluent times, but had forgotten about. He found none, which only served to escalate his anger and frustration.

He decided to take his mind off his situation and do something useful: he would clean and lubricate his private cache of weapons in anticipation of the upcoming mission he'd constructed for himself.

Viktor carefully laid the weapons out on his kitchen table. He first cleaned and oiled the Beretta, then reassembled it.

Next he worked on his favorite among all his weapons, the VSS Vintorez sniper rifle, the one known as the *thread cutter*. This weapon was issued primarily to Spetsnaz special forces units for undercover operations, but also sometimes to the special shooters units, such as the one Viktor had belonged to in the Afghan and Chechen wars.

The *thread cutter* fired a heavy, slow 9x39mm SP-5 cartridge to avoid creating a telltale sonic boom. The rifle had a folding stock, a scope that detached easily for transport, and an integrated silencer and muzzle flash suppressor that wrapped around its barrel. The VSS was sturdy, especially its stock, which had a rubber shoulder pad.

This weapon had served Viktor well in Chechnya. When fired, the VSS made little noise, and had an accurate range of three hundred meters. It was perfect for urban combat because of its short range, low-velocity, quiet cartridges, and the ease with which it broke down for transport in a specially fitted briefcase.

Viktor cleaned and lubricated the *thread cutter*, then reassembled it. Next he stripped down his Dragunov sniper rifle, the long barreled rifle used for long distance kills. Unlike the *thread cutter*, this weapon was considered too unwieldy for urban combat. Certainly too unwieldy for the Quarantine Zone. Or was it?

Viktor, in both the Afghan and Chechen wars, had found this weapon to be perfectly suited for his occasional urban-based assignments.

The Dragunov was considered to be a marksman's weapon, a military unit's support weapon. In Russia, every infantry unit had at least one person who carried a Dragunov and was proficient with it. The weapon was sturdy, but lightweight, fired a deadly round, and, overall, was extremely reliable.

Viktor decided that both the *thread cutter* and the Dragunov would suit him fine for what he had in mind to do in the Quarantine Zone, in this American gulag. He would use one or the other of these weapons once he'd selected his targets and had determined where he would exercise his trained talents to reject this American-made internment camp he now found himself imprisoned in.

For the first time in many days, as Viktor contemplated becoming a shooter again, he smiled.

CHAPTER 82

Quarantine
Day 28

T RACE, IBRAHIM, AND THEIR DARKLY-CLAD escorts kept
close to the shadowed shelter of houses and other buildings
as they moved through the streets of Fort Lauderdale.

The cloud-covered night became their ally.

All street lights remained dark for curfew, but a small
measure of light leaked from houses, traveling up to the dense
cloud ceiling and then rebounding to Earth, passing back
through air thick with humidity and salt. It seemed to Trace he
was seeing neighborhoods through gauzy eyes shrouded with
well-developed cataracts.

After walking a little more than one hour, they arrived at a
highway overpass and stood at the side of the road looking
down into a culvert.

Trace and Ibrahim fell into a single-file line with their
escorts, and then tentatively side-stepped with them toward the
bottom of the hill.

As Trace's eyes adjusted to the dim light away from the

street, he saw armed guards posted along both slopes, north to south.

Down in the culvert, again walking single file, the escorts led Trace and Ibrahim along the bottom crease of the culvert, traveling four or five city blocks from the overpass.

"This should do," one of the escorts said. "Let's sit."

They arranged themselves on the ground in a circle as if they were a Boy Scout troop sitting around a campfire. The escorts remained masked.

"We're Friday's Progeny," one black-clad person said, speaking through his mask. His voice was muffled by his mask and difficult to understand.

Trace and Ibrahim turned and looked at one another, then turned back to the speaker.

Trace said, "You're the bandits we heard about on the TV newscast."

"We're not bandits."

Trace said, "Do we have to stay in these?" He pointed at his black, wool ski mask. "They're uncomfortable. You know who we are even if we don't know you. I'm hot, and I'm going to take this off." Before anyone could respond, Trace grabbed the bottom of his mask and started to roll it up over his face and head.

The speaker who had just identified the group as Friday's Progeny answered Trace by holding up his palm to stop him. Then he lowered his own chin to his chest, temporarily hiding his face. He grabbed the base of his own ski mask and slowly pulled it up until it came all the way off his face and head.

He raised his face and looked directly at Trace.

"Remember me?"

CHAPTER 83

Quarantine
Day 28

"Y ou've got to be kidding me," Trace said to the unmasked speaker. "Of course, I remember you, but I thought you were just a college jock on a spring break fling."

Alex shrugged. "I was, but things changed. We do what we have to do."

Trace stared briefly at Alex, then nodded.

"Where does your cousin fit in? Is Jenna part of this?" he said, sweeping his arm to take in the nearby people in black. "And Ibrahim?" he added, looking over at Ibrahim.

"We recruited Jenna early on," Alex said. "I knew I could trust her. I've known her all her life. She's our eyes and ears."

Alex paused. "He's not part of this," he said, nodding at Ibrahim.

Trace looked at Ibrahim, who shrugged.

"Then you came along. Jenna filled us in on you," Alex said. "And so here we are."

"You're terrorists," Trace said. "Vigilantes, looters, bandits, black marketers. Whatever you want to call yourselves. Pick the name that suits you." He paused to collect his thoughts.

"How did you find us? How'd you know we were at that house?" Trace said.

"We've been watching you ever since we met at the hotel," Alex said.

What do you want with us?"

Alex ignored Trace's question, and said, "We're none of those things. We're ordinary people caught up in circumstances, people who want to survive until the quarantine ends, then go back to our normal lives. Like I told you at the hotel, we can help each other."

"What's the name Friday's Progeny mean?" Trace asked.

"Some of us were tourists trapped here, some snow-birds left over from up north for the season. A few of us live here year round. We even have some people who work for the county and city governments."

"That doesn't answer my question," Trace said.

Alex nodded. "We're like the character Friday in Defoe's *robinson Crusoe*. We help each other. We share our knowledge and skills to survive on this island now defined by barbed wire." He paused. "We're the spiritual children, the progeny so to speak, of Crusoe's island companion, Friday."

"How clever," Trace said. "I don't think Crusoe and Friday broke any laws to survive."

"Nor do we," Alex said, "if we can avoid it."

"You're outlaws no matter what you call yourselves," Trace said. "Dress it up any way you want. It doesn't change the facts. You represent everything I've been trained to oppose."

"I don't think you're against surviving, are you?" Alex said. "You call us outlaws? Well, doesn't that depend on your point of view? You're a fugitive, aren't you? You assaulted a soldier. Does that make you an outlaw?"

"Point taken," Trace answered.

"We get together after curfew if we can find a safe place and have a specific mission in mind," Alex said. "During the day we spread out among different hotels, squatting alone or in small groups."

"Why'd you bring us here?" Trace said, nodding toward Ibrahim.

"We don't talk about Friday's Progeny during the day when we're away from encampment. Not at all. Not to anyone. Not even to each other. It's safer that way."

"Answer my question," Trace said. "Why'd you bring us here?"

Alex continued. "I'm getting to that. On any given day when we have a reason for getting together, I'm the only one at first who knows where we'll meet. I don't tell anyone until the last minute. Then I send a coded text message to group leaders. If I don't get back an *all clear* from every group leader within ten minutes, I know someone's been compromised or taken. If that happens, I have to decide if we'll meet anyway or if I should send out another code canceling the meeting, alerting everyone to stay put."

Alex paused to let his words sink in. Then he said to Trace, "What was your question?"

Trace narrowed his eyes. This kid enjoys playing war too much. "Why'd you bring us here?"

"To have you join us."

"Meaning what?"

"Meaning, have you help us and have us help you survive during the occupation. Pretty much what I said to you when we met at the hotel."

"How do we do that?"

"We can talk more about it tomorrow night."

"What about my wife? If I decide to stay, I'll want her with me."

"Jenna, too," Ibrahim said. "She also should be with us. I'll join if Trace does."

"Your wife and Jenna will come from the hotel tonight or tomorrow night. Depends on when Jenna thinks it's safe to move out after curfew."

Trace nodded.

"I'll send her a text message," Alex said, "and let Jenna know you're both with us. Then we'll see."

CHAPTER 84

Quarantine
Day 29

"GOOD EVENING, LADIES AND GENTLEMEN. Derek Peterson here for CNN."

He paused and looked at four soldiers — each dressed in MOP gear — who had stopped their patrol of the street to watch him broadcast.

"We have a follow-up to the report we brought you earlier this week concerning the apparent leveling off in the number of new cases of people infected with Melioidosis. The CDC has now advised us that the earlier report is no longer considered accurate.

"Further investigation by the CDC has disclosed that the number of new cases is still increasing. The good news, however, is that the rate of increase seems to be slowing."

He glanced over at the soldiers watching him.

"The CDC states that its prior report, in which it indicated that the number of new cases had leveled off, likely resulted not from fewer new cases, but from the existence of fewer reports of new cases as people stopped taking the newly-ill to doctors, hospitals and clinics because medicine is no longer available at these sources. As a result, healthcare workers are not seeing new cases to report to the CDC."

I need to wrap this up without putting my viewers into a state of panic.

"The CDC will continue to monitor the situation by going house-to-house in the Quarantine Zone and removing people for testing and possible isolation who might be carrying the infection. It's important that you cooperate with the authorities when they visit you.

"We will bring you the results of this continuing assessment as we learn more."

CHAPTER 85

Quarantine
Day 29

VIKTOR PLOTTED HIS NEWLY CONCEIVED mission as carefully as if he still was on active duty in Chechnya. His Fort Lauderdale undertaking consisted of four phases.

Phase One involved meticulously planning, mapping and practicing getting to and escaping from areas of the Quarantine Zone where he would target and randomly kill adults who happen to wander into his cross-hairs. Viktor's goal in Phase One was to strike terror in the civilian population and thereby frustrate and punish the authorities who were operating this Fort Lauderdale internment camp. Randomly and frequently killing civilians, he believed, would achieve that result.

Phase Two would ratchet up the stakes by having him randomly shoot children to generate fear in parents in the Quarantine Zone, showing the authorities how helpless they were to protect those among them most needing protection.

Phrase Three would involve the periodic shooting of police and soldiers at night during the curfew to show the authorities that not even the nighttime restriction could impair the will of a dedicated, trained, disciplined professional shooter.

And Phase Four, the most interesting step, would involve the recruiting of other shooters from among the disaffected in the Quarantine Zone, briefly training them, and sending them out to find and eliminate wide-spread targets of every type, thereby virally spreading his reign of fear.

Just thinking about this plan caused Viktor to feel better about his unexpected confinement in the American gulag.

Viktor's first day of shooting went well. His first victim was an elderly man who was in an empty parking lot counting used aluminum soda cans he'd extracted from a garbage bag he carried with him.

Viktor used the Dragunov for this kill from an easy distance of two hundred-fifty meters. It's probably overkill for that mere distance, Viktor thought, as he laughed at his wordplay in his adopted language.

He also used the Dragunov for his second and third kills, which occurred one hour and three hours, respectively, after the first one — the hit of a young woman who had been walking through a park, and the shooting of a middle-aged man who had been up on a ladder repairing a rain spout on the side of a house. In each instance Viktor escaped without any problems along his predetermined escape routes.

For variety, one day later Viktor took the *thread cutter* with him. He used it first to shoot and kill a young man who rode his mountain bike across Viktor's cross-hairs, and next to kill a 20s-something pregnant woman as she left a house and stepped out onto the sidewalk along 67th Street.

CHAPTER 86

Quarantine
Day 29

ALEX PLACED HIS HAND ON Trace's shoulder.

Trace bolted awake, confused at first, but then memory seeped back in. "What's wrong?" he said, rubbing his eyes and looking around, finally settling his gaze on Alex. "Is Isabella here?"

"No," Alex said, "they didn't show. I assume Jenna will try again tonight. We have to leave now. The sun will be up soon."

"Why didn't they show up?"

"We'll stay at the Atlantic Beach Hotel today. Let's get going." He paused, then added, "I don't know why they're not here. Ask your wife or Jenna when you see them tonight."

———— ⊁—⊁—⊁—⊁—⊁ ————

That night, shortly after the start of curfew, after spending the day in the lobby of the Atlantic Beach Hotel, Trace, Alex and Ibrahim left the hotel for that night's rendezvous with other members of Friday's Progeny.

Fifteen minutes later they arrived at the outskirts of Port Everglades, Fort Lauderdale's deep water port. Everyone who received Alex's coded text message showed up by 10:00 p.m. Everyone except Jenna and Isabella.

Trace, Alex and Ibrahim sat on the grass under a palm tree. Several other members of the cell sat close by. Others took their turns at sentry duty.

The night was very dark with thick, low cloud cover.

"We'll meet with a small group of farmers tonight," Alex said, "in three groups, then all come back here."

"Did you send tonight's rendezvous location to Jenna?" Trace asked.

Alex glared at Trace, said nothing, then turned back to the group. "We need to convince the farmers to withhold their crops from the authorities, to give them to us to distribute free."

"What about my wife?" Trace said. "Is she on her way here?"

Alex again looked at Trace, but held up his finger to signal, *Just a minute.*

Trace said, "No, Alex, you wait a minute. Answer me. What about my wife and Jenna? Are they on their way here? Stop avoiding my question."

"No, they're not here," Alex said. "They'll be here later tonight when we get back," he said.

Well, maybe they'll be here, he thought.

CHAPTER 87

Quarantine
Day 30

B Y 2:00 A.M., TRACE, ALEX and Ibrahim had finished their meetings with the farmers and had returned to Port Everglades. They were exhausted, mentally and physically, but elated because they had convinced the farmers to hide their meager harvests from the authorities and to donate the crops to Friday's Progeny.

Trace walked from one end of the camp site to the other looking for Isabella or Jenna. He didn't see them.

He went looking for Alex.

"Isabella's not here," Trace said. "Where are they?"

"I know they're not," Alex said.

"What do you mean, you know? What's going on, Alex? Where's my wife?"

"I know because I looked around the camp when we returned here and didn't see your wife or Jenna. I don't know why they're not here."

"Send another message. I want to know what's going on."

"Trace," Alex said, "I sent another message as soon as I realized they weren't here. I haven't heard anything back yet."

"I'm going to the hotel to find them," Trace said.

"That would be stupid. We don't know why they're not here. Maybe they never left the hotel, but maybe they did leave and something happened to them on the way. All you'll do by going to the hotel is put all of us at risk. That won't help your wife."

Trace knew Alex was right. "I need to think about this," he said. "I'm going to take a walk around the encampment and think. I'll be back."

Trace walked to the far end of the encampment, spotted a large tree, and sat down at its base. He took out a cigarette and his lighter.

As he put the flame to the cigarette, he saw a male emerge from behind a nearby tree and sit down at its base, facing him. The man nodded at Trace.

"Evening," the man said.

"Evening," Trace responded.

"Can you spare cigarette," the man asked in a Slavic accent. "My pack is empty."

Trace stood up, walked over to the man, and offered him his softpack. He held his lighter, waiting for the man to lip the smoke and lean forward to catch the flame.

"Thank you. My name is Viktor," the man said, as he nodded.

"You're welcome. I'm Trace." They shook hands.

Trace returned to the base of his tree, sat, and resumed working on his cigarette.

"You have the bearing of military man," Viktor said. "Are you soldier?"

Trace shook his head. "No, I'm not. I'm former military, but retired now for many years. And you?"

"No more. Was in Soviet, then Russian, military many years ago. Am private citizen now, am citizen of America now, just like you."

"You're part of Friday's Progeny?" Trace said.

Viktor shrugged. "Not really. I don't want to insult you, but these people are like children playing war games. I don't take these juveniles seriously. I come sometimes to eat. These people provide food to its members."

Trace said, "I agree with your assessment of them based on what I've seen so far, but I might need these people to help me rescue my wife from the authorities, so I'm here for now."

"Why do the authorities hold your wife?" Viktor said. "Is she terrorist?"

"To use her as bait to lure me in so they can arrest me."

"Are you terrorist or criminal?"

Trace shook his head. "No, not by my standards, but yes, based on their rules, I guess you could say that."

"You don't look like terrorist or criminal to me. Should I be afraid of you?"

Trace chuckled and shook his head. "Not so far. We're doing fine."

CHAPTER 88

Quarantine
Day 30

WHEN TRACE LEFT VIKTOR AND returned to the center of the encampment, he sought out Alex.

Alex looked hard at Trace, wondering if he still intended to go to Jenna's and Isabella's hotel to retrieve the women.

"I'm out of here," Trace said. "Don't worry, I won't give you away if I'm picked up."

He waited for a response. None came.

"I plan to be back with my wife before sunrise. With Jenna, too, if she's with Isabella."

Alex held up his palm.

"First, Trace, we need to find out if this still is necessary. I'll send Jenna another text message. We'll see if she answers. Sit tight and wait for now. Another half hour or so won't make any difference."

Trace wanted to say they were wasting time, that another text message probably wouldn't be answered, but he didn't say anything. He knew from his stint in the SEALs that careful preparation and proper timing usually meant the difference between a successful mission and disaster.

He nodded at Alex, and sat down.

Ibrahim walked over.

"What's up?" he asked.

"I'm going to look for Isabella."

"What about Jenna?"

"I assume they're together." Trace said.

"What if they're not?"

"Then I'll figure out what to do about that. For now, I'm assuming they're together."

Twenty minutes later, with no text message back from Jenna, Trace decided it was time to go. But first, he had one more thing he needed to do.

He retraced his steps to the tree he'd sat under, hoping to find Viktor still nearby. He was in luck.

Viktor looked up as Trace approached him.

"You're back. Did you forget something over there?" he said, as he canted his head toward the tree Trace had sat under.

"I've come to ask you a favor," Trace said.

He explained the situation to Viktor, telling him that he wanted to go to a hotel to retrieve Bella.

"And what do you want from me?" Viktor said.

"I want you to act as my spotter while I check out the building, cover my back," Trace said.

"No problem," Viktor said. "I can do that. It would relieve my boredom for a while."

Trace and Viktor walked away from the encampment. They moved out under a commercial wharf, then walked along a narrow street lined with warehouses on both sides. They stayed close to the aging structures as they made their way toward the Hotel Carlota, blending into the dark irregular shapes and shadows cast by buildings, dumpsters, crates, rusted-out steel barrels, and scattered stacks of wood pallets.

Behind them, silently keeping a vigil over the idle port, four praying-mantis-like cranes, each silhouetted against the dark sky, brooded above the horizon, their metal sentinel necks and heads extended high into the night.

Trace and Viktor threaded their way through streets and alleys until they arrived across the street from the Hotel Carlota.

Neither Viktor nor Trace spoke as they settled into prone positions behind a thick Rosemary Scrub hedge and watched the hotel's entrance.

The street and sidewalks — now well into the evening's curfew — were generally empty. There were no civilians they could see. They only occasionally saw or heard soldiers.

Nothing about the silent street suggested to Viktor or Trace that anything was amiss, that their presence was known or anticipated.

CHAPTER 89

Quarantine Day 30

A NTHONY VISTA WAS FURIOUS. HE grabbed the chain-link collar around his boxer's neck and yanked him away from the foot of the desk chair. Vista sat down.

Not only did he have to contend with vigilante groups and the likes of Trace Austin and his wife, but now he also had a sniper on his hands who was terrorizing Fort Lauderdale's civilian population.

And as if that wasn't enough to contend with, this morning he received strange instructions from the Pentagon ordering him not to pursue the sniper too vigorously.

What the hell does that mean and why would some moron in Washington give him that order? he wondered.

"What do you have on the sniper, Major," Vista said.

"He killed two more civilians this morning. Both under fifteen years old. A boy and a young woman. That makes six kills in the past two days."

"I asked what you have on him," Vista said, "not his scorecard."

"Yes, Sir. Ballistics says there were two weapons used. Both Russian manufactured rifles."

This was Vista's worst nightmare. "One more time, Major. What do we know about the shooter?"

"We don't have enough evidence yet to put together a portrait of the shooter or shooters. He, or perhaps, they, are very careful. We haven't even been able to establish a pattern of targets they seek or to pin down their shooting nests or find any spent cartridges anywhere," the major said. "We're dealing with a pro — or pros — who, I would suggest, have been trained by the military."

Vista stood up from his desk, then immediately sat again. "What are you doing about grabbing him or them?" he said.

"We've stepped up patrols all over the Quarantine Zone and have warned people to be on the lookout for anyone or anything suspicious. We've set up a hotline for people to call.

"We've also increased the number of drone flights so we have more eyes in the sky looking for him or them," the major said.

Vista looked at the blotter on his desk and said nothing.

Should I follow my orders and relax my search? No, that would be stupid. Instead, I will find the sniper and eliminate him. I'll worry about my orders after I've extinguished the problem. It will be easier for me to obtain forgiveness if I succeed than to obtain permission up front.

The major remained at attention, not relieved and put at ease by the general, as he would have expected before the start of a discussion such as this one.

Vista had an idea. He could follow the Pentagon's order to the letter and ease up on his search for the sniper, but still make it hard for the sniper to succeed.

"When you leave here, Major, tell Sergeant McElroy I am revising Field Order No. 2 to reduce the number of people who can lawfully congregate in public places from two to one. We will reduce the number of targets available to the shooter.

"Tell McElroy to distribute the revised Field Order among the troops and throughout the city, and to be sure that the CNN news broadcaster — Peterson's his name — discusses this change on his show for a few days, starting today. Then we'll see how much terror this shooter, without targets, can stir up before we catch him."

CHAPTER 90

Quarantine Day 30

TRACE AND VIKTOR STAYED OUT-OF-SIGHT behind the hedge for another twenty minutes watching the hotel. Nothing significant changed during that time. The night remained quiet under its curfew.

Trace lifted himself onto one elbow and wiped sweat from his forehead and eyes with the back of his other hand. He climbed up onto one knee and looked up and down the street.

"Let's go," he said. "The street's clear. There'll never be a better time." He nodded at Viktor. "You go first. When you get to the bushes in front of the patio," he said, pointing, "I'll follow."

Viktor took off running across the street, crouching low. He slowed as he bulled his way behind the Saw Palmetto bush.

Trace watched and waited. He could tell from the cautious way Viktor moved across the street that he'd had special military training.

The street and sidewalks remained empty.

Trace took off, crouching low, running.

They waited behind the bushes, watching the patio and the hotel's entrance.

"We should to go in," Trace said."

Viktor started to straighten up. "Okay. There's no time like—"

Trace put up his palm to stop Viktor, and sniffed. He thought he smelled something, but he could not locate. His senses were smothered by the fragrance of the bushes he and Viktor hid behind. But he knew someone was there, unseen.

Then the air current delivered the scent directly to Trace and he knew what it was he'd smelled. It was the faintest whiff of cigarette smoke.

Trace grabbed Viktor's shoulder, making the *shhhh* sign with his finger raised to his lips as he guided Viktor back down behind the shrubbery. He pointed toward the steps just as a soldier walked from around the corner of the building, heading toward the patio, his head bowed. The soldier stopped near the bottom of the steps, took a final pull on his cigarette, then flicked it onto the lawn. He turned and walked away into the dark.

Viktor looked at Trace, raised his eyebrows, then nodded.

They waited five more minutes, then stepped from behind the shrub, crouched, and scampered up onto the patio heading for the Hotel Carlota's entrance.

They knew this was the time they were most vulnerable to discovery and arrest. If they were noticed at this late hour they would not be able to explain why they were coming back into the hotel during curfew.

But they had no choice. They had to enter the hotel, take their chances, and hope for the best. Going in amounted to a crapshoot with the dice loaded in favor of the house. Trace knew this and Viktor knew this, but they prudently let it sit unstated between them.

They paused just inside the entryway and listened to the sounds coming from the hotel. When they'd satisfied themselves they had not been seen, Trace stepped in and sauntered through the hotel's entrance, followed by Viktor.

Trace winced at the malodorous, uncirculated air, the groans of too many uprooted people crammed into too small a space, and the chaotic movements of the swarming resident-squatters who seemed to him to be in constant, random motion notwithstanding the early-morning hour.

He hesitated, but knew he should not remain standing in the framed doorway where he would attract attention. He took a slow, deep breath through his mouth, controlled but did not conquer his offended olfactory senses, and walked into the hallway.

Viktor had already moved across the hall to the entrance to the main lobby. Trace walked over and joined him.

"Let's look in here first," Trace said, pointing to the expansive lobby.

Viktor nodded.

They stood just inside the lobby entrance and looked around, Trace's eyes examining the crowd, looking for the familiar face of Isabella or Jenna. He didn't see either woman.

Trace slowly walked from the front of the room to the back. Viktor trailed close behind him.

No one seemed to pay attention to them. It was as if the

hotel's squatter population was used to people roaming the public areas at all hours of the night.

Trace's eyes scanned the human muddle, his head sweeping like a radar antennae as he and Viktor headed toward the far side of the lobby.

When they reached the wall, Trace said, "I want to check the meeting rooms."

They started to walk back to the lobby entrance when Trace grabbed Viktor's arm.

"Hold on," he said.

"What's the matter?" Viktor asked. He stiffened and quickly looked around trying to spot the problem that had grabbed Trace's attention.

Trace remained silent.

"What's wrong?" Viktor again said. "Tell me."

Trace still said nothing. He walked over to a woman who sat on the floor, about fifteen feet away. He stopped in front of her, menacingly close, but outside the boundary of her instinctual, personal space, her bodily territory. Trace intended to rattle her, but not terrify her.

She looked up at him and quickly crab-crawled backward across the floor, keeping her eyes on Trace as she moved away, stopping about ten feet from him.

"What do you want, Mister?" she said to Trace. "I'm trying to get some rest."

"That blouse. Where'd you get it?"

She pulled in her legs, raising her knees to her chin. She wrapped her arms around her legs and leaned into them, hiding much of the blouse.

"It's mine," she said. She squinted and wrinkled her forehead, glanced around as if looking for a friendly, familiar face, then looked back at Trace. "I didn't steal it or nothin'. You can't have it."

"I don't want it. Just tell me where you got it," Trace said. He gentled his voice and face, using body language signals he had learned in SEALs' training intended to relax and draw in a person being interrogated.

"I found it," the woman said. "It's mine." She relaxed her arms around her body, but did not let go of her legs.

Trace took a long step backward away from the woman, then kneeled on one knee. Now at her face level, he spoke softly, nodding his head repeatedly as he talked, trying to establish some measure of rapport with the woman.

"I know the blouse is yours, and I don't want it. But it reminds me of one I bought my wife. It even has her initials." He paused to let this sink in.

"Please tell me. Did you see my wife here? A tall woman with dark hair, thin body? Her name's Isabella. All I want is to know. Nothing else. The blouse is yours to keep in any event." He nodded and smiled as warmly as he could under the circumstances.

The woman relaxed her arms, dropping them to her sides. She folded one leg under the other.

"I keep the blouse?"

Trace nodded. "Yes, keep it," he said, "it's yours now. Just tell me what you know about the woman who had the blouse before you."

"I found it in another room in a shopping bag. After the soldiers came. I didn't steal it."

"What soldiers?" Trace said. He felt his stomach roil. "Did they take the lady with them?"

"You know . . . army men. Soldier men. Five, six, with

guns. They was wearing those white space suits like the men who walked on the Moon." She stared at Trace.

"They put the two womens' arms behind them," she said, "and tied them with plastic bracelets like on the cop shows on TV. The soldiers took the womens away. I don't know where." She shrugged.

"Did the soldiers say anything? Try to remember," Trace said. "It could be important. Anything at all?"

The woman shook her head. "I went with other people after they left. We looked at the womens stuff in the other room. That's when I found the blouse there. They couldn't use it no more so you can't say I stole it."

"Did the soldiers say anything?" Trace asked again.

The woman shook her head.

Trace looked at Viktor.

Viktor motioned with his head toward the entrance and started walking.

Trace thanked the woman and left the Hotel Carlota with Viktor. They retraced their steps back to Port Everglades.

Back at Port Everglades, Trace and Viktor sat side-by-side under a tree, both silent, both smoking cigarettes, each in his own world contemplating the events at the hotel.

"You handled woman well," Viktor said. "In my country, we would have pressured her to tell us what she knew without dancing around as you did."

Trace nodded. "I need to find my wife and break her loose from the military."

"You come up with plan, then I help you," Viktor said.

Trace looked hard at Viktor. "Why?" he asked. "You barely know me."

"I'm bored. And because we both were military men. Different sides, but same code. We are brothers that way. I can be useful to you."

Trace paused to think about what Viktor offered. "I'll consider it. If I need my back protected, I'll find you."

Viktor nodded.

Trace stood up and turned to leave.

"Hey, Mr. ex-Military Man," Viktor called to Trace, "Good luck. Don't take any shit from the occupiers.

Trace turned back to face Viktor. "Right you are, Brother."

CHAPTER 91

Quarantine
Day 31
4:12 a.m.

Trace and Viktor made it back from the Hotel Carlota without incident.

As they entered the Port Everglades encampment, Ibrahim rushed over. He ignored Viktor.

"Where's Jenna?"

"Arrested. Taken away with my wife by soldiers."

"What?" Ibrahim looked back and forth between Viktor and Trace. He did not ask Trace who Viktor was.

"Soldiers showed up at the hotel and arrested them," Trace said. "We don't know where they are."

"What're we going to do?" Ibrahim said. "We can't just leave them."

"We're going to get them back," Trace said quietly.

Ibrahim said, "Okay. How? When?"

———✶——✶——✶——✶——✶———

Trace left Viktor and Ibrahim, and searched the encampment for Alex. When he found him, he said, "I need a wireless device of some kind. My son's laptop is in a safe deposit box back at the Palm Court Hotel. Is there something here I can use?"

"I'll see what I can find," Alex said.

Ten minutes later Trace leaned back against a palm tree and booted up the iPad Alex had borrowed for him. He clicked the wireless network icon to connect to some nearby public hotspot. It took him a few minutes to find a connection with a strong signal. He settled on an unsecured site called Rainbow. He had no idea who operated the hotspot, and under the circumstances he didn't care. Right now he would gladly make do with an unsecured wireless network just to have online access.

Trace decided to send two e-mail messages. He would use an anonymous router just as he and Pete had used to update Trace's stale hacking skills when they were away on their fishing trip.

As for the first message, the world could see it for all Trace cared. Its text would be designed to fire-up Admiral Max Tyler's juices. No one else would understand its significance.

As for the second message, the follow-up e-mail to Max, Trace also did not care who might read it. The message would be encrypted using a protocol known only to Trace and the men in his and Max's SEAL team. Trace would further protect himself by using a coded ID for both messages.

Trace located an e-mail service that allowed users to send anonymous e-mails. He took a few minutes to set up his free anonymous account. Then he typed the first message to Max.

To: mtyler@navy.pentagon.mil
From: mailer@anonymous.sum.to
Time: 3:20 a.m. EST

Your friendship desperately needed.

OPERATION JUST CAUSE protocol only.

Highly vulnerable.

Will await confirmation.

Regards from your Pappy.

Trace had no idea if Max still maintained this e-mail account. He waited a few minutes, then checked his own account to see if the message had bounced back as undeliverable. It had not. With luck, then, Max would see the message first thing in the morning and get right back to him.

Trace broke-off the wireless connection and tucked the borrowed iPad under his arm. He would check his e-mail account every fifteen minutes for a response, although he didn't expect an answer before late morning.

Max's confirmation e-mail message came in at 5:10 a.m. Trace was surprised Max was up and checking his mail at that hour. He'd have to ask him about this the next time they saw one another. In the meantime, he was glad Max had responded to him so quickly.

Trace returned to the base of the palm tree and typed his

reply to Max. Then he applied the OPERATION JUST CAUSE protocol to encrypt his message.

> To: mtyler@navy.pentagon.mil
>
> From: mailer@anonymous.sum.to
> Protocol: OPERATION JUST CAUSE
> Time: 5:20 a.m. EST
>
> Family and I caught in the Quarantine Zone while on vacation in Fort Lauderdale, Florida. Pete dead from terrorists' disease. Isabella's mother, too.
>
> Isabella taken prisoner by District Military Commander's troops. Do not know why. I am in hiding after a physical confrontation with a soldier during a non-routine stop. Am on the run from authorities.
>
> Need to know our official status, mine and Bella's. Need to know, too, location of Isabella.
>
> Also find out status/whereabouts, etc., of young woman named Jenna Burke. She has ROTC background. She was taken prisoner with Isabella. She might be an Unfriendly.
>
> Pappy.

Two hours later Max's reply e-mail arrived.

CHAPTER 92

Quarantine
Day 31
Morning

"LADIES AND GENTLEMEN, PLEASE LISTEN to this important announcement from the Office of the District Military Commander." Derek paused.

"You are warned to be on the lookout for a very dangerous man wanted by the authorities. The fugitive's name is Trace Austin. He is 6'1" tall, approximately 180 to 190 lbs. He has brown hair and green eyes. He is forty-nine years old.

"If you see him, or someone you think might be him, do not approach him or try to apprehend him. He is considered dangerous, and might be armed. Report him immediately to the authorities.

"I repeat. Do not approach him. Call the telephone number now showing at the bottom of your television screen. You will be well rewarded if your information leads to his capture."

On another important matter, the Fort Lauderdale sniper has been shooting again since my broadcast yesterday, and has taken the lives of three more innocent people. You are urged to stay at home unless you must go out, and, if you do go out, you are asked to report anyone or anything suspicious.

"General Vista has advised this reporter that anyone who makes a report of a suspicious person or circumstance concerning the sniper or the fugitive Austin will not be entered into the ODMC database for that reason alone.

"General Vista has also instructed me to tell you that Field Order No. 2 has been amended to temporarily deal with the sniper situation. It will no longer be acceptable for two people over the age of thirteen to be in public areas together.

"Until the sniper has been apprehended or neutralized, everyone will be required to venture about the Quarantine Zone alone. Until further notice, any two or more people over the age of thirteen out together will be in violation of the Field Order and will be dealt with accordingly.

"It is the intent of this new, temporary requirement to reduce the number of targets available to the sniper until he is caught or killed. When that occurs, General Vista has advised this reporter, the Field Order will be amended to again permit up to two people to congregate together in public."

"Ladies and gentlemen, this reporter must close with this obvious question: Is the fugitive Trace Austin, the man we asked you to be on the lookout for, the Quarantine Zone sniper?

Derek nodded at his cameraman.

"Now, back to today's other news programming . . . ."

CHAPTER 93

Quarantine
Day 31
Early afternoon

"So, Mrs. Austin," Vista said, "we finally meet. I apologize for the wrist restraints. It's standard procedure. I'll have them removed immediately."

Isabella nodded and remained silent.

A few minutes later Vista said, "Have a seat." He pointed to the chair in front of his desk.

Isabella lowered herself into the chair, her back rigid, her hands together on her lap as if they were still shackled. Once seated, she turned her head from side-to-side, looking around the office. Pictures of Vista in civilian clothes, standing with other people, covered much of one wall. Framed certificates and plaques dominated another.

A trophy collector, she thought.

Isabella turned back to face the officer. He had settled into his chair behind his desk and was staring at her.

Isabella looked at the name plate on his desk. It read, GENERAL ANTHONY VISTA.

"How did you find me?" Isabella said.

"Someone at the hotel reported you. Your photo was on the news. No one can hide from us."

"Why'd you bring me here?" Isabella looked directly into the general's eyes as she questioned him.

"We want to give you the opportunity to save your husband's life."

Isabella's jaw clenched. Her spine tightened. She drew in a short gulp of air. Her eyes and her posture, both carefully watched by the general, appeared to be impervious to his implied threat.

"You could have asked me to come in voluntarily," she said, trying to control her voice to mask her apprehension. "I would have cooperated."

"That's all we want, Mrs. Austin. Your cooperation. And your husband's, too, of course."

"My husband wouldn't appreciate knowing you brought me here in restraints like a common criminal."

"Your husband is a criminal," the general said. "He assaulted one of my men. That's a felony. To add to his problems, now your husband also is a fugitive." He paused to let this sink in. "Where is he?"

"If my husband did what you say, he must've had a good reason."

"Why did your husband quit the SEALs?" Vista said.

Isabella stiffened, surprised by the question. "What's that have to do with anything?"

"I asked you a question. Answer it."

"Ask my husband if you want to know. I don't discuss his personal business with other people."

"When did your husband become disloyal to the United States military?"

"That's ridiculous," Isabella said, slowly shaking her head and chuckling out loud. "My husband's loyal to our country. He's an ex-SEAL, a patriot, a decorated war hero. Are you a war hero, General? Have you been decorated for valor as my husband was?"

Vista frowned, but let the question pass.

"I'm sure my husband will answer all your questions if he thinks they're appropriate, General. I want to see him."

"As do I, Mrs. Austin, as do I. Your husband needs to come in. He's in danger every minute he's out there." He paused, then said, "People are looking for him. We *will* get him, you know, one way or another."

"You'll have to let him know that, General."

"I want you to persuade him to turn himself in. It's for his own good and for yours, believe me."

"My husband won't appreciate knowing you're threatening us."

"It's no threat, Mrs. Austin. Just a fact, stated for your edification, to keep you informed of the possibilities. I can't guaranty your husband's safety while he's a fugitive. His safety, right now, is up to you."

"Where's Jenna, the young woman arrested with me?" Isabella said. "I want to see her."

"You really should be more concerned about yourself and your husband."

"More implied threats?" Isabella slowly shook her head, answering him in a tone of voice that was as mild as Vista's had been impatient. "I have nothing more to say to you, General. I want to go back to the hotel."

"I'm afraid that's not possible. Perhaps later if you change your mind and cooperate."

"I demand to be set free," she said. Her eyes narrowed as she stared at Vista.

"That would suit us fine, Mrs. Austin. All you have to do is tell your husband to give himself up. We won't harm him, and when he arrives, you may leave if you wish. Otherwise, who knows?"

Isabella hesitated and looked at the general, trying to read him by looking at his eyes.

"He'll be protected if he comes in?" she said. "You give me your word as an officer?"

"Absolutely."

"He won't be harmed? He'll leave with me when I leave?"

"You have my word."

Isabella remained silent, considering the alternatives.

General Vista stood, leaned toward her, and placed his palms flat on his desk.

"Make your decision, Mrs. Austin. Make it now. Your husband doesn't have much time. His safety, his very life, are in your hands."

CHAPTER 94

Quarantine
Day 31

T RACE STARED AT THE iPAD'S screen and reread
Max's response.

To: mailer@anonymous.sum.to
From: mtyler@navy.pentagon.mil
Protocol: OPERATION JUST CAUSE
Time: 6:28 a.m. EST

You called it right, ol' buddy. You're in
deep trouble.

Isabella's being held as a material witness
against you. You're the subject of a fugitive
warrant. There's an All Points out on you with
an "armed and dangerous" alert.

Isabella's being held at the headquarters of the
District Military Commander. Assume you

will find that location. No write-up yet on disposition of her status.

Other subject, Jenna Burke, is fourth year college student. Majoring in international relations. Will be cadre second lieutenant after ROTC. Has received several student ROTC merit citations. Clean record. Nothing on her in FBI or INTERPOL databases. Will check other sources if you want. Her mother is active member of DAR. Her father, now deceased, was active in American Legion.

Apprise me of your intended course of action. I will assist if I am able under the circumstances, but it will be difficult penetrating the Quarantine Zone from my office at the Pentagon.

Keep your spirits up. My love to Isabella when you rescue her.

Trace deleted the email, powered off the iPad and closed the cover. He thought about what his next move should be.

He looked around for Alex and Ibrahim, but didn't see them. He started to walk to the entrance of the encampment, figuring he'd find them along the way.

His cell phone vibrated in a silent ring.

He was glad he had set the phone to vibrate since he didn't want any of Friday's Progeny knowing he had received a telephone call. Its presence, with its built-in GPS chip, was a weak link in the encampment's security, but as far as he was concerned, wasn't anyone's business. At least not yet.

He looked at the CallerID readout on his phone.

The call was coming from Pete's cell phone.

CHAPTER 95

Quarantine
Day 31

TRACE ANSWERED THE CALL COMING from Pete's cell phone.

"Trace, is that you? Thank God."

"Bella? Are you all right? Where are you?"

"Trace? I was so worried."

"Where are you? I'll come get you."

"I'm somewhere downtown in a hotel. I'm with an army officer. His nameplate reads GENERAL ANTHONY VISTA."

Bella's mention of Vista's name flooded him with all-too-recent unpleasant memories.

"Bella, are you under arrest?"

Isabella looked at Vista. "Am I under arrest?" she asked him.

"He says, no, I'm not under arrest. At least not yet." She looked again at Vista for confirmation.

He nodded.

"Trace, he wants you to give yourself up to him. He says you're in serious danger if you don't."

"He has to let you go first. Will he do that? What's he told you?"

"He made threats against us, if you don't give up." She paused and looked at Vista.

"Trace, listen carefully to me."

She looked over at Vista and locked her eyes on his as she slowly and deliberately spoke.

"I don't want you to surrender yourself. No matter what he promises or threatens. I don't care what happens to me. I don't trust him. He—"

Vista rushed over to Isabella and slammed his fist into her side, cracking her ribs.

Isabella screamed, dropped the cell phone, and fell to her knees. She clutched her side, gasping for breath. Her eyes filled with tears.

"That was stupid," Vista said, speaking in a low, measured tone. "Stand up now, damn you." He waited briefly, then added, "I said get up." Vista stooped down and picked up the cell phone. He looked at the readout. Then he raised the cell phone to his mouth.

"Come to me, Austin, if you value your wife's well-being. Come to me soon."

He ended the call and pocketed the phone. Then he turned his attention back to Isabella.

He moved in close to her, leaning in not more than ten inches from her face.

"Get up," he said.

Isabella stood up, trembling as she did, slightly hunched. She pressed her palm against her ribs, holding them in place. She breathed in short, rapid gasps. She felt a sharp, stabbing pain with each breath.

Isabella looked up at General Vista through rheumy eyes.

Vista placed the palm of his hand flat against Isabella's

chest and steadily pushed against her, forcing her, step-by-step, backward until she could not retreat any farther. Isabella shoulders blades stabbed the wall.

Vista moved in closer now, just inches away from her face.

Isabella could smell him, feel the heat of his fury.

Vista narrowed his eyes. Sweat beaded on his forehead and streamed down his cheeks and neck.

Isabella held her breath and waited.

Seconds passed.

Vista loomed over her.

More time passed. Still he said nothing.

Then he stepped back.

The dark red color gradually ebbed from his face and neck.

Vista spoke quietly now, menacingly enunciating each word, letting each phrase linger before he offered another.

He smiled a distorted smile.

Isabella recoiled from this anomaly.

"Now Mrs. Austin, you will have no one to blame but yourself when we kill your husband."

CHAPTER 96

Quarantine
Day 31

T RACE WALKED OVER TO WHERE Alex was sitting and dropped down onto the grass next to him.

"You seem bothered," Alex said.

"I've been better. I just talked to my wife."

"How'd you do that?"

"She called me. The District Military Commander, General Vista, has her."

Trace summarized his conversation with Isabella, adding, "I don't think it's safe to stay here now. They probably have a fix on our location from the cell phone."

Alex leaped to his feet. "Move it everybody," he shouted. "We've been compromised. Everybody, move out. Now."

He ran from one end of the encampment to the other rousting people. Within minutes, the Friday's Progeny encampment was deserted and its members disbursed into a dozen or more small groups, each headed in a different direction, moving stealthily into the night.

At Trace's suggestion, when they left the encampment, he, Alex and Ibrahim made their way to Pete's favorite eating spot in Fort Lauderdale for pizza and subs, an eat-in place called Everglade Harry's, located on 17th Street. This restaurant, like all commercial eating establishments in the Quarantine Zone, had closed almost immediately after the introduction of food rationing.

At the restaurant, once he was satisfied the property was abandoned for the time being, Trace used lock-pick tools Alex carried with him, and his SEAL-trained lock picking skills, to open the lock on the service-entrance door. They entered the restaurant for the night.

After they settled in, Trace said to Alex, "I'm going to rescue Isabella. There's no point trying to talk me out of it."

They sat in the dark in the dining area spread around a circular table large enough for eight or ten patrons, drinking warm beer they found stored under a counter.

"Really? How?" Alex said. His voice didn't betray his attitude, whether he was being sarcastic or merely curious.

"I know where she is, more or less. I'll figure it out as I go along."

"You mean you'll ignore the dictum: plan, practice and execute, the SEALs' mantra?" Alex said.

"More or less," Trace said. "I don't really have any other choice."

"Won't they be expecting you," Ibrahim said, "after the phone call from your wife?"

"Maybe not," Trace said, "They have no reason to think I'd

be stupid enough to walk into the lion's den at feeding hour. I'll have the element of surprise on my side."

"You won't get that chance," Alex said. "Ibrahim's right. They'll be expecting you. They've probably already moved your wife to another location. I would if I were them." He paused to let this sink in. Then he added, "It'll be a useless effort, maybe even a suicide mission for you. That won't help anyone."

"I'm getting my wife back."

"You will. I'll help you. So will Ibrahim," Alex said, nodding at Ibrahim. "But not yet."

Trace stood and started to pace.

"Trace, you *will* rescue her," Alex said. "But first we'll plan carefully so you have a decent shot at it."

Trace reluctantly sat down again.

"We'll get her back," Ibrahim said. He looked at Alex from the corner of his eyes, and licked his lips. We will, won't we? he wondered.

CHAPTER 97

Quarantine
Day 32

Anthony Vista slammed his office door and stomped back to his desk.

The major stood at attention facing him. Sweat ran down the back of his neck forming a dark "V" on his shirt between his shoulder blades.

"You really have no clue, Major? You're telling me you have no goddamn clue where they are? Is that the best you can do? They just vanished into the night?"

"I'm afraid that's correct, Sir" the major said. "The encampment was deserted when we got there."

"What about the surveillance tapes, Major? I assume you've reviewed the tapes or would that be asking too much"

"We have the tapes, Sir, but they weren't helpful. We could see groups of people moving around the city after curfew. Presumably they were the vigilantes moving from their most recent encampment. But the visual feedback was pixilated. It continuously tiled as we watched."

"That's just great," Vista muttered under his breath.

"Sir? Sorry, but I didn't hear you."

"What's being done to find Austin, Major?"

"We have a full alert out for him, Sir. We also have city-wide patrols looking. They've been ordered to report any unusual circumstances. We'll get him, Sir. I'm confident of that."

"I'm glad you are, Major. One of us has to be."

"Sir?"

"Any questions?"

"Yes, Sir. One. Will the general be releasing Austin's wife?" Or should we begin her interrogation?"

Vista shook his head and rolled his eyes. "Why would I release her? She's my bait. I'm still counting on her to lure in her husband since I can't count on you to bring him in."

CHAPTER 98

Quarantine
Day 32
Late Afternoon

"GOOD AFTERNOON, LADIES AND GENTLEMEN. This is Derek Peterson. I'm coming to you with a special late afternoon broadcast. Today is day thirty-two since the president announced the terrorists' bioweapon attack on our city and imposed quarantine and martial law on our community."

Derek wiped his face and forehead with his bandana and looked back at his invisible TV audience. He'd better get on with today's business — meaning, the business of the ODMC — if he wanted to be allowed to continue to broadcast day-after-day.

"Ladies and Gentlemen," he said, "I have an important announcement for you from the District Military Commander. Please pay careful attention to this.

"General Anthony Vista has instructed me to inform you that he has added a new aspect to the nightly curfew, an aspect you absolutely must heed to protect yourself and everyone else from the sniper, Trace Austin, who has been terrorizing our community — shooting innocent men, women and children, as well as police officers and soldiers — and who still is at large."

Derek wiped his face.

"This is what you must now know about the curfew," he said. "If you are discovered outdoors or in any enclosed public place during the hours of curfew, no matter what your reason, you will be assumed to be an enemy combatant or a terrorist. In that case, you will be shot on sight, without any warning. This is in response to the sniper who has been terrorizing innocent people."

Derek let this sink in.

"Now, Ladies and Gentlemen, having said that, I do have some good news for you. I am happy to pass along to you that the number of people the sniper has killed or attempted to kill the past three days is now zero. . . . None." He paused, then said, "That's right. None.

"The sniper appears to have stopped his reign of terror, thanks to the efforts of General Vista and his military unit, although Austin still is on the run from authorities. I think it is fair to say that the sniper shootings have ended."

CHAPTER 99

Quarantine
Day 32 8:00 p.m.

BRAHIM LEFT ALEX AND TRACE sitting at Everglade Harry's table and walked to the deserted lounge where he turned on the flat screen TV located in the corner above the bar. He watched a news broadcast for a few minutes and then ran back into the dining area.

"Alex, Trace, come with me. There's something on TV you should see."

He ran back into the lounge, climbed up onto a bar stool, and pointed to the TV.

"Listen to what this guy's saying."

"...and so this is Derek Peterson for CNN wrapping up our broadcast. To sum up and repeat our lead story, the Office of the District Military Commander announced this morning that the authorities will begin tomorrow taking into mandatory protective custody all persons from the Middle East, or who are descendants of persons from the Middle East, located in the Quarantine Zone.

"This also includes all other persons who practice the Islamic religion," Derek said. "In doing this, the ODMC hopes to protect such people from the attacks that have been occurring against them with increasing frequency in the Quarantine Zone.

"In the meantime the authorities are making every effort to identify the hooligans who are assaulting such people to bring them to justice."

Peterson continued, "Any Middle Eastern-type persons, including others who study Islam, who have failed to register as required by Field Order No. 2 will be subject to the penalties stated in the Field Order."

He waited a beat. "This is Derek Peterson signing off from this special broadcast announcement until 10:00 a.m. tomorrow morning."

The TV screen went dark. Ibrahim stood up on the bar stool, reached up to the TV and turned it off.

"You better lie low, my friend," Trace said. "Being a Syrian or, now, an Israeli won't help you in this climate. I assume you didn't register?"

"Of course I did," Ibrahim said, his feelings seemingly hurt. "Why wouldn't I? I'm a good American. If my government wants me to register, I register," he said. He clearly was put off by Trace's statement.

"I didn't mean to offend you, Ibrahim," Trace said. "Of course you're a good American. I was just being protective of you. Sorry I wasn't clear."

Trace and Alex looked at each other. Alex raised his eyebrows and slightly shrugged his shoulders.

Trace stared at Ibrahim for a few seconds but did not say anything. *I guess we're all getting touchy.*

CHAPTER 100

Quarantine
Day 33

TRACE, ALEX AND IBRAHIM SPENT the early morning at Everglade Harry's, then left the restaurant soon after curfew ended, each going out alone to a different, unspecified destination.

Trace headed toward the beach. He moved slowly among trees and other shelters, keeping out of sight as he walked.

He selected the Flamingo Beach Hotel on Ocean Drive as this day's sanctuary. He hadn't stayed there before so he doubted his presence would be noticed. He wanted to mentally regroup and take stock of his situation.

He settled into the back corner of the lobby, as far from the entrance door as he could get, and closed his eyes. He silently held a conversation with Isabella in which he explained to her why he hadn't yet rescued her, but in which he also assured her that he would come for her.

Trace's thoughts reverted to his elite SEAL military training, reminding himself that the successes and achievements of the

SEALs were due to the way the team members trained and conditioned their minds to pre-visualize a situation, plan for it, then resolve it. Make the unknown or unfamiliar become known and familiar through previsualization. He also thought through the SEALs' maxim which dictated that every physical operation must always begin with careful surveillance of the target.

The Navy had drilled into Trace and his SEAL teammates that many plans were created and developed or were abandoned during the long, dry periods of mind-numbing surveillance.

Trace spent almost a full hour walking the normal twenty minutes' distance to ODMC's headquarters, executing an SDR as he made his way to the headquarters building. He moved slowly and cautiously, remaining hidden from plain sight and from the ubiquitous surveillance cameras and occasional overhead drones he saw, and, he hoped, from the drones he couldn't see.

When he arrived, he stretched out on his stomach behind a thick hedge across the street from the headquarters' entrance. He knew he was at risk of being detected and arrested, and that the consequences of that would be catastrophic for him and Bella. But he didn't see that he had any other choice than to be here under these conditions.

Trace was used to taking risks. Facing danger had been what being a SEAL was all about. But the danger he'd faced as a SEAL, and the risk he'd exposed himself to then, were part of well-planned missions, not ad hoc projects, as today. His SEAL missions had been thoroughly thought through and rehearsed, not executed on the fly, as today.

He wasn't sure what he was looking for. He wasn't even

sure this was where Isabella still was being held, but if she was there he might notice it. Perhaps all he'd find was some peace of mind, knowing he was doing something to try to help her, however limited or futile his actions might be for now.

Peace of mind did not visit Trace that day.

After ninety minutes, he decided he had seen enough. He had watched soldiers enter and leave the building. He'd watched civilians come and go. He saw sentries change shifts. But nothing he observed either alarmed or surprised him. And nothing planted the seeds of a rescue plan or even informed him that Bella still was being held at this building.

CHAPTER 101

Quarantine
Day 33

SABELLA STEPPED INTO GENERAL VISTA'S office, but stopped just inside the door to wait for permission to enter further.

The general's orderly closed the door behind her.

"Please sit down, Mrs. Austin," Vista said. He swept his arm toward a small sofa on the far side of the room. "Make yourself comfortable." As before, he smiled with practiced malevolence.

Isabella frowned and looked at him, but she did as he told her.

She winced as she lowered herself onto the soft cushions, still feeling as if she was being poked in her left lung with a needle, notwithstanding the bandage that had been applied to hold her injured, floating ribs in place.

Isabella looked up at the general who now sat at the other end of the sofa, watching her, with one leg crossed over the other, his fingers inter-laced on his lap.

She linked her eyes with Vista's, refusing to break-off contact. She reminded herself that he had assaulted her and threatened Trace.

"May I get you anything, Mrs. Austin? A drink? Something

to eat? Something, perhaps, for your pain?" His voice assumed the tone of a well-disposed party host.

"I'm fine."

"I'm sorry about your ribs," he said, "but you brought that on yourself."

Isabella continued to watch his eyes. She did not rise to the bait and respond.

"It's foolish for you to think your husband can evade us indefinitely. It's just a matter of time, Mrs. Austin. We *will* get him, you know. It's just a question of how and when, a question whether we'll take him dead or alive." Vista paused and looked hard at her. Then he said, "And that, Mrs. Austin, will mostly be up to you."

Isabella took a deep breath and shuddered from the pain.

"Let's talk about this like reasonable people," Vista said. "I don't want to kill your husband even though some people suspect him of being the Quarantine Zone sniper." He paused, then said, "I don't think he's the sniper so I'm even willing to forgive him for assaulting my soldier, but only if he gives himself up. Otherwise, well . . . who knows?"

"What will happen if he comes in?"

"We'll question him about the vigilantes and his role with them. We'll also question him about the shootings to see if he's the sniper or to eliminate him as a suspect. We'll also ask him some routine questions.

"If he isn't the sniper and hasn't otherwise been involved in anything illegal or anything in violation of the Field Orders, he'll be allowed to leave, as I said before, when you leave."

"That's too vague, *not been involved*. That's a weasel phrase you can interpret any way you want. I won't ask him to come in based on that if that's the best you can do."

"What's it you want, Mrs. Austin? What will satisfy you and your husband, satisfy your propensity for legal niceties?"

"My husband won't surrender to you, not as long as he believes you'll harm us or keep us prisoner. He'll require guarantees of our safety and freedom. Why don't you show some good faith, General. Make a gesture."

"Such as?"

"Set me free. Then I'll talk to my husband about coming in, provided you make creditable promises of safe conduct and prompt, safe release."

Vista frowned and slowly shook his head. He stared hard at her. "I won't just turn you out, Mrs. Austin. I can't do that, although I don't blame you for asking."

He hesitated and looked at her before continuing. "But I'll do this for you," he said. "I'll promise you on my oath as an officer that your husband won't be harmed if he turns himself in, peacefully, that is."

"As I said, General, that's not good enough. My husband will require guarantees that we also won't be detained. He'll want full, blanket immunity, too, in writing. My husband's no fool, you know. Did I tell you he's an attorney? He knows how to protect us."

"You drive a good bargain, Mrs. Austin. I admire that in a woman."

He stood and walked over to the window and looked out. After a minute he turned back to her.

"All right, Mrs. Austin, I agree, provided he can convince me he's not the sniper. I just want to talk with him, that's all. No point in turning this into a federal case," he said. "After that, your husband can leave when you leave. Does that satisfy you?"

"Not quite."

Vista frowned. "Now what? This is becoming tedious."

"I want it all spelled-out in writing, signed by you before two witnesses who are not part of the military, and I want it notarized. Then I'll text a copy to one of my husband's law partners in Washington with instructions to give a copy to the *Washington Post* and *USA Today* for possible future publication if you or the Army renege. Then, and only then, will I talk to my husband about this."

"Anything else?"

"You need to understand, General, I can't guarantee my husband will agree to these terms."

"Understood."

Vista pushed the intercom button and called in his orderly.

"Major, our guest here will dictate a document to you."

He turned to Isabella. "The floor's yours, Mrs. Austin."

CHAPTER 102

Quarantine
Day 33

"Hello, Ladies and Gentlemen. Welcome to our 4:00 p.m. broadcast. I'm pleased to report that the sniper shootings have ended. General Vista's office has assured me that there have been no reports of more killings or even known attempts by the Quarantine Zone sniper.

"It seems that the mysterious sniper — assuming there was only one person — whoever he is and for whatever reason he started shooting our civilian citizens, our children, and our police and military personnel, has now come to his senses and ended his terrorist activities. We can thank General Vista and the good Lord for that," Derek said.

"I have no other news to report this afternoon. However, I've been asked to remind you that even though the sniper has stopped his terrorist activity for now, be sure to remember the new penalty I mentioned yesterday if you are caught violating the curfew. This still remains in effect.

"With that, Ladies and Gentlemen, I will now sign off until 10:00 a.m. tomorrow morning. We should all say a prayer of thanks that the sniper shootings have ended and—"

Derek's head exploded as he wrapped-up the broadcast with his familiar signing-off patter.

Blood, brain matter, and bone shards sprayed behind him as his television audience watched.

Viktor field stripped the *thread cutter*, put it into its briefcase, picked up the spent shell casing, and left the scene by his predetermined exit route.

"Tell me now, Mr. Television Newsreader," he said to no one as he hurried away, "do you still think the sniper shootings have ended?"

CHAPTER 103

Quarantine
Day 33

T RACE LEFT THE AREA FROM where he'd been watching
ODMC's headquarters and returned to the Palm Court
Hotel. The lights were turned down low. Dusk had visited
the lobby.

He headed for the manager's office to retrieve Pete's laptop
from the safe deposit box. Then he headed back to the Flamingo
Beach Hotel.

Trace booted up the laptop, double-clicked the Mozilla
Thunderbird e-mail program to open it, and configured
Thunderbird to retrieve his e-mail from the anonymous
mail server.

There were a few dozen unread e-mail messages waiting for
him. Mostly SPAM. He wondered how spammers targeted an
anonymous e-mail address. He also wondered why they did.

He scrolled to the top of the list to look for mail received
that day, and easily located Alex's messages among the e-mail.

Trace double-clicked the tag line and waited for the message to open and display itself on the monitor. Alex's message was brief and in simple code. It gave him the location for that night's rendezvous of Friday's Progeny.

Trace replied to Alex, also in code, TRIBECA, indicating he had received the message from Alex and had not been compromised. Then he waited thirty minutes and again checked his e-mail directory for a follow-up message from Alex aborting the meeting if someone else had been compromised. No abort message had come in. That night's meeting was on.

Trace was pleased. Tonight he would lay out the plan he'd formulated to rescue Isabella.

CHAPTER 104

Quarantine
Day 33

WHEN TRACE ARRIVED AT FRIDAY Progeny's encampment, he joined Ibrahim, and they then found Alex sitting against a tree.

"Have a plan yet?" Alex said to Trace.

Trace nodded. "I'll trade myself for Isabella. That seems to be what Vista wants anyway. Later I'll figure out how to talk Vista into releasing me."

"You're dreaming," Alex said. "He'll never release you. He won't have any reason to." He waited for Trace to say something. When it became clear that Trace was not going to respond, Alex added, "That's not much of a plan. More like a suicide mission."

Trace narrowed his eyes. "I don't understand why you're so negative," he said.

"You're not thinking clearly, Trace. What's the point of getting yourself captured? That won't help your wife."

"You don't know that," Trace said.

"Trace," Alex said, "this isn't a workable plan. It's not worth a damn. You're just setting up yourself and your wife for failure. You of all people, with your SEAL background, should know that."

Trace hesitated as if he was about to say something, but remained silent. He stood up, nodded at Alex, and said, "I'm going for a walk. You can plan your next adventure without me."

CHAPTER 105

Quarantine
Day 34

L ater that evening, Trace, with Ibrahim following close behind, left the encampment and returned to the Flamingo Beach Hotel. It was almost dawn.

They stopped under the archway leading into the lobby and looked around. More people were awake and milling about at this early hour than he expected.

Trace and Ibrahim started walking to the back of the lobby when Trace thought he noticed something strange happening around him.

Is it my imagination or are people turning and looking at me?

As he passed a young couple, he saw them look directly at him and whisper. When he caught the young man's eye, he abruptly turned away from Trace and said something to his companion.

Something's going on. Trace's senses switched to high alert.

He looked around the room, scanning the faces of those people he thought were paying attention to him. He saw one man point at him until he realized Trace was looking back at him. The man lowered his arm and turned away.

Trace turned back to face the young couple who, once again, looked away when he directed his gaze at them.

Trace took a step toward the couple. Their eyes opened wide, they looked at each other, then turned and bolted to the other side of the lobby.

He noticed a familiar young man staring at him, although he could not remember why he seemed familiar. The young man did not look away when Trace's eyes locked on his.

Trace nodded at him.

He nodded back.

Trace pointed toward the lobby's entrance and canted his head in its direction.

The young man indicated *yes* with his head and started walking across the lobby toward the doorway.

Trace and Ibrahim walked over, too, timing their arrival at the entrance to coincide with the young man's arrival. Trace struggled to place the young man's face, but wasn't able to remember him.

"The masses are restless," Trace said, as he thrust out his hand.

"With good reason," the young man said, "at least for now, Mr. Austin."

"How do you know my name?"

The young man glanced around furtively, then looked back at Trace, and said, "You're a celebrity around here. By the way, I'm Karl. We met through your son. I don't remember his name though."

Trace frowned. "His name was Pete. What do you mean I'm a celebrity? And where did we meet?"

"Your son, Pete, introduced us when I drove him back home from an Internet café. He and I played computer games a few times." He paused, waited a beat, then said, "As for the celebrity thing, there were soldiers here looking for you, an hour or so ago. They woke everyone up and searched the hotel. They asked us questions about you."

"What makes you think they were looking for me, not someone else?"

"It was you they were after, Mr. Austin. There's no question about it. Come with me, I'll show you."

CHAPTER 106

Quarantine
Day 33

T RACE STARED AT KARL, PUZZLED and made wary by his unequivocal statement. When Trace spoke again, he willed himself to speak softly and slowly to avoid spooking the kid. "Tell me what you mean, Karl," he said.

Karl shrugged his shoulders, looked from Trace to Ibrahim, then said again, "Follow me."

He turned, walked toward the hotel's central hall, and stopped when he reached an imitation Doric alabaster column that acted as an illusory vertical support for the high-entrance ceiling.

Karl pointed to a letter-size sheet of paper taped to the column. He swept his arm across the expanse of the room in a slow, dramatic, arcing gesture.

"They're all over the place, Mr. Austin," he said. "Look around. The soldiers taped them up."

Trace's eyes followed the sweep of Karl's arm, then settled on the poster nearest him. He looked at his photographic headshot beneath the highly legible word, wanted.

Trace looked around the room. It seemed to him that as

he did so everyone stopped talking, stopped moving, and now stared at him.

He reached out to the column and peeled the poster away, held it in both hands and looked at it.

The poster was a FBI-type *Ten Most Wanted*-type poster with a good likeness of Trace taken two years before when he, Isabella and Pete had played around with the digital camera they'd given Pete for Christmas. Isabella carried the photograph in her wallet.

Trace turned toward Karl.

"We're going now," Trace said. "Thanks for your help." He started toward the door.

"Wait a minute," Karl said. "You can't just walk out in broad daylight. You'll be a sitting duck."

"I can't stay here. I'll be reported, if I haven't been already," Trace said, as he and Ibrahim stepped through the door onto the patio.

Trace looked around. He didn't see any unusual activity.

He and Ibrahim cut over toward the side of the building, behind the bushes. They paused, out of sight, to gather their thoughts and plan their next step.

They began to work their way along the side of the building, moving parallel to the street, back toward Port Everglades, heading to an abandoned warehouse Alex had told Trace about.

Trace planned to hide himself and Ibrahim in the warehouse for the day, and sort through his thoughts, see how his plan to rescue Bella had evolved in his mind, and, hopefully, see if it seemed achievable.

He would continue the debate with Alex later that night at the rendezvous. Some discussion of my plan might prove useful, he thought.

CHAPTER 107

Quarantine
Day 34

VIKTOR LOCKED UP HIS WEAPONS for the afternoon, satisfied the tools of his trade were properly cleaned and oiled, ready for his next foray out into the night to kill unsuspecting policemen and soldiers.

His life had taken on a familiar and comforting rhythm now that he had upped the stakes and reintroduced some risk to himself by targeting the government, not only soft-target civilians. Kill civilians during the day to sow panic and discord among the population; kill policemen and soldiers at night during curfew to let the authorities know they, too, are vulnerable.

Not that the risk he now encountered was anything like the risk he'd known as an authentic shooter engaged in Afghanistan and Chechnya. Now that was invigorating risk, he thought. It kept you on high alert day in and day out. You slept with one eye open. Viktor beamed at the memory.

The risk Viktor experienced as a shooter in the Quarantine Zone, he decided, was akin to that he experienced when he'd ridden a roller coaster for the first time — a frightening sensation felt at the moment, but with the certain knowledge that the danger was contrived and managed by the ride's designer. Illusory danger, not really risk at all.

So be it, he thought. If this is the best Fort Lauderdale has to offer, I'll live with it until something better, something more perilous and interesting comes along.

CHAPTER 108

Quarantine
Day 34

TRACE AND IBRAHIM ENTERED THE warehouse through a side door. Trace easily picked the lock using Alex's tools he'd held onto after they had broken into Everglade Harry's. The air inside was heavy and stale. Trace could see dust floating in the light that filtered through grime-covered windows.

Trace looked around for a place to sit, somewhere he and Ibrahim could take advantage of the limited daylight squeezing into the building.

Trace settled onto a wooden pallet, opened Pete's laptop, and booted it up. Ibrahim stood behind him and looked over Trace's shoulder at the computer's screen.

After twenty minutes of watching Trace, Ibrahim said, "How's your son, Pete? Will I meet him? How come he's not been with you?"

Trace stopped what he was doing and said, "Pete died from the terrorists' disease." He turned his attention back to the laptop.

"Sorry," Ibrahim said. "I'll be quiet now."

A few minutes later, Ibrahim said, as he pointed to the computer, "What're you trying to do with the laptop?"

"Checking my e-mail."

"Can I see it when you're finished? The laptop, I mean, not your e-mail?" Ibrahim asked.

Trace nodded, said, "I'm finished for now," and passed the laptop over.

"Ever hack a network other than for the Israeli military?" Trace asked.

Ibrahim stilled his fingers on the keyboard, and looked up at Trace.

"Hacking's illegal," he answered. "Besides, I think you mean crack a network, not hack. They're different."

"Call it what you want. You know what I meant," Trace said. "That's a strange question. Are you a cop?"

"No, I'm not a cop, and not a federal agent or anything like that. I have my reasons for asking, personal reasons. So, what about it. Have you?"

"I might have, but I never did any damage. Never stole anything. If I broke in, it was only for bragging rights. Assuming I even did it in the first place, that is."

Where'd I ever hear that before? "Okay. So now we both know you've done it."

Ibrahim's face reddened, and he slowly nodded.

"I learned recently that my son, Pete, hacked systems. He said he did it for the same reasons you said, for the challenge, for peer recognition. Pete wasn't a criminal."

Ibrahim remained silent for a minute. Then he nodded at Trace. "What's your interest in hacking?"

"I need to get into a government network," Trace said, "to find a file so I can learn about my wife's imprisonment and, hopefully, use the information to free her. I need help getting into the system."

"You're talking major prison time when you're caught," Ibrahim said. "Notice, I said when, not if, you're caught."

He paused, waiting for Trace to respond. When Trace remained silent, Ibrahim said, "I don't do government computers."

"That's fine, Ibrahim, but I don't have a choice. I understand your reluctance to help me." He reached out to take back the laptop.

"Anyway, I can get along on my own," Trace said. "I had an assignment in the Navy similar to your Israeli Army assignment so I understand the fundamentals of hacking.

"Not only that," he said, "Pete showed me how to use some of the current, popular hacking tools so I'm pretty much up to date on the software used to penetrate networks."

"I said I don't hack government networks," Ibrahim said. "I didn't say I wouldn't help you other ways. There's a difference. And a condition."

"What's the condition?"

"It's simple. When the Feds bust you and want to know how you learned to hack, you tell them you learned from your son. You don't know me. Never heard of me. My name never comes up. As far as you're concerned, I don't exist. That's my condition."

Trace hesitated, not comfortable with the prospect of shifting blame to Pete, but said, "Fair enough."

CHAPTER 109

Quarantine
Day 34

"FIRST OFF," IBRAHIM SAID, I need to know what you know. Have you ever actually hacked a network since you left the Navy? Alone or with your son?"

"No," Trace said. "Pete showed me current keystrokes and explained some of the software tools. That being said, I do have a pretty good grasp of the concepts from my Navy days even if I haven't used them for years. I also have a master's degree in Computer Science and I'm a technology lawyer.

"Did Pete have hacking tools on this computer?" Ibrahim said, looking over at the laptop.

Trace nodded. "In a password protected directory. Here—" Trace said. as he double-clicked a folder Pete had named SAFECRACKER.

A text box popped up instructing Trace to enter the password. Trace typed it in. A list of twenty-three files scrolled down the screen.

Ibrahim leaned in close and examined the list.

"Good tools," he said. "I use most of these myself."

Trace couldn't help smiling at Pete's state-of-the-art preparation.

"I'll probably tell you things you already know from your Navy days or from Pete," Ibrahim said, "but bear with me. I don't want to assume you know every step and leave something out that will cause you to fail before you're caught, after I'm gone."

"The first thing we'd do in a real hack," Ibrahim said, "would be to find a target. We don't have to do that. I have one in mind for the lesson. I assume you know which federal target you want, but don't tell me. I don't want to know."

"Uh huh," Trace said. He wasn't going to reveal his target in any event.

"We'll hack into an easy target right now," Ibrahim said, "one of the corporations I sometimes poke around in. Based on my prior experience, we'll be able to do what we want there without being detected."

"Okay," Trace said, "but I thought you said—"

"I said I wouldn't mess with a government network. This is private, a business."

He pulled the laptop in close to him.

"I'll step you through the process. After that I'm out of here and you're on your own."

CHAPTER 110

Quarantine
Day 34

IBRAHIM PLACED THE COMPUTER ON his lap. "First we'll start by getting your target's IP address and host name."

He opened Pete's directory and scanned the list of hacking tools.

"For that we'll use the *whois* protocol tool to create a diagram of the network to show us how the network is organized. Then, with that information we'll examine the network for vulnerable ports. If we find an unprotected port, we'll enter the network there."

Trace said, "Okay." This all was familiar to him.

The *whois* tool did its work. In about thirty seconds it returned the specimen corporation's IP address and host name.

"Now, open the *QuaylsGuard* tool," Ibrahim said. "We'll use it to scan the corporation's IP ports."

After a few minutes *QuaylsGuard* highlighted two vulnerable ports. Ibrahim wrote down their identifying numbers — Ports 3702 and 3734.

Ibrahim said, "We'll first try to enter through Port 3702 using *Nmap*." He handed the laptop to Trace and said, "Open

Nmap and type "3702" into the text box . . . . Good. Now, click the run button."

They watched the monitor as *Nmap* did its job and infiltrated the network, entering the corporation's network through Port 3702.

"Good," Ibrahim said. "We're in. Now the fun starts. We'll monitor network traffic to identify some careless user whose UserID and password we can temporarily hijack."

Ibrahim again deployed *QuaylsGuard*, this time to monitor network traffic. He wanted to find an employee or a contractor whose user account was vulnerable, then glom onto the account and temporarily make it his own.

They were in luck, and soon had a UserID and password.

"With these," Ibrahim said, "we'll be able to pass through the firewall. We'll have this user's account privileges, such they are, as our entree, our first step into the network."

Trace nodded, then recorded the step in a notebook he carried with him.

"What we really want to do, as I'm sure you already know," Ibrahim said, "is leverage this user's privileges up to someone with privileges at the level of a system administrator. When we have that we'll seize root control and own the network."

Ibrahim waited while Trace wrote in his notebook.

"When you hack the government site, you'll need not only administrator's privileges, like we'll soon get here, but also the highest security-level clearance possible in case the files you're after are classified. You'll follow the same steps we're using now, but it'll take you several tries, a few passes to get through all the firewalls. That's when you'll be caught, if you haven't been already."

Trace shrugged. What choice did he have?

"Are you with me so far?"

"I am." He held up his notebook.

"Now we'll use the *DumpSec* tool. It will scan the network to learn the protocols and services that are running. It should also return a list of the required authentications, the users, groups, and file-sharing permissions we'll need."

Trace wrote furiously as he looked back and forth from the laptop's monitor to his notebook.

"Now we're going to sniff packets that are crossing the network," Ibrahim said.

"Our tool, *Ethereal*, will check each packet — sniff it — to locate the files we want," Ibrahim said. "But since we don't really want any files, we'll log off now and close up."

"That was helpful," Trace said. He closed his notebook.

"That was equivalent to elementary school compared to what you plan to do — a graduate school-level penetration. You'll not only have to penetrate several firewalls, but once you're in, assuming you get in, you'll have to detect several levels of UserIds and passwords to find and assign yourself a high-level security clearance. I don't think you can do it."

"Maybe, but I don't have a choice."

Ibrahim raised his eyebrows. "Do you think you understand what we just did well enough to replicate it?" he asked. When Trace nodded, Ibrahim said, "Okay, let's try another one of my private corporation targets. I'll watch while you hack into its system on your own."

Thirty minutes later Trace powered down the laptop and closed the lid.

"That was good. Better than I expected," Ibrahim said.

"It'll probably go all right for you until they detect you. Then the roof will come crashing in." He paused as if trying to remember something.

"Here's some advice for you," Ibrahim said. "Go slowly. Follow the steps I showed you. If anything unusual happens, anything at all, immediately break-off the network connection so they can't track it back to you.

"If in doubt, break off the connection. You can always come back another time. Your speed getting offline might just save you, though probably not." Ibrahim studied Trace's face for a second.

"You're going to get caught, you know. I'd bet on it," Ibrahim said.

Trace nodded.

"Remember our deal. Once I leave here, you're on your own. I don't exist."

CHAPTER 111

Quarantine
Day 34

T RACE TOOK HIS FIRST STEPS to break into ODMC's network. He thought about Pete's repeated admonition to him: to hack a system successfully, you have to think like a computer programmer who is writing software code to achieve a specific goal.

He could do that. This was the methodology he used with clients in his law practice. As a lawyer, he would first establish his client's goals; then he'd map a logical route to achieve them, anticipating or addressing and resolving obstacles as they surfaced along the way.

Pete had also drilled into Trace that it was stupid to engage in anything other than safe hacking, an oxymoronic phrase if ever I heard one, Trace now thought. It was essential, Pete had said at the start of each night's lesson, that the hacker disguise his identity and hide his location from prying eyes. His goal should always be to probe without being noticed, to penetrate the system's defenses in secret, spend time within the system unobserved, and then withdraw.

Be invisible at every step in the hack, Pete had said. Be a good runner who leaves no footprints.

Trace looked through the pages of his notebook and thought about how he would approach attacking ODMC's network. He did not have the benefit of knowing the names of ODMC's servers or the identities of its firewalls. He also did not know the identity of any authorized user whose account he could appropriate to crack the network.

Trace's assault on ODMC's protected network would have to be made directly, blindly, with what Pete had called brute force penetration. He would probe every possible avenue of entry until he found an open port and an available password or until they heard him coming, shut him out of the system, and stormed in and arrested him.

Pete's laptop searched the airwaves for a usable wireless connection. It located a hotspot called FRIEDA, and logged on to it. FRIEDA was an unsecured Wi-Fi network, like the old telephone party lines, operated by someone who generously or, more likely, unknowingly made the online connection available to anyone close enough to tap into it. FRIEDA was as public a wireless network source as Trace could find since the usual sources of public wireless hotspots — schools, libraries, airports, hotels and restaurants — were closed for the duration of the quarantine.

Trace looked again at his notes, took a deep breath, and embarked on his first step as a civilian network hacker.

CHAPTER 112

Quarantine
Day 34

U SING HIS NOTEBOOK AND HIS memory as guides, Trace stepped through the preliminary stages of hacking.

He quickly identified the IP address of ODMC's network, found three vulnerable ports, and lurked at one port long enough to capture the UserID and password of Major Michael Fowler (UserID: mfowler. Password: General*2B1Day#). Using this as his entrée, Trace then deployed the *Ethereal* tool to penetrate two firewalls.

He paused and reviewed his notes. He now needed to elevate his privileges from that of a user with ordinary, limited access to the level of a user having full administrative standing.

He examined the system's log files to see who had access to the server and to the various directories.

Well, well, well, Trace thought, isn't that interesting. He couldn't help smiling at his discovery.

I'll become General Anthony Vista today. He wrote down Anthony Vista's UserId (Wunderkind) and Vista's password @MyDogWaynes*Master). Then he entered the network as General Anthony Vista and looked for Isabella's file.

Trace spent twelve minutes, longer than he wanted to be in the network, and found nothing. Then he came across a password protected database called quarantine zone. Using Vista's logon information, he pulled up the list of files it contained.

There, among several thousand names, were two that interested him — Austin, Isabella MARY and Austin, Trace MICHAEL.

He downloaded both files to Pete's laptop so he could examine them later when he was safely offline. He logged off.

He was pleased with himself. Not only had he gotten in and out of ODMC's network without being discovered, at least as far as he knew, but he had found the files he was after.

A few minutes after having logged off ODMC's network, Trace turned back to Pete's laptop and opened Isabella's file.

It was a waste of time.

The file contained a typed note that Isabella was not known to have committed any crime, but was being held indefinitely as a reluctant informer with respect to crimes committed by her husband, fugitive sniper, Trace Austin.

Nothing else.

Trace closed her file and double-clicked his file to open it.

His file held even less information than Isabella's file, but it was much more illuminating. His file contained a single note stating that his case had been removed from the custody of the ODMC and transferred to the Pentagon Forces' watch list.

Other than that notation, Trace's digital file folder was empty.

Trace's curiosity spiked. Why'd they transfer my file to the Pentagon?

He decided to explore this.

He composed an encrypted e-mail message to Max Tyler, sent it off and waited. Ten minutes later he had his reply.

> To: Pappy@anonymous.sum.to
> From: Offspring@anonymous.sum.to
> Protocol: OPERATION JUST CAUSE
>
> Unable to learn anything to satisfy your request.
> Subject is classified in the Pentagon's database.
>
> Sorry, Ol' Buddy.
>
> Watch your back.
>
> One of your offspring

"Damn," Trace said softly to himself. "The answers are out there. If it does nothing else right, the military keeps detailed records of absolutely everything it touches."

Trace realized he had no choice now. He could not operate in the dark. If he was to have any chance of rescuing Isabella, he first had to know how they intended to deal with him. That knowledge might eliminate some options, and he needed to know that in advance. He had to get hold of his file.

To do that, he would have to break into the Pentagon's secure, trusted network.

CHAPTER 113

Quarantine
Day 34

T HE FIRST THING TRACE DID to embark on his hack of the Pentagon's trusted network was to log on to several known public message boards operated by hackers. He hoped to find sources describing the Pentagon's network, its IP address, and its host name.

He was able to grab this information on the second message board he tried. The posting also provided maps of the Pentagon's *Sleeping Giant* network showing how it was physically and logically organized.

Trace then replicated the steps he had followed when he'd penetrated ODMC's security and network.

Trace expected the Pentagon's trusted system to be harder to crack than ODMC's network, but it was not since he already had a UserId and password he'd recovered.

Trace logged on to the Pentagon's system using General Vista's identity. Now he would see if Vista had sufficient privileges at this network level to enable him to find Trace's own file.

Trace opened the file search text box on the main screen

and typed Trace Austin into the keyword space. He pressed the Enter button to search the network for everything containing his name.

One file popped up.

Trace walked through the steps necessary to download the file to the laptop's hard drive, but the file would not download. Instead, a pop-up message appeared on the screen informing him, as General Vista, that the file could not be downloaded because he did not have the required clearance privileges, that the file was read only.

"Okay," Trace said to himself, "I'll read it. I don't need a copy. I just need information."

Trace double-clicked the file to open it. The system now returned the message that Vista did not have adequate privileges to open this file to read it, and that he should not again attempt to open this file or he would risk losing all his network privileges.

Trace read the message. He could not help smiling. This is almost too tempting to resist, he thought. Wouldn't it be a kick if Vista was to wake up tomorrow and find that I have locked him out of the entire network, stripped him of his privileges.

Trace logged off. He had to think of another way to get into the protected file.

Twenty minutes later Trace started again. He retraced his earlier steps in his digital disguise as Vista, and penetrated the Pentagon's network.

Trace then turned to *Ethereal* to sniff packets, to find a UserId and a password having TOP SECRET/SECRET COMPARTMENTED INFORMATION level clearance —

the highest level of clearance — so he could download his file. The tool took less than one minute to return a usable identity and password at the TS/SCI level of secrecy.

Trace located his file again and, using his new, purloined online identity, downloaded this file to his hard drive.

He would look at his file later. For now, he would poke around in the network to see what else he could find that might be useful to him in dealing with Vista. Then he would quit the network and not return.

Trace used the same TS/SCI UserID and password he had just used successfully to perform a keyword search of the Pentagon's entire network. He entered into the search field the keyword phrases, Trace Austin, Isabella Austin, Peter Austin, bioterror, bioterrorists, bioweapon, bioagent, biological warfare, MELIOIDOSIS, pentagon, fort lauderdale, BROWARD COUNTY, quarantine, ANTHONY VISTA, GENERAL VISTA, DISTRICT MILITARY COMMANDER, and martial law. Then he directed the program, first, to search through all the Pentagon's files and databases, at every level of clearance, using these phrases, and then to automatically download to Pete's laptop any files it found meeting these criteria.

Trace sat back and waited while the search engine did its work. He was now as vulnerable to detection and arrest as he ever would be.

CHAPTER 114

Quarantine
Day 34

TRACE'S MULTIPLE SEARCH CRITERIA RETURNED and downloaded too many files for him to look through immediately. To deal with this, he created five descriptive folders on Pete's hard drive to dump the files into for later review: Family; City; TerroristS' Attack; TERRORISTS' Disease; SECRETARY OF DEFENSE; and MISCELLANEOUS.

He moved each file into its appropriate folder. Then he logged off and shut down the computer.

Later that evening, in a corner in the back of a meeting room in the hotel he'd selected to squat in that night, Trace set up the laptop on the floor in front of himself and began the tedious task of looking through the downloaded files.

He started with the directories called City and TerroristS' Attack. Nothing in either folder interested him. Next, he looked at the files in the TerroristS' Disease directory. He was surprised to learn the extent to which the population was infected by

Melioidosis. It was much more devastating than either CNN or the authorities had admitted to the public, he thought.

The next directory he opened, designated SECRETARY OF DEFENCE, contained only one file. It was marked Secret Compartmented Information. This, in and of itself, did not arouse Trace's interest since he expected to find files spanning the whole range of security classifications. What caught his eye, however, was the notice in the file's name that the file was "Eyes Only, Copy 2 of 2, Report to the President of the United States Concerning OPERATION TESTING GROUND: Proposed U.S. DOMESTIC BIOWEAPON Attack on A designated united states city."

Trace moved the cursor over the file's name and allowed it to hover there.

Maybe I should leave this alone, he thought. Breaking into the secretary of defense's file would be fundamentally wrong, unpatriotic, at best. Maybe even worse. After all, he said out loud, this *is* a cabinet officer, not some passed-over-for-promotion pissant colonel who's been exiled to the Pentagon.

But what about that reference to a proposed U.S. domestic bioweapon terrorist attack? he thought.

He took a deep breath and stared across the room, looking through the warehouse's hazy, ambient night light.

I'm already in for one or more felonies, he thought. How much more can they do to me if I'm caught? If the file contains nothing relevant, I'll forget I ever saw it. No one will ever know.

He wiped his forehead with his sleeve. Then he double-clicked the file, entered the stolen TS/SCI level UserID and password he'd appropriated, and looked on as the file opened.

He skimmed the entire file, all eighteen pages of the *Report to the President.*

Then he read it again, slowly.

"Holy sweet Jesus," he said out loud.

He leaned over and looked again at the first page, the Report's Executive Summary.

"I don't believe this. How could they?"

Trace thought about what he knew from television specials and other sources he'd read over the years. The government is capable of doing this, he thought. It's done it before on a smaller scale on innocent populations. Several times, in fact. It's well documented.

He recalled the government's Tuskegee experiment where the Public Health Department allowed syphilis, affecting hundreds of African-Americans, to go untreated for forty years, even after a cure for syphilis had been discovered.

He also thought back to the government's public apology in 1993 in which it admitted that during the Cold War it had conducted the Tennessee experiment in which designated slums of that state, because they physically resembled Russian cities that the United States might attack, were sprayed with radioactive zinc cadmium sulfide, a fine fluorescent powder, to see the effects of the attack on the population. He also recalled a similar admission and apology in 1994 when the government admitted doing the same thing in various slums outside St. Louis.

Trace slammed his fist down on the floor. "What will I tell Isabella — that the president, the man she voted for, killed Pete and Nanna?"

The next thing Trace did was take a thumb drive from the laptop's case and make a backup copy of the file. He would take the backup copy to the hotel safe deposit box where he'd kept the laptop and leave the thumb drive there so he would not have it with him if he was picked up by the authorities.

CHAPTER 115

Quarantine
Day 34
The Pentagon
Arlington, Virginia

"WE HAVE AN INTRUDER, SIR," the sergeant said.
"Lock him out. Grab his identity, locate him, then arrest the bastard."

"I've already closed the vulnerable port and broken-off the connection, Sir. I'm starting the probe back to him now, pinging him as we speak."

The sergeant used the same packet sniffer *Ethereal* software that Trace had used to now ping Trace's computer and to identify his IP address. Then, armed with the address, the sergeant let *VisualRoute* software work its magic backwards.

VisualRoute utilized the *whois* and *traceit* tools to identify the path followed by the packet of data from Pete's laptop to the Pentagon. *VisualRoute* identified every network device exploited by the fugitive packet on its journey to the Pentagon, then created a reverse map of the intruder's route from the Pentagon's network back to the originating laptop.

"We'll have his name, physical location, and a map of his trail in just a few minutes, Sir."

"We have him, Sir. And I've taken control of his computer," the sergeant said.

"Examine his hard drive. I want to know if he's taken anything or was just snooping. If he's taken anything, I want to know what it was."

"His name's Peter Austin, Sir. He's in Fort Lauderdale. We're running a profile and a GPS location on him. Just a few more minutes and we'll have it all."

We have his profile and the description of his activity in the network," the sergeant said, holding up a printout.

He paused to read the printout, then turned to the colonel.

"Here are the files Austin downloaded," he said, handing over the printout.

The colonel looked at the list and handed it back to the sergeant.

"Notify the District Military Commander in Fort Lauderdale to pick up Peter Austin and hold him. Instruct him to get the hard drive from his computer."

PART FOUR

CHAPTER 116

Quarantine
Day 34

GENERAL VISTA PACED IN FRONT of his desk.

Wayne, the general's boxer, sat by the desk, his sloping golden back rigid, his head up. His affect was that of a sitting mountain lion with a black snout. His eyes kept pace with Vista's steps as if the dog was watching a child on a carnival merry-go-round ride.

"Austin hacked into the Pentagon's trusted network using my ID and password," Vista said to his dog. "That bastard. And they've cut off my privileges, my access to the network because of him. He's messing with my career."

He leaned over and scratched Wayne's head.

"So the IT nerds at the Pentagon think they're going to take Peter Austin as their prisoner. Ha! Not likely unless I find him in the mass grave and pack his ashes in a bottle for the top brass." He laughed.

Wayne quit his regal pose, lowered himself to the floor, and curled up at the foot of the desk's chair, his jaw resting on his crossed paws.

"I'll give them an Austin all right, but it won't be Peter. I can't wait to see Austin's face when I arrest him."

CHAPTER 117

Quarantine
Day 34

EARLY THAT SAME EVENING TRACE composed an encrypted
e-mail using the Panama mission's OPERATION JUST
CAUSE encryption protocol, and sent it to his former
SEAL friend who now was at the Pentagon, Admiral Max Tyler.

To: **mtyler@navy.pentagon.mil**
From: mailer@anonymous.sum.to
Protocol: OPERATION JUST CAUSE

Desperately need your friendship, help, and
unquestioning trust.

Upon your reply e-mail confirming your
agreement to the terms below, I will send you
a follow-up e-mail with a file attachment I
have encrypted with the OPERATION JUST
CAUSE algorithm.

Bury the file in deep cover. Do not resurrect it

unless something happens to me or Isabella — not even if I, in person or otherwise, request that you return the file to me. In that event, you must assume coercion.

If anything happens to me or Isabella other than death by unequivocal natural causes, contact my law partner, Harlan Crockett, at the law firm of Clayton, Patton, Morris & Rome, in Washington. He will deliver the KEY to you upon your statement to him of the phrase, "JUST CAUSE".

In that event, deliver the file and the KEY to the Managing Editors of Huffington Post, Politico, the *New York Times, Fox News,* and the *Washington Post* for publication. First make a backup copy for yourself.

Under no circumstances are you to attempt to open and examine the file. Knowing its contents would pose grave danger to you and your loved ones.

Confirm by return e-mail that these terms are acceptable to you. Or, confirm that you will not accept them. In either case you should destroy this e-mail to protect yourself.

Offspring, your Pappy desperately needs your help. Don't let me down.

Trace sent the e-mail.

Next, he composed and sent an e-mail to Harlan Crockett. Since his law partner had no knowledge of the OPERATION JUST CAUSE encryption key, Trace encrypted his e-mail to Crockett using only the law firm's Blowfish code.

> To: **hcrockett@dclawyers.com**
> From: **mailer@anonymous.sum.to**
> Subject: Firm Billings
> Protocol: Blowfish
>
> Harlan,
>
> I need your help. If you are agreeable to the terms I state below I will send you a follow-up e-mail with an encryption KEY attachment. Place the digital copy of the KEY in the same place we maintain clients' deep-cover files.
>
> Do nothing with the KEY unless you are contacted by a person who uses the phrase "JUST CAUSE" as a password. In that event, deliver the KEY to him.
>
> This request has no time limitation. It is absolutely confidential. Sorry I cannot tell you more. Rush your reply. Trace.

When he finished, Trace ran one of Pete's sophisticated software file-shredding programs. It was, ironically, the same

software program used by the Department of Defense —
available online to the general public — to destroy everything
on the laptop's hard drive. This involved making seven slow
electronic passes shredding files, and took just over two hours
to complete.

When this program finished its destruction, Trace opened
the laptop, removed the drive, and broke it into two pieces.
He planned to toss one piece into the Intracoastal Waterway at
one location and toss the second section into the Intracoastal
Waterway at some other location. Then he would take the
cannibalized laptop case and place it back in the hotel's safe
deposit box where it would not be found.

Trace received both reply e-mails within an hour of his messages.
Both men agreed to his terms and, as he expected, did not ask
any questions.

Trace responded to the e-mails by immediately sending
each man his respective digital file — the encrypted Report to
the President to Max and the encryption KEY to unlock that
file to Harlan.

He took a deep breath, slowly let it out, and smiled for
the first time in many hours. He now had his plan and his
insurance policy. He would be able to rescue Isabella, and then
he and she would be safe from government retribution.

CHAPTER 118

Quarantine
Day 34

L ATER THAT NIGHT AFTER CURFEW, Trace sat under a tree
with Alex, Jenna and Ibrahim at that evening's Friday's
Progeny's encampment. A thicket of Jacaranda trees on one
side and the Intracoastal Waterway on their other side sheltered
the encampment from sight.

"I've decided what I need to do to rescue my wife," Trace
said, looking at Alex. "I'll trade for Isabella, like you suggested
before, but I won't trade me for her."

Alex squinted and looked skeptically at Trace. "Then what
do you have to trade they'd want if not you?"

"I can't tell you."

Alex looked annoyed. He started to say something, caught
himself, and just nodded.

"Anyway, I'm out of here," Trace said, as he stood up. "See
you all one day if all goes well."

He turned from the group, left the encampment, and
headed to the Pelican Cove Hotel.

The man stayed well back from Trace as he watched him enter the hotel. Then he pushed the CALL button on his cell phone.

"Austin just entered the Pelican Cove Hotel," he said. "I'm across the street."

"Good work," General Vista said. "Stay put. My men will be there in less than ten minutes."

Inside the hotel, Trace settled onto the floor with his back against the wall, off by himself at the far end of the lobby.

He considered his plan to release Bella, and ran it through various hypothetical obstacles he'd set up trying to spot a weakness in it. The plan seemed solid. The one catch was that he could not yet come up with a way of presenting the plan to the authorities without placing himself at risk of being captured before he could implement the plan.

Trace looked around the room. Most people seemed to be sleeping. A few adults and some children were awake and talking softly. The overall ambiance of the lobby was marked by a state of tranquil repose.

He put his cheek against one knee, yawned, closed his eyes, and drifted off into sleep.

Trace bolted awake, jarred into foggy consciousness by a sharp pain in his ribs. He felt as if he had been poked by something knifelike and hard.

He jumped to his feet, his adrenalin propelling him out of his fog, his instincts on high alert.

Soldiers, dressed in MOP gear, formed a semi-circle around him, stretching from the wall on one side of him, back to the wall on his other side. They faced Trace with automatic assault weapons.

Other soldiers, also in MOP suits, stood back, away from Trace, in a second phalanx, some pointing weapons at him, others keeping the small crowd away.

The soldiers put Trace on his stomach, searched him, and flex-cuffed his hands behind his back. Then they hauled him up onto his feet and put a short ankle chain on both his legs.

Within minutes, he was on his way to General Vista.

CHAPTER 119

Quarantine
Day 35

THE NEXT MORNING, AFTER HAVING spent the night in a cell and having had his blood tested to see if he was infected and contagious, Trace, not having shown any symptoms of Melioidosis, was taken to General Vista's office. He still was manacled, but now with his arms in front.

Vista stood behind his desk facing the doorway, holding a lit cigar. He stared into Trace's eyes as Trace entered the room. A slow grin carved itself into his face.

Trace couldn't read the general's expression, especially his anomalous smile.

"Sit," Vista said, nodding at a chair in front of his desk.

Trace sat.

"Leave us," Vista ordered the guards.

Trace looked around the office to the limited extent he could see by shifting his eyes without turning his head. He continued to face Vista head-on, even as he strained to survey his surroundings.

He could just make out the presence of another person behind his back and far off to his left, leaning against the wall.

He couldn't identify the person without turning his head, but he refused to do that.

"Welcome, Mr. Austin. You've been a difficult man to catch up with. You're fortunate you weren't shot on sight."

Trace remained silent.

"I believe you already know my colleague, Alex," Vista said, looking beyond Trace at the wall to Trace's left.

This time Trace turned his head to look.

"Apparently I didn't know him as well as I thought," Trace said.

"Now, now, Mr. Austin. Don't be so self-righteous. We all do what we must when our country's at war. Alex was being a good soldier."

Trace shook his head in disgust. "Jenna, too, I suppose," he said.

Alex looked at the general and raised his eyebrows.

Vista nodded his permission to speak.

"Jenna was the initiating force behind your involvement," Alex said. "When she met you and learned about your SEALs' background, she called me."

"She's not your cousin, right?" Trace said.

"Actually, she is my cousin. That's how I recruited her," Alex said.

"And Ibrahim? Was he part of it, too?"

"Ibrahim's a nice kid and a good patriot. He seems to love his adopted country. But, no, he wasn't part of it, as you describe us. He was Jenna's cover although he didn't know it."

Trace turned back and faced Vista.

"I want to see my wife," he said.

"In due time, Mr. Austin. First I have some questions."

"No," Trace said. "I want to see her now. I have nothing to say until I see her and see she's all right."

"This is becoming tiresome, Mr. Austin." He paused as if considering Trace's demand. "Very well, have it your way. You can see her now. But afterward, you *will* talk to me."

———✻——✻——✻——✻——✻——

A few minutes later Trace and Isabella stood in front of Vista's desk. They were not left alone. Two guards and Vista kept watch over them.

Trace thought Isabella looked haggard and worried, but, he was happy to see, she did not seem frightened by the circumstances. Her left eye wasn't twitching as it always did when she was frightened.

Vista started interrogating Trace immediately after Isabella arrived.

"What part did you have in the terrorists' bioweapon attack?" Vista said.

"That's ridiculous," Isabella said. "My husband would not—"

Vista whipped his head around toward Isabella. "I'm not speaking to you. Be quiet or I'll have you removed."

He looked back at Trace. "I asked you a question."

"No part. To quote my wife," Trace said, "that's ridiculous. I'm here on vacation with my family, with what's left of my family."

"Good cover, but transparent," Vista said.

Trace remained silent.

"You've committed several felonies, Mr. Austin, at least those we know about. Maybe others, too. Let's see . . . Assault on a federal employee. Breaking into a federal computer. Who knows what else. You'll be going away to prison for a very long time, Mr. Austin . . . Mr. ex-SEAL."

"I demand to go before a civilian judge," Trace said.

"Forget your demands, Austin. Civilian law doesn't apply here during martial law. I'm the judge and jury for now."

Trace looked directly into Vista's eyes and smiled. A big smile.

"Don't get your hopes up, General, not if you don't want to be disappointed," Trace said. "There's more to this than you could ever know."

He turned his head slightly toward Isabella and caught her eyes with his. He nodded slightly.

She frowned and raised her eyebrows, silently asking Trace what he was talking about?

"I demand," Trace said softly, looking back at Vista, "to speak to someone in authority, someone higher up the chain of command than you." He paused to let his statement sink in.

"What I have to say affects national security and will significantly affect the well-being of the president. I have nothing more to say to you. Until I talk with your superiors, I'm done here."

"At the risk of sounding like a cliché, Austin, we can make you talk," Vista said. "Don't be naïve."

"Listen, General," Trace snapped, his eyes narrowing and his voice becoming sharper, "forget your threats and your tough-guy bullshit. If you harm me or my wife, in fact, if you even threaten us again, you'll regret it. I promise you that. Your superiors will see to it when I insist upon it. And, General, that's not a threat. It's my promise to you."

"My husband always keeps his promises, General," Isabella said. "He's fanatical about it. You'd be wise to listen to him."

Vista frowned. Strange response. My superiors? He'll insist on it? What can he have in mind? Must be his macho SEAL training surfacing.

"Now, General," Trace said, his voice deliberately softening, becoming almost conspiratorial in tone, "I'm going to do you one favor, but only one. So listen carefully. I won't repeat this."

He looked over at Isabella and winked, then turned back to Vista.

"If you value your career, General, if you don't want to come out of this scenario busted down to sergeant, you will stop wasting my time. You'll arrange for me to talk to someone substantially higher in authority than you about a national security matter of the highest priority."

He paused to let this sink in.

"Until then, General, my wife and I are finished with you."

Trace turned toward Isabella and threw her a mock-kiss with his lips.

Bella smiled and nodded slightly.

"Yes, Sir, that's exactly what Austin said, word for word. I have it on tape if you'd like to hear it," Vista said. "No, Sir, I just thought—"

He patted Wayne's head.

"Yes, Sir, right away. I'll prepare a complete report and have it on your desk by 0800 tomorrow. Thank you, Sir."

CHAPTER 120

Quarantine Day 36
3:00 a.m.

T HE NEXT NIGHT THE DEPUTY secretary of defense, acting
under orders from his boss, the secretary of defense, came
to the Quarantine Zone. He'd been secretly transported
from the Pentagon to Fort Lauderdale's civilian airport in an
unmarked fixed-wing aircraft, then flown from the airport to
ODMC's headquarters building in a Blackhawk helicopter
which landed on the building's front lawn. The deputy secretary
of defense had disguised himself as an Army colonel.

Vista was waiting for him. He took the deputy secretary
directly to a room where, notwithstanding the late hour, Trace
was awake and waiting for him, with two guards standing by.

— ✕ — ✕ — ✕ — ✕ — ✕

"Mr. Austin," the deputy said as he walked quickly into the
room, not greeting Trace or introducing himself, "you're in
serious trouble. We take a dim view of people breaking into
classified federal computers."

Trace nodded. "As well you should, Sir."

"Why'd you do it?"

"Looking for something, obviously."

"It must have been a very important *something* for you to be willing to go to prison for a very long time just to find it."

"It was, Sir, but I won't be going to prison." He waited a beat, then said, "Now, Sir, why don't you stop wasting your time and mine. I want to speak with the president."

"What were you looking for?"

Trace shrugged slightly. "Okay, have it your way. My file and my wife's file. The ones created and kept by the Office of the District Military Commander."

"I hope what you found was worth it to you."

"I didn't find anything worthwhile in our files," Trace said. "But, yes, Sir, what I ultimately found definitely was worth it."

"You'll be going to prison for the next twenty-five years."

"I seriously doubt that," Trace said. "Not with what I found."

"And what was that, Mr. Austin?"

"I found a Get-Out-Of-Jail-Free card. But I'll only tell the president, in person, what I discovered. No cut-outs. Not you, not anyone else."

"That's not possible. Tell me what you found."

"Only the president."

The deputy turned away from Trace and walked to the far end of the room, paused briefly, then turned and walked back.

"What is it you ultimately want, Mr. Austin?"

"Considering this is bigger than Watergate, and that Watergate brought down a president, I think this president will want to talk with me," Trace said. "That's what I want, for now, to talk privately with the president."

"I'll need more than that to take to my boss, Mr. Austin, to convince him to take this to the president. Give me something I can work with."

"Tell the secretary of defense to tell the president I read and copied the REPORT ON OPERATION TESTING GROUND. The president will know what I'm talking about. Now, Sir, that's all I have to say to you."

The deputy took two rapid steps over to Trace and stopped just one foot away, facing him. He narrowed his eyes, pointed his finger at Trace's chest, almost touching Trace's shirt, and looked directly at the bridge of Trace's nose.

"Mr. Austin, the federal government does not appreciate threats, especially threats made against the president. That utterance is another felony committed by you. You're digging your hole deeper." He paused a beat, then added, "We can cause you and your family more harm than you can possibly imagine."

He continued to stare at Trace, continued to point his finger, and waited for Trace to reveal some sign he was intimidated by this staged show of righteous, patriotic indignation.

Trace remained silent and inscrutable.

"With just a few taps at a keyboard, we can irrevocably ruin your life, Mr. Austin, destroy your credit, render you forever unemployable, seize all your assets, and turn you into such a pariah you won't be able to find a doorway to sleep in. And that's after you finish your long prison term."

He paused to gauge Trace's reaction, then said, "Don't fuck with us, Austin. I'm warning you."

Trace looked at him and slowly shook his head.

"I'm finished here," Trace said. "You have my terms." He started to turn away.

"Reconsider, Mr. Austin. You won't get another chance. Think of your wife, if not yourself."

Trace spun around to face the deputy and took a quick step toward him. The deputy back-peddled away.

Trace pulled up, and said, "Listen here, you pissant, two-bit bureaucrat. I know you can do those things to me, even worse if you want. But I can bring down the president of the United States even as you do your worst to me. And I will, believe me, I will, if anything at all happens to me or my wife. It's arranged, even if we're dead or missing. It's unstoppable. So take your threats and shove them."

The deputy said nothing in response. He turned and walked away, over to the sofa, sat down, and crossed his legs. He folded his hands together on his lap and looked at Trace. He took a long breath, sighed, then let his breath out.

"Okay, Mr. Austin," he said, speaking from the neutral distance of his seat across the room, "let's both of us calm down and start over." He nodded and smiled as he said this.

"Speaking hypothetically, Mr. Austin, what's it you want from the president? Be specific so I can pass it on to my boss. You have to help me here so I can help you."

"I have conditions. If they're met, I'll keep the secret of what I found. If they're not met, or if anything happens to me or my wife — ever — the secret will be turned loose by third parties.

"In that case the president, and everyone involved with him in this matter, will fall, will likely go to federal prison. Tell that to your boss, Mr. Deputy Secretary." Trace paused, then added, "That should be enough help for you."

Trace waited a few seconds, then added, "And, by the way, Mr. Deputy Secretary, in spite of this so-called hypothetical exercise of yours, that part's not hypothetical. It's my promise."

The deputy frowned. "Still speaking hypothetically, if you

will, Mr. Austin, if you don't get to speak to the president, then what?"

Trace paused, looked at the him, and said, "In that case, here's what I expect. My wife and I will be removed from the Quarantine Zone, back to our home in Washington, immediately. We'll have full immunity for any crimes we committed or the government thinks we might have committed. That's absolute, blanket immunity, in writing from the president himself. Nothing less."

He waited while the deputy made a note on his iPad.

"I want an ironclad guarantee of our safety forever. I want it all in writing signed by the president."

"I don't know if we can do that."

"There's one more condition."

"Another?"

"One more."

"What is it?"

"I'll tell this one only to the president. So, you see, he does need to speak with me."

The deputy looked at Trace, started to say something, but stopped himself. He briefly looked off in space, then refocused and looked back at Trace. "I'll get back to you as soon as I can, Mr. Austin," he said. "Sit tight."

CHAPTER 121

Quarantine
Day 36

VIKTOR SAT AT HIS KITCHEN table staring at the black market bottle of vodka he'd just emptied. He was feeling unusually content.

He opened his notebook and added two strokes to its left hand column, making the total for that column — the number of policemen or soldiers he'd killed after curfew — six in all.

Not bad, but just the beginning.

He looked at the right hand column — the number of civilians killed during the day — and thought, nine is good in such a short time. It will strike terror in the heart of this gulag.

Viktor stood up, went to the cabinet over the sink, and pulled down a fresh bottle of vodka.

As he poured it into a tumbler, he thought, Not as interesting or challenging as Chechnya or Afghanistan, but better than nothing.

He had already resolved that he would keep hunting targets — civilian and the fascist police and soldiers — until he was caught or until martial law ended. He didn't care which. He was having too much fun to stop now, and the hunt relieved his boredom.

CHAPTER 122

Quarantine
Day 37

THE DAY AFTER TRACE MET with the deputy secretary of defense, he was taken to an empty office at ODMC's Headquarters where he waited for the deputy to return to meet with him.

This time he wasn't handcuffed or wearing leg chains, and he no longer was guarded. That meant, he figured, that for now they were accepting his demands and statements at face value.

Trace looked up when the door opened.

The deputy walked in followed by General Vista. There were no guards this time.

Trace resisted the urge to stand as they approached.

"Good morning, Mr. Austin," the deputy said. "I hope you had a restful night."

Trace nodded. "All things considered, Sir."

"I have some news. The secretary of defense has agreed to meet briefly with you and listen to your story. Not that he believes your innuendo. He's curious, however, and feels he owes it to the president and to the country to hear you out."

"We'll fly you to the Pentagon in about one hour, so get

yourself ready. You're not to tell your wife or anyone else where you're going or, on your return, where you've been. Understood?"

"Understood," Trace said. "But first you need to do something for me."

"What's that?"

"I want my wife flown immediately to the Mayo Clinic for a complete physical, treatment for her hives, and treatment for anything else she needs, without limitation. All on the government's nickel. First class all the way."

"No problem."

The deputy turned to Vista. "Make it happen, General."

"I'll talk to my wife," Trace said. "Pick me up when we're ready to leave. I'll see that she's ready for her trip. I'll be ready for mine."

The Blackhawk landed at a heliport located between the Pentagon and the parking lot designated as the North Parking Area. As a security precaution, the Pentagon Forces had declared the North Parking Area off-limits to all vehicles and pedestrians for the day.

A black Ford Expedition with heavily tinted windows waited for Trace and the deputy at the heliport. As soon as they were hustled aboard, it drove them into a secure tunnel leading to a staging area deep below the Pentagon.

The first thing that occurred was that Trace's blood was drawn to determine if he had developed any Melioidosis antibodies since his last test. His results were back in forty minutes. He tested negative. The meeting would go forward.

Trace and the secretary of defense did not meet in the secretary's office. Instead, Trace was led to a room that lacked the trappings of power Trace expected to find in a cabinet-level secretary's office. The room had no trophy wall of photographs and certificates; no large American flag; and no executive desk, among other missing power indicia. But when the office door opened and the secretary of defense strode in, Trace had no doubt he was in the presence of understated, but genuine power.

The secretary seemed to Trace just as he appeared on TV, but thinner and taller. His actual presence intimidated Trace who, as a former SEAL, still had great respect for federal authority and the chain of command.

The man's swagger as he entered the office and stepped across the room was theatrical. But his cold, unblinking stare as he approached Trace, and his impeccable grooming, all demanded attention and commanded deference.

"Hello, Mr. Austin," he said, as he approached Trace. He smiled with what to Trace seemed to be a well-practiced smile, and extended his hand to shake.

Trace hesitated, originally intending to salute the secretary, but then shook hands instead.

"Why don't we sit," the secretary said, sweeping his arm toward a sofa and two cushioned chairs surrounding a low coffee table. "I appreciate you taking your time to come to see me."

"Thank you, Sir."

They settled in, Trace low on the sofa and the secretary slightly higher on an elevated chair.

"It seems we have an important matter to deal with, Mr. Austin. I'm sure we can work this out. After all, we're both reasonable men and patriots."

"Yes, Mr. Secretary, I'd like to think we are." Trace waited, but did not smile back. He would not speak first, not bid against himself in this game of high-stakes bridge they were playing.

When Trace did not pick up the cue, the secretary nodded at Trace, silently commanding him, Trace realized, to speak first. He yielded to his trained respect for the higher authority.

"Mr. Secretary, I have some conditions to be met. They're very important to me. I don't think you should have any problem with them." He took a slow, deep breath and continued.

"But I'll need absolute assurances my conditions will be fulfilled, with appropriate safeguards to protect me and my wife. If the president can accommodate us on those matters, Sir, we'll all do just fine."

The secretary looked hard at Trace, then said, "What is it you think you've found, Mr. Austin, that gives you any right to make any demands on your country's president?"

CHAPTER 123

Quarantine
Day 37

TRACE THOUGHT ABOUT THE SECRETARY'S provocative, but fair question, and said, "I'm sorry, Sir, but I can't tell you. As you probably know, it has to do with something I found, but I'll only tell what that was to the president, in person."

The secretary glared at Trace. "That's nonsense, Mr. Austin. I have the highest possible security clearance and the full confidence of the president."

"With all due respect, Sir, not for this you don't. You're not cleared to see this." At least I hope you're not, Trace thought.

Trace continued. "Once you and I have an agreement on my conditions, I'll disclose my discovery to the president. Only to him. If he chooses to bring you into the loop, that's up to him. I won't do it on my own." He paused, then said, "That's non-negotiable, Mr. Secretary."

The secretary face darkened. He wasn't used to being talked to this way. On the other hand, on balance, he definitely liked this response. It made him feel a little more secure, even with the secret being out there, because this man before him seemed to have a measure of honor.

"Let's talk about your conditions, Mr. Austin. What do you want from your president?"

Trace repeated his conditions, this time adding Ibrahim and, after considering Viktor's offer to help him rescue Bella, also adding Viktor to the list of people he'd require be extricated from the Quarantine Zone. He had considered including Jenna, too, but decided that the military would have to determine her fate as part of her ROTC responsibility. He did not mention her to the secretary.

Then he added, "There's another condition, Sir. I didn't raise it with your deputy, but it's just as important as the others for reasons I hope you'll accept on trust, without my disclosure of it to you."

"Now what is it, Mr. Austin?" the secretary said, his impatience asserting itself. "I hope this is the last stipulation you have. You can't keep piling on every time we talk with you."

"That wasn't my intent, Sir, and that's not the case now. I assure you it will be the last condition. I just didn't feel it was appropriate to tell your subordinate because of its implications. It might not even be right to raise this with you rather than with the president." He paused to let this sink in.

"Tell me now, Mr. Austin," the secretary said. "This is becoming irksome."

Trace hesitated, then said, "All right. In addition to what I've already told you, we want a large, lump-sum, tax-free payment as monetary compensation for the deaths of our son and my mother-in-law in the Quarantine Zone."

"Why should we agree to that, Mr. Austin? Many unfortunate people have lost loved ones during the terrorists' attack and the quarantine. I sympathize with your losses, but why should your government compensate you, but not compensate everyone else who suffered a family loss?" He shook his head and glared at Trace.

"Perhaps the government *should* compensate everyone, Mr. Secretary, for reasons I won't disclose to you. But, Sir, my only concern has to be for me and my wife. As for why the government should compensate us, I won't tell you. You'll just have to accept that as my last condition. I assure you, Mr. Secretary, that the president will understand this condition."

The secretary frowned, then nodded. *He knows.* Somehow he found my file — my insurance policy against the president — when he penetrated the Pentagon's network.

Trace watched the secretary nod once, and thought, He's agreed to my last condition.

"Let's talk about your other conditions, Mr. Austin. Assuming we agree to them, we'll need the originals and all copies of the files you stole given back to us. I gather from what you've hinted that they're the source of your perceived leverage over the president."

"One original file is all, Sir, not files, and one copy. But I won't hand them over, Mr. Secretary. These files are the only means I have to protect my wife and me from harm, protect us from future retribution. It's our insurance policy, Sir. I won't budge on that."

"How will we know we can trust you not to disclose its contents sometime in the future. Maybe when you're elderly and at the end of your days?"

"I'll give you my word as a decorated former SEAL and as a citizen patriot. If that's not good enough for you, consider the practical side. If I ever disclose the contents of the file, I'll have given up my family's only protection against harm, even if I'm gone."

He paused to let this sink in.

Trace continued, "Although the government would be harmed by the disclosure, it would survive. But there's no measure to how much injury the government then would be able to do to us and our heirs.

"But the bottom line, Mr. Secretary, is trust. You and the president have to trust my integrity and my loyalty to our country, respect my patriotism — the same patriotism I showed as a Navy SEAL. That's what it's all about, Sir, in the end."

The secretary looked at him for almost a full minute, saying nothing, his face impassive.

Trace stared back.

The secretary finally spoke.

"You wait here, Mr. Austin. I'll get back to you."

He stood, turned away from Trace, not offering his hand this time, and left the room.

Just over two hours later, the door opened.

Trace stood up as the secretary of defense walked back in.

CHAPTER 124

Quarantine
Day 37

THE SECRETARY OF DEFENSE ENTERED the room alone and quickly walked over to the same chair he'd left hours earlier. He had a grim look on his face. This time he ignored Trace completely as he settled himself. Then he looked over at Trace.

"Let's get started," he said. "I have a busy day ahead of me."

Trace wondered about the secretary's change in demeanor, but dismissed this concern as irrelevant. What counted now was to get as much for himself and Isabella as he could, and to arrange to have Ibrahim and Viktor allowed to leave the Quarantine Zone. Anything else was just ego.

"First off," the secretary said, "the president will not meet with you. That's final. And furthermore, he has no idea what you're referring to, and no time to lay on his hands to bless your wild, implicit assertions."

He paused to let this sink in.

"The president instructed me to tell you either deal directly with me or there won't be any dealing."

Trace was stunned. He had not expected this. He cleared his throat.

"Let's take that condition off the table for the time being then, Mr. Secretary. Let's see how we come out on the other conditions. If we can reach accommodation on those, I might be able to forego meeting with the president."

The secretary reached inside his suit jacket and pulled out a slip of paper. He looked at it for a few seconds, then crumbled it into a ball and put it back into his jacket's side pocket.

"Here's what we're willing to do and here are our conditions for doing it, Mr. Austin."

He paused and stared hard into Trace's eyes. Then he said, "I will add, by the way, that we're agreeing to some of your conditions only to avoid wasting any more valuable government time. If I had my way, Mr. Austin, we'd hold you under the Patriot Act and lock you away so deeply inside a maximum security military prison you'd feel like you're Dumas' man in the iron mask."

The secretary shifted in his seat. "We will fulfill all but one of your conditions. In return, you will turn the original and all copies of the files over to us.

"You and your wife and those other two people will sign oaths that none of you will ever, under any circumstances, disclose either the existence or the contents of the files or the existence of our agreement here. Not ever. Not even if a court orders you to disclose them. Not even if your silence will land you in prison for contempt of court."

He waited a few seconds while he studied Trace's face to discern his reaction. Then he continued.

"You all will support cover stories we'll create for you explaining how you were able to leave the Quarantine Zone before the lifting of the quarantine. In the alternative, you will take on new identities we will create for you. It's up to each of you which one you choose."

He continued to look at Trace.

"One more thing," he said. "There won't be any lump sum payment to you, tax free or otherwise. Your request offends your president."

Trace nodded. *I guess there has to be some horse-trading.*

"That's the price of your freedom and peace of mind," the secretary said. "I suggest you accept it."

Trace rose from the chair, then immediately sat back down.

"I'll accept the oath requirement for me and my wife. I assume Ibrahim and Viktor will also accept that condition, although they will not understand why they are being let out from the Quarantine Zone or why they must remain silent about it. But they both have military experience so I expect they will go along. The government will have to deal with them on that matter.

"I will not return the file or the copy, however, under any circumstances. And if anything ever happens to me or my wife, the files will be sent by third parties, who have copies, to national news organizations. I already told you, this has been arranged to protect us and is not negotiable. It's not on the table."

"I'll also want the president's word, in writing, that Ibrahim and Viktor will not be harmed since they have no idea what this is about." Trace paused, then added, "I know I can't enforce this condition, but I hope the president will be a man of honor concerning it."

The secretary stared at Trace for a beat, then said, "Go on."

"As for your cover story versus a new identity, I'll have to talk to my wife. Either's fine with me, but I'll defer to her on that. Also, someone from the government will have to talk to Ibrahim and Viktor about this condition and let them decide for themselves.

"Finally, my wife and I will want blanket immunity for any crimes we may have committed in connection with this matter, as well as a full pardon from the president with respect to any such crimes. All in writing, of course."

"All right, then," the secretary said. "I'll go along with your refusal to turn over the files. Frankly, I don't blame you if they are as important as you've hinted."

The secretary continued, "We'll have to work out the details of the oath, the punishment if any of you violates it, and the terms of your immunity, the pardon, and the guarantees of safety. My deputy will meet with you later today to go over this. We'll deal separately with your friends."

"I'll be here."

"As far as your government is concerned, Mr. Austin, your oath of silence begins immediately, as soon as I leave this room."

He started to walk away, but then turned back and looked at Trace.

"Mr. Austin—"

"Sir?"

"Good luck."

CHAPTER 125

Washington, DC The present

ISABELLA AND TRACE KEPT THEIR old identities after they were clandestinely extricated from the Quarantine Zone and had returned home to Washington.

Ibrahim, once he was given a plausible, but false reason by ODMC explaining why he'd been removed from the Quarantine Zone and why he would need a cover story, bought into the scheme and performed his role like the well-trained ex-Israeli soldier he was.

Viktor, however, elected to remain in the Quarantine Zone. He gave as his reason that he wanted to remain near his sister, not abandon her to the conditions of martial law. In fact, he stayed because he wanted to continue his life as the Quarantine Zone sniper. After all, he thought, he hadn't felt so alive in years, not since he'd been discharged from the Russian military.

The cover story created for Trace and Isabella was simple enough to be believable: the story stated that Trace and Bella had left Fort Lauderdale for a few days, without Pete and Nanna, to rejuvenate their marriage with a simulated second honeymoon. While they were gone, the president announced the imposition of the quarantine and martial law so that Trace and Isabella were barred from reentering Fort Lauderdale.

According to the cover story, they then waited in a nearby town for the quarantine and martial law to end, expecting to rejoin Pete and Nanna when they were permitted to do so, but that plan did not work out. Instead, according to their cover story, when they hadn't heard from Pete and Nanna, Trace and Isabella asked Trace's friend at the Pentagon, Admiral Max Tyler, to use his military connections to contact them in Fort Lauderdale. When Max reported — so the cover story went — that Pete and Nanna had died from the terrorists' disease, Trace and Isabella returned to Washington.

Their friends, Trace's law partners, and their neighbors seemed to accept the story at face value.

Life in the Quarantine Zone continued as it had before the government extracted Trace, Isabella and Ibrahim.

General Vista remained as the District Military Commander, ruling the Quarantine Zone with an iron fist until martial law ended.

Viktor, meanwhile, continued his reign of terror, shooting civilians by day and the authorities after dark. He intended to cease this activity when the quarantine ended. He would then seek compensation from the government for his guns that had been confiscated and would reopen his gun shop.

Alex and Jenna performed their duties as soldier and ROTC cadet, respectively, assisting ODMC when called upon. Both survived the quarantine.

Gradually, as the period of martial law entered its three months' anniversary, the Pentagon eased the pressure on the

Quarantine Zone. It now regularly delivered food, medicine and various amenities to the Quarantine Zone's occupants. It also relaxed the enforcement of the Field Orders and removed the quarantine in measured phases. The architects of the experiment had learned all they believed they could learn from OPERATION TESTING GROUND.

CHAPTER 126

Washington, DC The present

O NE SATURDAY MORNING IN OCTOBER as Trace dusted
Pete's bedroom, Isabella entered the room for the first time
since she and Trace had returned to Washington.

She said nothing to Trace, but walked directly to Pete's
desk and picked up a baseball sitting in a display stand on one
corner. The ball had been autographed for Trace, when he was a
teenager, by now long-deceased ballplayer, Ted Williams. Trace
had given the ball to Pete when Pete became a Red Sox fan in
his teens. Now, Bella held the ball in her palms and looked at
it as if she were gazing into a crystal ball. After a few minutes,
she put the ball back on the desk and left the room. She never
said a word.

This is progress, Trace thought. Bella has come back into
Pete's bedroom.

A few weeks later, as he walked down the hallway, Trace
noticed that Pete's door was open. He stopped at the doorway
and looked in.

Isabella was sitting on the edge of the bed staring at Pete's
corkboard hanging on the wall, with its many reminders of
Pete's presence.

She looked over when Trace filled the doorway. She held out her hand to beckon him in.

Trace sat close to Isabella and put his arm around her waist, pulling her in to him. He kissed her.

"I miss him so much. I don't know what I'm going to do," Isabella said.

"I miss him, too, all the time."

She put her head on Trace's shoulder and cried, so softly that Trace could only feel her anguish against his body; he could not hear it.

Trace eventually convinced Isabella to help him go through Pete's closet to sort out clothing to give to Goodwill. It had taken him the past two weeks of gently nudging her along this path, but, to Isabella's credit, she eventually overcame her resistance and worked with him to take this step. As a result, Trace began to relax his concern for Isabella's emotional well-being.

On the last Saturday of the month, Trace stretched out on the sofa and soon slipped into that state of consciousness somewhere between dozing and wakefulness, thinking about Pete, thinking especially about their time together fishing in Key West.

He listened to the news on the radio as he lay on the sofa. The newsreader's headline stated that the president, just that morning, had ended the quarantine and martial law in Fort Lauderdale. He added that federal aid was poised to pour into the city to help the people who'd been trapped there and to help rebuild the city and its local economy.

I'd like to think that I had some role in hastening the end of OPERATION TESTING GROUND, Trace thought.

Then his reverie screeched to a halt.

Isabella called him from the kitchen, yanking Trace from his daydream. Something in her tone put Trace on high alert.

He sat up as Isabella rushed in from the kitchen holding that morning's early edition of the *Washington Post*.

"You need to see this," she said. She pointed to an article as she handed Trace the paper.

Trace glanced at the article's headline. Then he looked up at Isabella.

She made a face, and said, "I'm sorry, Trace."

Trace pushed back into the cushions and read the article.

NAVY OFFICER DIES IN CAR CRASH

Rear Admiral Max Tyler died yesterday when the car he was driving crashed into a tree in Rock Creek Park. Admiral Tyler was alone at the time of the accident which occurred at approximately 4:00 a.m., Friday morning.

The preliminary results of the toxicology report indicate that at the time of the fatal accident Admiral Tyler had a blood alcohol concentration of 1.10%, which is significantly above the 0.08% legal limit for driving in the District of Columbia.

Admiral Tyler is survived by his wife, Carole, and their two children.

In an unrelated event, Admiral Tyler's home in Chevy Chase, Maryland, caught fire this morning and burned to the ground. No one was home at the time and there are no casualties reported. The cause of the fire has not yet been determined, but fire department inspectors said the cause was suspicious, and would require further investigation.

[Please turn to page B3]

Trace folded the newspaper and placed it onto his lap. He looked at Isabella.

"Maybe he outgrew his alcohol allergy," Isabella said, "and we just didn't know. It's been years since we've been out with him and Carole."

"No," Trace said, "he didn't outgrow it. He joked about it when he called me for my birthday, kidded about still not being able to have a birthday drink with his best middle-aged SEAL buddy."

"Then why would he drink and drive?"

"He wouldn't," Trace said. "He didn't. Not voluntarily."

CHAPTER 127

Washington, DC The present

FOUR DAYS LATER TRACE ANSWERED his cell phone as he and Isabella were coming in through the front door, returning from Max's funeral.

He was in no mood to talk to anyone. He debated letting the call go to voice mail, but decided to take it when he saw the identity of the caller on the phone's screen.

As he pressed the TALK button with one hand, he used his other hand to loosen the knot on his only black necktie.

"This is Trace," he said.

"Hello, Trace. It's Aaron Weiss. Very sorry about Pete. He was a good kid. Hope you're doing all right under the circumstances."

"Thanks, Aaron. I'm a little better each day. In fact, I've been meaning to call you," Trace said. "I've been thinking about returning to my law practice soon."

"Well, you might have to delay your return for a while," Aaron said. "That's why I'm calling, to give you a heads-up." He paused.

Trace waited, then he thought, That was a strange response, and this pause is too long.

Trace waited two more beats, then said, "Aaron, you called me."

"Yes. Well . . . Trace, the reason I'm calling might undo your peace of mind. I almost didn't call."

"What is it?"

"It's not public yet, but Harlan Crockett, his wife and kids, and two of Harlan's friends, disappeared a few days ago while on vacation. Their chartered sailboat went missing in the Caribbean.

"This morning," Aaron said, "the Coast Guard found some of the boat's wreckage. They said the boat had been destroyed by an explosion of unknown origin. The Coast Guard hasn't found any survivors or bodies, but from the extensive damage to the boat, they presume everyone on board was killed."

Trace said nothing.

"Trace. Are you there?"

"Are you sure it was Harlan? Is there any chance it wasn't him? Any possibility he wasn't aboard?"

"It was Harlan's charter all right." Aaron paused. "They recovered the registration number from a piece of the boat. No doubt about it. The dock master also reported helping Harlan, his family, and guests get settled aboard that same morning and watching them cast off."

"What does that have to do with delaying my return to the firm?" Trace said.

"There's something else," Aaron said.

Trace didn't say anything at first. Then he said, "Tell me."

"The day after Harlan went missing," Aaron said, "his house and our firm's office burned down. Both deliberately torched, the fire marshal said." He paused to let Trace say something, but Trace remained silent.

"Fortunately," Aaron said, "it was in the middle of the night for both. No one was home at Harlan's house, of course, and no one was at the law office that late, so no one was hurt, but our law practice is in chaos. We're trying to find temporary office space and to reconstruct our active, missing files."

Trace thought about the file — the encryption KEY — he'd given Harlan for safekeeping, and wondered if it was among the casualties of the arson. Doesn't matter. Harlan will never use it now, he thought.

He assumed the file was the target of the two fires and was destroyed in one or the other. He couldn't reasonably assume otherwise.

Trace said, "I've got to go, Aaron. I'll call you later."

He ended the call, placed the cell phone in his pocket, and walked to the kitchen to tell Bella what he'd just learned.

CHAPTER 128

Washington, DC

T RACE LED BELLA INTO THE living room, over to the sofa, and held both her hands on his lap as he recounted Aaron's conversation to her. When he finished, he nodded once to indicate he'd finished, and waited for Bella to say something. The color had drained from her face.

"First Max, now Harlan," she said. "What's it mean?"

"It means somehow the government identified them as our insurance policy, and found out about the file and encryption KEY they were holding for us, then eliminated them and the files as threats."

"Why didn't they kill us, too?"

"Probably because they aren't sure Max and Harlan were our only backup."

"Are there others? You never said."

Trace put his finger to his lips to indicate that Bella should be quiet. Then he led her by the hand to the bathroom, and turned the water on in the sink and shower.

He whispered, "No other people, but, yes, another backup thumb drive, although the government doesn't know that." Trace took his finger and stroked Isabella's cheek.

"What's going to happen to us, Trace?"

He leaned in to Bella so his lips lightly touched her ear. "I'm going to contact the secretary of defense and let him know how pissed off I am about Max and Harlan. I'll say I had given another copy of the file to someone else because we anticipated this possibility. I'll rant and rave how I don't care what they do to us now, that I'm going public with the file."

He continued softly, "Even if he doesn't believe I have another insurance policy, he'll have no choice but to proceed as if he does believe me. He'll start by trying to calm me down."

"But won't he eventually figure out you're bluffing?" Bell whispered to him.

Trace nodded. "Possibly, but they will leave us alone anyway because we've kept our end of the bargain and because they can't be certain we're bluffing."

Isabella put her head on Trace's shoulder and hugged him tightly. "Those bastards," she said. "Poor Max and Harlan, and their families."

"Bella," Trace said, as he pulled away from her to look into her eyes, "I *will* keep us safe. I promise."

Isabella kissed him on the cheek, and said, "I know you will."

Trace kissed the top of her head, and said, "I'll go make the call to the secretary of defense to set up the meeting."

THE END

Please Review NO SAFE PLACE
If you enjoyed NO SAFE PLACE, please leave a
review on Amazon at www.Amazon.com [Type into
the search box: Roth NO SAFE PLACE] and/or leave
a review at your other favorite online retailer.

Reviews not only help me, but help other readers
decide if they want to read my book.

Thanks.

**Free Copies of the Report to the
President and the Field Orders**
If you would like to read the summary of the report given to
the president by the secretary of defense in which the secretary
recommended that the president implement OPERATION
TESTING GROUND, and if you would like to see the
Field Orders put in place by General Vista during martial
law, you can download them for free by going to this link:
http://dl.bookfunnel.com/kj9zbc2v4b

Visit my web site: www.stevenmroth.com

Coming soon. The second Trace Austin suspense novel:
NO PLACE TO HIDE
And
The third Socrates Cheng mystery novel:
THE COUNTERFEIT TWIN

Sign-up for my book updates sending you information
about these and my other upcoming books:
http://eepurl.com/chLiUD

Visit my web site at www.stevenmroth.com